# Griffin Academy 2

*A LitRPG Progression Fantasy*

Knights of War
Book 2

Travis Dean

## Chapter One

A BONE-SHAKING RUMBLE SHOOK THE ARENA floor. Narrow fissures spiderwebbed out across packed dirt as a luminous sphere exploded from the hole, blasting out of the arena and into the morning sky. I counted to four before hissing came from the direction of the academy lake.

I shook my head and exchanged barely suppressed giggles with Sienna and Elandra as Brom, Fitmigar, and Mallen appeared from the hole, coughing.

They trudged across the arena floor toward where we sat, their expressions downcast. Drizzle smeared the soot that plastered their faces further across their features, and a tendril of steam arose from Fitmigar's long braid. Mallen's ponytail was tucked inside his shirt like he'd expected the outcome all along.

"Any luck?" I asked Brom as they neared, trying to keep a straight face.

"Nothing," he grumbled, dropping down next to me in the wooden arena seats and shaking his head, small water droplets flying free. "Feels like we're just throwing fuckin' spells against it for the sake of it now."

My friend had a point.

"Impressive result, though..." I told him, throwing in an exaggerated wink. "Guess it's our turn again now."

I pushed myself to my feet and waited a moment for Sienna and Elandra to do the same. We walked across the damp arena floor toward the center where rope had been used to cordon off the recently uncovered stone door buried below the surface.

After we'd traveled to Atania's northern border and dealt with the threat of the shapeshifting mage Geilazar, we'd hurried back to the academy. We had pushed ourselves and our bonded griffins to our physical limits after the dean's message alerted us to events here in our absence.

That had been three days ago, and our frustration had only grown as we had come no closer to uncovering the mysteries behind this magical doorway—despite our daily attempts.

Dean Hallow had all fourth-year students taking turns to try and bust the door open through any means that came to mind. Approaches varied from brute force to groups 'somewhat carefully' flinging spell after spell at the door in varying sequences. Others worked in the library on deciphering the strange symbols etched into its surface.

I nodded to the couple of guards currently stationed at the cordon. They had sensibly taken a few steps back today, ensuring they were under the cover of the open-sided tent erected over the hole, keeping them out of the near-constant rain. A tent that now had a smoldering hole through the center of it.

King Aarlan had sent eight of his men down from his seat at Olnfast upon hearing of the door's discovery. They were running rotating shifts, watching over what currently amounted to not much more than a large hole in our arena floor.

The guards were not the most talkative, but both nodded in return and stepped aside to let us pass, their light armor jangling as they moved.

I paused at the edge of the hole. It was hard to believe that Rivers, a four-foot-tall beastkin, had managed to partially excavate this hole with no assistance before being discovered. He had dug it out with one side resembling a semi-walkable ramp down to the base, albeit a relatively steep one.

The hole had since been enlarged to fully uncover a stone doorway eight feet wide and twice that in length, the entire surface of the stone engraved with mysterious symbols.

To think that everyone had been unaware that this was under our feet all this time.

It was pure chance that Master Froom had risen pre-dawn and decided to get a head start on his day, beginning with the arena stalls. I hadn't been made privy to all that had happened, but the head of the stables had somehow managed to subdue the traitorous beastkin despite being struck several times with a metal shovel. After tying Rivers up, Froom had alerted Tad, and the smithy had delivered the beastkin to the dean.

"After you, ladies," I said, turning to the two beautiful girls at my side.

Sienna smiled, her blue eyes sparkling as she took Elandra's hand, and they slowly made their way down the side of the hole toward the stone door at the bottom. I followed, careful to watch my footing as I descended.

"Is there anything left that we haven't tried?" Elandra asked, turning to me at the bottom. The soft light made her light-brown skin somehow even more perfect and gave her dark-brown eyes a downright mesmerizing twinkle.

"Baring attempting to merge more of my spells together to create something new, I'm not sure," I admitted, shaking my head. I'd been making a little progress on that front, but without knowing exactly how to open the door, it seemed almost foolhardy to settle on a second merged spell after [Fire Wall*]

We had discovered after I merged [Fireball] and [Wind Wall] on the way north that I could create new spells by combining different elements. What we weren't sure of was just how many of these new spells I could create. Thus, I wanted to be sure of exactly what I needed before confirming any second new multi-element spell.

Sienna crouched and ran a hand over the carvings in the large stone door at our feet. "It would help if we had an idea of what any of these symbols mean."

None of the symbols etched into the stone door appeared even remotely related to any of the written languages of the continent that we knew of.

I smiled to reassure her. "Sars will find something, I'm sure."

Our Darkbrand friend had locked himself in the library on our return and hardly left since, other than to eat and sleep. He'd had Brom and me copy down the symbols and run them up to him, and that was the last thing of note we'd heard on the matter.

Sienna nodded. "Maybe one of us should stop by on the way back up and see how he's getting on?"

"That might be best." I effortlessly pushed mana from my core as I spoke, creating a two-inch-tall fire elemental in the palm of my hand. I crouched next to her, and the tiny elemental hopped off my palm and landed, knees bent, on the edge of the stone doorway.

We watched it slowly move around the perimeter of the door on its tiny legs. It paused every now and again, lowering a small, fiery hand as though checking the seam, searching for any weakness in the spell that continued to keep us out.

Elandra crouched down next to us and released a similar-sized elemental. Her tightly pursed lips already told me she doubted this would be any different from our previous failed attempts.

Besides having us fling magic at it, Tad had also tried prying the stone up using some of his smithing tools and the help of the strongest fourth years. But, one after the next, the tools snapped without the door so much as budging an inch.

As we continued to push mana out into our spells, our elementals took an opposite edge of the stone door. With mana being pushed into them, they grew in size while attempting to superheat the stone beneath them. When the ambient temperature started getting sweaty, Sienna raised [Wind Wall] to keep the building heat away from us, and we watched on.

"Feels like we've tried everything," Elandra said, shaking her head in frustration. "We've tried spells both individually and together. Tried weakening all areas and then attempting to push other spells through, but nothing. Not one chink of light. Not one hint of success to give us any hope that we can get this damn thing open." She huffed and stood up, turning away from us and kicking at the loose dirt.

I rose back to my feet and put a hand on her shoulder. "I know it's frustrating, Elandra, but all it takes is one discovery, one small reaction, and we might get it open."

"We don't even know what's behind it," she continued. "Why are we wasting time with a door that might have an ancient bathroom behind it for all we know?"

"It must be something important," I reassured her, "for Rivers to go through all that subterfuge before attempting to uncover it."

Sienna rose to join us. "Still can't believe he was a spy."

"It's been a few years since he arrived. Surely, he would have done something before now if he was an enemy from the start." I shrugged. "Guess we could try and get some time in with him to grill him."

"No harm in asking," Sienna agreed as Elandra remained sullen beside us, arms crossed.

A couple of puffs of smoke then caught my attention as our elementals dispersed, leaving us still no closer to the secrets beyond the spell-warded door.

"How about we call it a day and head back up to the courtyard?" I gave Elandra a gentle nudge and a smile that I hoped would ease her frustration. We'd already had a couple of attempts earlier in the morning, so it made no sense to drag this last effort out.

"If it gets us away from this damn door, I'd love to." A tired smile appeared on her face.

"Yeah, let's grab the others," Sienna added, and I nodded in agreement.

I gestured for Sienna to go first and slipped my hand into Elandra's, giving it a light squeeze of encouragement. "Shall we?"

She nodded, and the three of us headed back across to the others who sat waiting patiently for us to finish up our latest futile attempt.

We must have just missed the end of a joke as all three were chuckling away when we reached them. I gave Brom a questioning look, but he shook his head, his soot-covered face grinning.

Sienna leaned close to whisper. "Amazing how being away from that door cheers everyone up."

"Isn't it." I doubted there was a magical aspect to it, likely just the frustration easing, but it might be worth looking into. Another thing to mention to Sars.

We waited in the rain at the base of the tarp-covered arena seats for the three to join us and then took the winding path up through the gardens. Before we'd departed for the northern border, the late-flowering plants had been in bloom. Now, only a layer of mushy brown leaves carpeted the ground.

"Anyone else hungry?" Brom asked, scrubbing his face with rainwater as he walked. There were washing facilities on the way into the food hall, but Brom clearly didn't want to arrive all covered in soot.

"I could eat." Fitmigar nudged him playfully.

Everyone else nodded in silent agreement. Nothing built an appetite like frustration it seemed.

"I'm just going to stop by and see Sars, and then I'll join you." I kissed Sienna and Elandra and turned toward the library.

Warmth and the scent of old paper welcomed me out of the rain when I entered the library building. Sars was a creature of habit, so I headed straight for the spiraling stairs that would take me up to the fourth floor of the ex-griffin roost. Due to the cloud cover, the stained-glass windows were dull today, but I still marveled at their intricacy and workmanship as I took the stairs two at a time.

I soon reached the top floor and found it surprisingly busy. The rain must've driven most people inside. Skirting a bunch of lower-year students crowded near the entrance, I found Sars seated behind piles of books in the far corner, a low-burning sconce casting a soft glow across his table.

"How's it going, buddy?" I asked, dropping into a chair at his side and brushing some of the rainwater from my hair.

He startled. "Oh, hi, Jadyn. I never saw you approach."

"Might be something to do with this fort you've built around yourself," I suggested, laughing.

"True." He acknowledged my comment without humor before placing a marker in the open book before him and closing it over.

I leaned closer. "So... any luck?"

"With which one?"

"Either." Only now did I notice how the books were clearly separated into two distinct piles.

"Well, let us start with the door first."

I nodded in agreement, and my friend picked up a sheet of notes from the top of the right-hand pile. He smoothed it out multiple times before speaking.

"There is little to tell you, I am afraid." I made sure to not sigh. Sars was our best hope of cracking this mystery. "The symbols are not of this continent. At least, not in any present or recent scripts."

"So, they might be from an earlier time, or they might be from across the seas?" I asked, making sure I was following my friend's train of thought.

"That is about right. I am inclined to believe that it is the former rather than the latter, though there is a chance that it is both."

My mouth dropped open in surprise. "Ancient script?"

"It appears so. I must admit to being unable to decipher it at present, though there have been hints, clues in passages I have read."

"So, there might be answers somewhere in these books?" I gestured to the two piles on the table, but I knew there were plenty of other books that Sars would have lined up after these.

"That is the hope."

I nodded, deep in thought. "Would it help if we joined you?"

"I would rather work alone if you do not mind. I have a structure, a method, and I fear more hands would only confuse matters."

His mood seemed low, his eyes barely meeting mine, and that brought me on to the second matter. "How goes the other search?"

He lowered his gaze further, pausing and taking a deep breath before answering, shifting uncomfortably in his seat as he did so. "I fear the damage is too great, and was left too long, for me to be able to reverse it sufficiently."

He was referring to the severe acid burns to his left arm that he'd received from the wyrm under Brickblade Fort. The adrenaline had carried him through at the time, but, despite all our efforts, his mood had sunk lower and lower during our journey home and the days that followed as he found no cure for the extensive damage he'd received.

"No new salves to try? No new ideas from Madame Summerstone or Elmar?" I asked, referring to our resident potion-making teacher and her young, flighty assistant.

"A couple. But I am not holding out much hope."

"If I can help in any way, just let me know."

He lowered his voice. "Will do."

"Oh," I started, remembering another reason I had come to see my friend, "everyone is eating now if you want to grab a bite?"

"I have already eaten something, but thank you..."

I wasn't sure I believed him, but I chose not to press the matter. "You want me to stay with you for a while?" I was already fairly sure of his response, but I wanted to offer still.

"No, you are good, Jadyn." He fussed to fix his hair, though I hadn't noticed a single strand out of place. "Go and get some food. I will catch up with you later."

I knew better than to argue with Sars when he'd made up his mind, so I rose from my seat, said a quick goodbye, and headed back down the library stairs. Only at the bottom of the stairs did I remember I was supposed to have checked on whether the frustrated feelings we experienced at the stone door could be magical in origin. I debated heading back up, but then with what little Sars currently knew about the door, it would likely be a wasted trip.

I was about to head back out into the courtyard, ready to join the others for lunch, when a shout caught my attention. Turning, I saw Dean Hallow waving from the other end of the main hall, beyond the pews, beckoning me over.

I jogged across the hall, pulling up before the small, bespeckled man.

"Morning, Dean Hallow."

The dean smiled. "Good morning, Jadyn. What wonderful timing."

"How so?"

"I was just about to go and look for you."

Okay. Maybe he had some new information from his latest interrogation of Rivers. A reason for his actions.

A hint at what might lie beyond the door. Anything would be useful right now. "Is it to do with the door?" I asked, hopeful.

"Not this time, Jadyn." I must have looked confused because he offered me a reassuring smile.

"How can I help then, sir?"

"I just have a couple of people in my office who I'd like you to meet."

Any attempt on my part to learn more was immediately rebuffed as the dean turned and headed back toward his office, correctly assuming I would follow.

At the top of the stairs, I paused briefly as I caught movement from the far end of the hallway. With the sound of shuffling feet swiftly following, I realized it was just Beralda going about her nursing day, and I switched my concentration back to the dean's retreating form.

He paused at his office door, his hand on the knob, waiting for me to join him.

"Ready?" he asked.

"Of course, sir."

He smiled, turned the knob, and pushed the door inwards. I immediately noticed two figures sitting facing away from the doorway. As we entered, the first stood and turned to greet us.

My eyes widened. "Nerimyn?"

The senior elven ranger smiled.

The second figure then rose and turned. Her blonde hair was pulled back into a tight ponytail, several strands tumbled beside her face, and a few were tucked behind her long, pointy ears. A soft, almost nervous smile appeared on her face as her piercing blue eyes met mine.

"Ella?"

I turned to the dean. "What's going on?"

## Chapter Two

Dean Hallow waited while we shook hands and exchanged greetings. He then gestured toward the two seats opposite the rangers. Ella continued to beam a small smile at me, which I couldn't help but return.

"Nerimyn, why don't you fill young Jadyn in," the dean said, and my attention flicked from the pretty girl to the senior elven ranger.

"Certainly, Dean Hallow." The ranger turned to me and smiled. "Jadyn, it's good to see you again."

"And you, Nerimyn," I replied. The senior ranger had been stern and a little standoffish when we first met, but he'd softened somewhat and been a great help to us north of the Lower Helerean Forest in our recent travails.

"Well, to give you the short version, Ella is going to be joining you here at the academy."

My mouth dropped open, and I flicked my gaze across to the beautiful blonde-haired elf sitting beside him. She sat upright, formal, though there was still a flicker of nerves evident.

"That's great news," I said, a broad smile breaking out on my face. I'd enjoyed her company recently, despite the situation, and both her tracking and shapeshifting skills would be a great asset to the academy.

Ella visibly relaxed, and I continued.

"As a student?"

Nerimyn looked to the dean, and Hallow took over. "We will be working on bonding Ella with a griffin and hopefully bringing her fully into the fold, yes. That being said, Ella has missed much of the earlier learnings you have been subject to, so I would like you to work closely with her to bring her up to speed as quickly as possible. She will also receive some additional tuition when available."

Almost four years of learning. Not much then...

Despite the enormity of the task before me, I readily accepted. "Not a problem, sir."

"However," the dean continued, "before you can do that, I'd very much like it if you could give Ella a tour of the academy."

I saw no reason why not. "Absolutely. Now?"

"If you are able, yes."

I rose from my chair. Ella stood, too, and we made our way across the room.

"Anything else you need to know about the arrangement, Ella will be able to fill you in," Nerimyn added as I held the door open for the shapeshifting elf.

"That's great. Thank you." I turned to Ella at my side. "Ready?"

"When you are, Jadyn."

I smiled at her formal yet friendly tone, and we headed out into the hall, pulling the dean's door closed behind us.

"So, where to first?" she asked.

I paused to consider it. It didn't really matter the route we took; we'd either finish up at the stables or the arena, down by the lake. I decided I'd had enough of the arena for a few hours, so I settled on leaving that until last.

Before we headed back down the hallway side by side, I took a moment to point out Beralda and the academy's small infirmary as the elderly nurse went about her day at the end of the hallway.

A look of confusion crossed Ella's face. "Does she always shuffle like that?"

I stifled a chuckle. "She does, but you get used to it."

She smiled again, a little less nervous than before. She was loosening up as we walked, taking the stairs down to the main hall.

Walking at her side, I found myself barely able to keep my eyes focused ahead. I'd glanced across at her at one point and glimpsed a pronounced chest, pushed up by the strapless brown leather bodice she currently wore. I had quickly looked away, but I could have sworn she was barely suppressing a grin. I'd been caught.

Reaching the bottom of the stairs, I led us past the rows of wooden pews at this end of the main hall before guiding Ella into the library, talking her through the decimal classification system Miss Benner had recently introduced. In an effort not to bore her senseless, I also told her what I knew of the various scenes depicted in the stained-glass windows.

*Nice one, Jadyn, that's much more exciting...*

The top floor revealed Sars still deep in thought behind his towering book fort, but other than a cursory wave, we left him to it—I'd only just disturbed him as it was. He didn't even seem that surprised by Ella's appearance. Did he already know she would be joining us?

We spent a few minutes talking with Miss Benner, the librarian happy to point out various sections that could be useful to Ella in catching up on our studies as quickly as possible. Once done, we headed back out and around the main hall to the potions workshop annexed on the side.

After a quick introduction to Madame Summerstone and a reacquaintance with Elmar, we headed back out into the drizzle. I guided Ella to the stables along the winding path, bypassing entering the smithy on the way after pausing and finding it silent. Tad was likely grabbing a bite to eat.

We reached the stable yard soon after, and Master Froom nodded in greeting as we passed, the head of the stables vigorously brushing the courtyard clear of fallen leaves. He still sported the bandage Beralda had affixed after he'd been injured apprehending Rivers, but he hadn't slowed down on his work.

Heading over to the individual stables, a soft chirp reached my ears before I'd even had a chance to open Hestia's door.

"Hey, girl." I ran a hand down her neck and ruffled her dark brown feathers. "You remember Ella, right?"

Hestia chirped again, lowering her head and nuzzling Ella's neck, cooing in recognition as the nine-foot-tall griffin towered over the tall elven girl.

"Hello again." She chuckled softly. My bonded griffin nudged her gently, wrapping a wing around the elf and pulling her into a greeting she usually reserved only for me.

"I see how it is." I crossed my arms and feigned jealousy. Hestia's other wing unfurled, wrapping around me and pulling me close, and I chuckled.

We stayed that way for a while, enjoying the pure-hearted animal's love. The warmth of Hestia's body even dried out some of the dampness from the drizzle that covered our clothes.

I closed my eyes for a moment, appreciating the comfort, but Ella's voice soon brought me back to alertness.

"Is Kelia here?"

Kelia had been Oscar's bonded griffin. She'd been pining ever since her rider lost his life in our recent battle. If she didn't bond again soon, she'd likely leave to join those griffins that never bonded, a few days' travel toward the capital.

"She certainly is." I patted Hestia goodbye and led Ella out of the stall. The elf had taken the time to comfort Kelia after the battle, and I hoped she could do likewise again.

We searched for a few minutes, eventually discovering Kelia out in the paddock behind the stables. She was not even making the effort the stay out of the worsening rain and sat in the center of the field, drenched. To my surprise, Ella vaulted over the three-rail fence and strode across the paddock, crouching beside the solemn-looking griffin while I waited at the railing.

I couldn't hear what Ella was saying, but I noticed how Kelia visibly relaxed in her presence. I hoped Ella could help the griffin overcome its sorrow, perhaps even bond with her. There was a moment, while Ella rested her head on Kestia's side, that I could have sworn I saw a ripple in the color of the griffin's feathers, but I shook my head, putting it down to the sun trying to burn through the rainclouds above.

By the time Ella rose to say her goodbyes, water was running down the back of my shirt, and my blond hair was stuck plastered against my forehead no matter how many times I attempted to brush the water free.

As the elf approached me, my gaze faltered again. The rain had soaked her white top, and stiff nipples with pink areolas were visible through the film of transparent cloth.

I averted my gaze to admire the rain-blurred silhouette of the academy buildings very intensely and tried to maintain my wits. A slight grin appeared on her face again, or was I imagining it?

We needed to get out of this awful weather.

"Are you hungry?"

Ella nodded. "I could eat."

"Perfect. It'll give us the chance to dry off some."

Our walk to the food hall took us between the dormitories, so I nipped inside and found a soft woolen blanket for Ella to wrap around herself. It was partly to keep her better protected against the rain, but I also needed to rein in my roving gaze.

Alas, my eyes quickly found themselves dipping towards the skintight pants that framed her athletic elven legs and sporty, pert rear. Thankfully, my eyes and I did find some form of agreement and only peeked *very* respectfully when we were absolutely certain Ella was not watching.

We entered the food hall just as the rest of my squad was leaving, Sars the only absentee. Looks of surprise and glee spread across their faces as they saw who accompanied me.

Sienna came over and pulled the elf into a warm embrace. "Hi, Ella, what a lovely surprise."

"What's brought you here?" Mallen lifted a hand in greeting.

"I'm going to be joining you all. Jadyn is showing me around," she explained.

The group blanketed her in welcomes. While the girls hugged her in turn, I didn't miss Brom smirking and waggling his eyebrows, to which I returned my best withering glare. I swear he thought I wanted to bang anything that moved.

Ella was very stunning, there was no denying the fact, but I hardly knew her. I wasn't about to start chasing anyone new when I already had Sienna and Elandra. If it ever was going to happen, it would happen naturally. I didn't need to go around forcing things.

"We were about to eat. Are you all heading out?" Ella asked, and I stepped to the side to pull Sienna into a kiss.

"Aye," Fitmigar confirmed. "Got a potions lesson."

I begrudgingly pulled back from Sienna's lips to say, "Can you let Madame Summerstone know that I won't be present?"

"Of course." Sienna pushed those strands of raven-black hair behind her ear again. I think she knew I found it super cute.

"Thanks." I then pulled Elandra in to press my lips hard against hers. She murmured and arched her back, her hand gripping my ass.

"Gonna miss you," she told me, her voice breathless.

"We'll all catch up later if that works?"

"Molerat?" Brom suggested from my right, and I nodded.

"That'll work."

The others said their goodbyes, and Elandra reluctantly released me. Ella and I then grabbed a plate of food each and wandered over to find a seat in the pretty empty hall.

"So, what brings you here to enroll?" I asked, placing my food down and dropping into a chair. She'd not mentioned doing so a few days ago.

Ella sat across from me, carefully placing her own food down. "It had been on my mind for a while, for reasons I won't go into right now, but after working with you all recently, I thought now could be the perfect time."

"Perfect time to...?"

"Learn more about my magic. I've been taught all my people could teach me about my shapeshifting abilities back in Birchvale—hence why I was already out with the rangers."

I could understand that. The wealth of information here at the academy was significant, and if Ella had thought she needed to know more... well, this was the perfect place to enroll.

We continued to discuss the academy while we ate, but Ella never delved too deep into her exact reasons for joining us here. I felt she was holding back but didn't try to pry. My job here was to give her a tour and warm welcome, not uncover her deepest, darkest secrets.

Once we finished eating and had dried out sufficiently, we headed back out to the courtyard. I noticed Ella smile as she noted the rain had finally stopped. The sun threatened to peek through the light clouds at any moment.

She turned on the spot. "Where to next?"

"We could head over to stores, but there isn't much to see. You can see the building just down the track there." I pointed past the food hall, showing the large warehouse-sized building in the near distance.

"The shower block is that way, too," I added, my mind momentarily taking me back to my first time with Sienna a few weeks back.

Ella's voice nudged me back to the present. "Okay. And what's this large stone building here?"

"That's the combat hall," I explained, following her gaze. "We take our combat classes there, with melee in the front and then jousting and archery in the rear. That's also where our weapons are stored."

"Can we take a look?"

I didn't see why not. "Sure. As long as it's not currently being used for a class."

We walked up to the courtyard-facing, high-beamed, grey stone hall. Its thatched roof glistened after the rain. The large double oak doors were closed, but I eased one back and peered inside. Empty.

"Come on." I pushed the door fully open and tossed a small [Fireball] onto the closest wall sconce. The room burst into light as the sconces around the room lit up.

The dirt-packed floor was covered in the usual dueling circles, and I noticed Ella gazing around, wide-eyed, taking everything in as we headed across the main hall toward the back and on through the archway to the jousting practice area.

Growing up in the forest, Ella would have undoubtedly learned hand-to-hand combat, and I knew firsthand that her archery skills were substantial, but this would be the area she wouldn't be well-practiced in. Fighting from horseback was a world of difference to fighting from griffinback.

Ella seemed to be thinking the same. She turned to me and said, "I've got a lot to learn here, haven't I?"

I didn't want to sugarcoat anything. "You have, but Galen is a patient teacher. And if Mirek returns, I'm sure he'll be only too pleased to assist."

Mirek had traveled home rather than back to the academy after the battle at the border. We thought he'd been mind-controlled by Geilazar, but the dark mage himself was found to be under someone else's influence, so we couldn't really be sure of who had actually controlled him anymore.

Mirek had decided to take a break, and no one was really sure if he'd come back in the future or not. A part of him seemed too guilt-stricken for 'failing his duty' as he put it despite us assuring him there wasn't anything he could've done.

A smile blossomed on Ella's face as we moved on into the archery range.

"More familiar?" I asked.

"The layout is different to what I'm used to, but yeah, it looks good. It's nice to have something where I won't feel like I'm having to rush to catch up."

"I can understand that." I'd turned up at the academy behind everyone else having had no one to teach me the basics of magic. Wendia had passed before I showed any signs of the magical core within me, and it took most of the first year for me to feel like I belonged and wasn't just holding others back.

After I pointed out where the weapons were safely stored, we headed back through the main combat hall and outside. I closed the large double doors again and led her through the gardens leading to the arena. As we walked, I found myself wishing I could have shown Ella the gardens a few months back when they were in full summer bloom. I bet the sight would've brought out that gorgeous smile of hers.

*Why the hells would I wish that? What is going on?*

I cleared my thoughts away as the imposing stone arena rose before us. Ella gasped as we drew closer. There couldn't have been many buildings as large as the arena within her forest home.

As I guided her through the entrance, her gaze was immediately drawn toward the cordoned-off area in the center of the arena floor. Two unfamiliar guards now stood there, the ones from earlier having changed shifts since the morning. They'd even replaced the damaged tent.

The guard on the left was a tall, thin man with a mop of red hair. The second was shorter, portlier, and his reddened cheeks suggested he liked an ale or ten. Both men wore the light armor of the king.

Ella leaned closer to whisper at my side. "Is that the stone door they are guarding?"

"It is." I looked around. No students were currently here giving the opening a go. "Want to take a look?"

The elf hesitated. "If that's okay?"

"Sure. I don't see any harm in it."

Passing the guards and exchanging subtle nods, we paused briefly at the edge of the hole before descending the steep dirt slope. Ella skidded down the uneven ground effortlessly as if she was skating downhill, while I took my time following behind her.

The elf dropped to a crouch at the bottom and studied the doorway, casting her gaze over the symbols carved into the stone.

"Recognize any?" I asked, praying to all that she did.

She shook her head. "No, I can't say I do."

It had been worth a shot.

She continued inspecting it for a few minutes, running her fingers over the symbols in much the same way that Sienna had earlier.

Finally, she shrugged and rose to her feet.

"Well, that's the grand finale of our tour I suppose. We might as well head back up to the dean's office now if that's okay?"

A soft smile appeared on Ella's face. "Sure. Thanks for showing me around, Jadyn."

"No problem at all, Ella."

We reached Dean Hallow's office a few minutes later. The door was closed, but we could hear the dean and Nerimyn deep in conversation beyond. I resisted the urge to eavesdrop and knocked twice on the door.

"Come in!"

Twisting the doorknob, I pushed the door open and led Ella back into the office.

"All done?" the dean asked, looking up from the same seat we'd left him in. A tray of beverages and small cakes sat on the low wooden table before him.

"We are."

Nerimyn immediately rose to his feet from opposite the dean.

"I'll take Ella of your hands then, Jadyn. We need to unload her things and get her located. Thank you."

"No trouble at all, Nerimyn." I nodded to the pair as they left the office. "Is that everything?" I asked Dean Hallow, turning to leave.

"Just one more thing." He gestured to the seat at his side.

I turned back and took the seat offered. "How can I help?"

"It's to do with the squads," he started, and I nodded in understanding. "We're going to be making a few changes due to the numbers lost from Bernolir's squad."

That made sense. We had started with four squads of ten students when we traveled north. We'd returned with three tens and a six. The losses had hit us all hard. If it hadn't felt real before, it certainly did after those four lost their lives at Brickblade Fort.

"Not a problem, sir. Just let me know what you need me to do."

The dean paused a moment as if still mulling things over, though I suspected he had long since made up his mind.

"I think it's best if we change to three squads of twelve."

OK... so that meant we were losing a squad leader. I thought I knew where this might be going.

The dean must have realized, too, because he went straight into it. "Bernolir will be stepping back from squad leader duties for the foreseeable."

I paused and waited for him to continue.

"He came to see me. The losses were all from his squad, and he admitted that he feels responsible, despite my efforts to assure the boy that he did well, all things considered. No leader, no matter how great, can ever control the war around them."

"I've done the same," I told the dean. "There was no way we could have predicted that the beasts would leave the front line, throwing their full force at his squad's rear as they tried to secure the fort's doors."

"Exactly what I explained." The dean pushed his dark-rimmed glasses up onto the bridge of his nose. "But he has made his mind up."

"So... myself, Enallo, and Lana?"

"Correct. Of the squad we are dividing up, Bernolir will be joining your squad, Jadyn, and Charn is moving across from Enallo's. Plus, there will be one other."

Those were the two students with the single highest-leveled spells in the academy—Bernolir with his [Rock Fall], and Charn with his [Ballad Boost]. It didn't escape my attention that Dean Hallow was entrusting a fragile Bernolir to my care. "One other, sir?"

"Yes, Ella will also be joining you."

I held back a smile. That was great news. Ella was the only shapeshifter at the academy, and I really liked her company besides. It would also make it easier for me to bring her skills up to speed as we were often divided into squads during classes.

"Thank you. I appreciate the faith you are showing in me."

"You've stood out for all the right reasons, Jadyn. Your actions have not gone unnoticed—both here and in the capital.

*Wow. High praise indeed.*

"I'll do my best to not let everyone down then, sir."

Dean Harrow smiled and leaned over. "Of that, I have no doubt."

"Is there anything else?"

"No, Jadyn. That will be all. Maybe get your squad together this evening and bond over a drink or two?"

"A fine plan, sir." I'd have to be careful that Bernolir didn't drink too much in his present state of mind, and Sars might not show, but I'd do my best to boost the morale of any that did choose to join me.

With the conversation over, I pushed myself to my feet, wished the dean a good day, and headed off to round up the others.

# Chapter Three

I'd managed to catch up with everyone at dinner. As expected, Sars had declined the invitation, but the others had all readily agreed. Now, as the sun disappeared behind the combat hall, the light of day waning, we stood in the courtyard ready to head off for an evening at the Wandering Molerat.

The journey along the track to the inn was a short one. I fell into step beside Sienna and Elandra, linking arms and pulling them closer. Already the gentle post-rain shower warmth of the day had departed, a chill now penetrating the exposed skin of my arms. *Blasted cold.*

A feminine laugh caught my attention, and I lifted my gaze. Ella had managed to get her things away in the room she would be sharing with Fitmigar, and now, she walked ahead, deep in conversation with her roommate, Brom, and Mallen. I hoped it would do Mallen some good to have another elf in our squad.

"How did the tour with Ella go?" Sienna asked, noticing the direction of my gaze.

"Good. I think she quickly realized the scope of how much catching up she has to do, though."

"We can help with that," Elandra offered from my left.

"I hoped you would," I admitted. "With everything that's happened recently, the sooner she's up to speed, the better."

"Sure," she agreed, "we're a team, a squad, after all."

I gave her hand a squeeze and continued on, deep in thought. "You think we should be worried about Sars?"

A slightly puzzled look crossed Sienna's features. "How so?"

"He just seems... troubled? It's the acid damage more than the search for answers behind the door I think."

"Well, wouldn't you be?" Elandra interjected.

I thought on it for a little while. We had all returned changed. We'd seen things. All of us had. But Sars was the only one with a lasting physical reminder of the troubles. Rammy had already healed from his cut, thanks to the copious health potions we'd fed him, and soon only a light scar would remain, but Sars' damage was significant. It was also likely permanent.

There was no point in hiding anything. "I would. If he doesn't find anything to reverse the damage, we'll have to be there for him. Mobility and strength in his left arm haven't recovered, and that could mean relearning skills. It's far from ideal." I knew I'd not find it easy in his position.

"It would have been nice if he could have joined us tonight," Sienna said.

I nodded in agreement. "I did try. He's just so focused on both tasks right now."

Sienna's reply was softer. "Maybe next time."

"Yeah, I hope so."

We continued to walk on in silence, and I found myself pulling both girls closer to my side.

The inn soon came into view, and I jogged ahead to hold the wooden door open as everyone filed in. I'd barely shut it before I heard Joff's voice booming across the room.

"Ho, Jadyn!"

I smiled and looked down the left-hand side of the room. The tall, short-bearded man was already pulling ales for Brom from behind the bar. I swore nothing moved faster than my friend to an ale.

"Joff," I returned, approaching the bar, "great to see you again."

"You, too, youngster. I've heard a few tales already of your adventures from Tad. Maybe you'll find time tonight to pass on more?"

"Of course," I told him, only too happy to talk about our time away. Partly because I was proud of what we'd achieved, but also because the danger wasn't over, and the more who knew that the better.

I scanned the room. The flickering glow of the fires revealed a few Persham locals at the far end, but otherwise, we had the place pretty much to ourselves. Helstrom, Syl, and Rammy had already pushed four tables together, and everyone was taking a seat.

Brom, Fitmigar, and Mallen had the ales covered, so after adding a couple more logs to the closest fire, I walked over and dropped down between Sienna and Elandra. Mallen placed a drink down in front of me a moment later, foam sloshing over the edge of the tankard.

I took a deep pull on my drink and let out a long, satisfied breath. The last lingering frustrations over that damn impossible door left my mind as I let myself enjoy sipping on a drink, surrounded by friends.

"How 'bout a song, Charn?" Helstrom called across the table, and the sandy-haired wind mage grinned at the dwarf in response.

"Any requests?"

Brom sat up, knocking his tankard with a flailing arm but managing to steady it before it spilled. "How about The Venereal Tales of—"

The table groaned as one.

"Do you not know any other songs?" Syl asked, shaking his head.

"Well, there's The Hard-Riding Maiden of Erbury, and then there's The Voluptuous—"

"Seriously, man?" I said, trying to hold back a chuckle. "Nothing for polite company?"

My friend grinned as he scanned around the table. "And where would I find that?"

Laughter and mock outrage broke out, and it felt good to see everyone relax. Charn decided in the end to go with something a little less bawdy. As his voice drifted over us, gifting us a barely noticeable boost, I leaned back and draped an arm around each of my girls, pulling them close.

It hadn't escaped my attention that Bernolir hadn't joined in with the cheers and goofs. The dwarf swirled his ale around, appearing deep in thought. I made a quick mental note to chat with him shortly. For now, though, I closed my eyes and appreciated the sound of my squad relaxing around me.

A few songs later, Bernolir stood and ambled over to the bar, so I pushed myself to my feet and went after him, keen to catch up with him away from the others.

As Joff set about pouring the drinks the dwarf had requested, I leaned in close to the former squad leader at my side.

"How are you doing, brother?" I asked.

He stared intensely at the counter while scuffing his boots up against the base of the bar. "Can't get their screams outta me mind."

The four knights we'd lost had all met their end in proximity to their squad leader. I'd likely be no different to Bernolir were the situation reversed. He was blaming himself for something beyond his control, but he'd never see it that way.

It wasn't quite the same, but when the sea drake struck at the Yorn crossing and we lost elves, I'd felt responsible. If not for the reassurances of my friends, I doubt I'd have been able to move on without carrying something heavy with me. "You did your best. They wouldn't blame you." I rested a hand on his shoulder.

"Part a me knows that," he said, briefly catching my eye, "but I wasn't prepared."

"We're fourth-year academy students. Nothing was going to prepare us for what we witnessed."

He nodded but didn't reply.

"Look," I told him, squeezing his shoulder, "it will get easier. The screams will quieten. The images will fade. Just know that we're all here for you, and no one blames you for anything."

The brown-haired dwarf nodded again. "Thanks, Jadyn. Appreciate ya."

He didn't sound entirely convinced yet, but he did offer me a weak smile, which I took as a step in the right direction.

"Anytime, buddy. You ever need an ear to just pour out whatever comes, I'll listen. No judgment. No pressure. Now, what's say we get back to the others and play some games?"

"Games sound good. Good distraction." He nodded, grabbing a handful of ales and moving to head back over to the table. "Con?"

"If you want," I agreed, the game one we were all familiar with.

As I picked up the other drinks, Joff gave me a nod of respect. "Nicely done, young one."

"Thanks. I'm trying. He doesn't deserve to feel responsible for anything that happened at the fort."

"I agree, and with you all around him, he'll get there."

"I hope so," I told the barman, turning and heading back to join the others.

I placed the ales down on the table and dropped back into my seat, pleased to see Bernolir a bit more upbeat. He was having to force it a little, but it was a start. I'd have to keep an eye on him if Helstrom, Fitmigar, or Brom tempted him into their drinking challenges, but I doubted he'd agree in the first place.

The next few hours passed by in a blur as laughter mingled with increasingly slurred singing reverberated around our end of the bar. The locals had already disappeared for the night, and now only we remained, some more intoxicated than others.

I was already relaxed before I noticed a hand rest on my left thigh and squeeze. I turned to Sienna, and she smiled, her hand easing higher.

A second hand brushed my right leg, and I turned again, Elandra's full, dark lips broadening into a huge grin. *Those lips...*

She leaned closer, resting her head on my shoulder. "We've missed you..." Her hand slid higher to the point she cupped my balls through my pants.

"Really missed you," Sienna added from my left, tugging at the waistband of my pants under the table. I found myself beginning to harden against them.

I was only gone for the afternoon!

Not that I was complaining, though. I'd enjoyed showing Ella the ropes, but I missed my girls being by my side while I did it.

Elandra pulled me in for a deep kiss as Sienna freed my cock under the table, gently trailing her fingers down my length, and I felt myself fully harden under her grip. She slid her fingers fully around my shaft, tightened her grip, and began to pump me up and down.

Elandra's hand remained on my balls, massaging them, leaving me struggling to maintain a straight face as my tongue explored her mouth.

Elandra pulled away from our kiss, gave me a devilish grin, and started to slide under the table, running her tongue seductively over her lips as she went. I liked where this was going.

She'd barely got her perfect ass off her seat before the door flew open. Sars charged in, a bundle of papers and books threatening to fall from his right arm, his left hanging loosely at his side.

"I have found something!" he shouted.

Charn cut short his latest rendition and drunkenly tumbled off his chair in the process, crashing to the floor and sending Brom into a series of booming guffaws.

This was amazing news, but I still struggled to contain a groan of disappointment. Elandra pouted at my side, puppy-dog eyes on full display as she lifted herself back onto her chair.

Sienna managed to fumble my pants back up as she whispered in my ear, "To be continued, Jadyn. You can't escape us for long."

"When was I planning on escaping?" I asked, kissing her.

Sars dropped his bundle on the table before us, several scrolls threatening to roll off the other side until Syl drunkenly threw out a hand to stop them.

"Good arm!" Helstrom shouted beside him, the blond-haired dwarf playfully punching his friend in the shoulder and roaring with approval.

These guys were *hammered*.

Sars must have realized the same because he shook his head in frustration before catching my eye. The best plan here might be to take this to the other end of the bar.

A quick scan around the table told me that Helstrom, Syl, Rammy, Brom, and Fitmigar were all well past the point of being useful tonight, and Charn was only now staggering up from the floor, one hand rubbing the side of his head. After making sure the wind mage was OK, the rest of us collected the information Sars had brought and headed to the other end of the inn.

I got there first, and after stoking the fire, I pulled a couple of tables together before we placed everything down and took seats.

"OK," I started, "what have you got for us, buddy?"

Sars was fidgety, anxious to start explaining. He even had the glimmer of a smile for the first time in days.

"Okay, so it is not the complete answer, but I have made some progress."

He paused to shuffle some papers around, searching for one in particular it seemed.

"Ah, here we go." He plucked up a couple of sheets with handwritten notes on them, his usual perfect penmanship replaced by the slanted scribble he could manage post-acid attack.

"I managed to locate a book that references the evolution of language on the continent." He pulled a heavy-looking tome from the books on the table. "This one here."

He had marked a particular section and flipped through to find what he needed.

"Here!" His finger pointed halfway down the page.

The rest of us leaned closer despite having no real chance of making anything out clearly in the flickering firelight.

"The author, a scholar named Tilo, references an ancient language here, including several symbols that you might recognize."

I peered closer, vaguely recognizing the cursive script. "Go on."

He picked up a second book, the cover battered and torn. "This is added to by Tadrur, and he includes a couple of different symbols and his rough translations, though I can't confirm the accuracy, of course."

Sars then grabbed a third book, quickly flicking through to his desired page. "Then here—and this is regarding a possible destination beyond—Ansell, in his book on ancient myths, mentions an underground building, a vault of some sort. He is not clear other than he talks of a wealth of information being stored there. It is rumored to be accessed through a doorway guarded by ancient magics. Then a series of challenges beyond."

"And how sure are you that it's the doorway in the arena floor he speaks of?" I asked.

"Currently, I am not. Sure, that is." He unrolled a scroll, revealing a basic map lacking much of anything to confirm locations. "I have narrowed down the area he speaks of to this area of the kingdom, though, so I feel like there is a good chance it might be."

"So, we have a potential start on the language and a potential destination beyond it?" Mallen asked, resting his chin on his hand.

Sars nodded. "That is about the size of it. But it is progress, right?"

"Of course, it is, Sars," Sienna said, and he smiled.

I noticed a few tired-looking faces around me. "How about we go through everything in the morning."

"There's the room next to the dean's we could use," Mallen added.

"Great idea. That work for you, Sars?"

He nodded, already starting to collect his things.

"What are we going to do about the others?" Bernolir asked, nodding towards the other end of the inn.

I looked across to see Fitmigar and Helstrom face-down on the table, Brom staggering back from the bar, both hands clutching multiple ales.

"Yeah, we'll see how they're doing in the morning. Anyone feeling up to it can join us. We don't have a lesson until after lunch, so we'll have a few hours at least."

With everything set, we helped Sars gather his books and papers and bid a goodnight to Joff on the way out, letting him know we'd be back to fill him in on the stories we'd promised another night.

The walk back was brisk, and soon Sienna, Elandra, and I were saying goodnight to Ella. Sienna and

Elandra hugged the beautiful blonde-haired elf, and then I nodded a goodnight.

As pre-arranged, Brom would be staying in our room tonight with Fitmigar—if they even made it out of the inn—and I would be right where I wanted to be. Here, with my girls at my side.

Tomorrow, maybe we'd uncover the secret behind getting the door open, but now was time to let my girls know just how much I needed them.

As the door closed, I moved toward Sienna, looking to pull her into a kiss, but she stepped back, standing at Elandra's side. "Not yet."

Elandra grinned, clearly enjoying my confusion. "Yeah, Jadyn. How about you head on over to the bed, lie down, and close your eyes tight. We've got a surprise for you."

*OK. This should be fun.*

I smiled, turned, and headed over to the bed, dropping down onto the covers and placing my hands over my eyes.

"No peeking!" Elandra called, and I heard them both giggle from over by the wardrobe.

A couple of minutes followed full of laughter, curses, and more than a couple of things knocked to the floor, before I heard a couple of sets of footsteps move around the room.

A soft call reached my ear. "Open your eyes, Jadyn."

I pulled my hands back and opened my eyes as I sat up, my mouth dropping open as I took in the girls before me. They'd managed to get hold of a couple of the academy maids' uniforms, made a few alterations, and now stood together, holding hands, leaning toward me.

The dresses were both black, with sets of white string crisscrossing and pulled tight across the stomach like corsets, pushing both girls' chests up to where frilly lace framed them in perfection.

They had pulled long white stockings up to just below their knees, and the hem of the dress reached barely below their waist. My cock was instantly hard, pressing against my pants as Sienna beckoned me over with a single finger.

As I approached, both girls pulled dusting feathers from behind their backs and split up, pretending to clean around the room as I decided who to follow.

Elandra giggled as she knocked over a stool. Bending over, she gave me a clear view that she wore nothing beneath the dress. "Oops."

I growled and moved behind her, running my hands over her ass as she looked back at me over her shoulder.

"Are you here to help?" she asked seductively, and I grinned, slapping her gently across her ass, causing her to groan in pleasure.

"Something like that."

She lifted her ass higher, and I slid my fingers down and between her legs, finding her already moist and ready for me. I pushed a finger in past her folds, and she pushed back against my hand, urging me to push deeper.

Movement caught my eye, and I looked left to see Sienna prowling toward me across the room on all fours, pretending to clean the wooden floor, her breasts threatening to tumble free at any moment from the low-cut maid's outfit she wore as she swayed her ass from side to side.

As I slipped a second finger inside Elandra's pussy, feeling her juices soaking against my skin, Sienna reached us, pulling up on my pant leg as she lifted herself to my side, running her hand across my chest as she rose.

My fingers continued to slide in and out of Elandra's soaking pussy as I turned my head and kissed Sienna, my tongue slipping between her lips, exploring her warm mouth.

Pulling away, she kissed my neck, her warm breath intoxicating, before she lowered herself down again. She eased my shirt apart, revealing my chest, and left a trail of kisses down to my waist.

Sienna tugged at my waistband as my cock strained for release. A soft giggle came from her as she tugged my pants down, my cock springing free, bouncing before her eyes.

Still, Elandra bucked against my hand, her moans increasing in volume as I pushed deeper into her, my fingers curling, pushing against her soaking walls and bringing her closer to release.

"Here." Sienna gestured at Elandra and passed me her duster as she took my shaft in her hands, fingers gripping tightly as she began to pump my cock, smiling as I groaned.

Slipping my fingers free from Elandra, I took the duster and tapped it across her ass.

"Mmmm... harder, Jadyn."

I grinned, feeling Sienna's hand pump faster as I tapped harder across Elandra's ass, a thin red line appearing across her perfect light-brown cheeks as she moaned in delight.

"Fuck, yeah, Jadyn. Again!"

I tapped again, harder still, the clapping sound making Sienna moan in unison as Elandra's back arched, the dress riding higher, the perfect skin of her lower back glistening with a light sheen of sweat.

Sienna smiled and eased the top of her dress down. Her tits fell free, and my eyes widened as she took them in her hands. She then slipped her lips over my cock and ran her tongue along my shaft, lubricating me for what would come next.

Pulling her lips away, she leaned closer, easing my cock between her tits and then rocking in place, a shudder of ecstasy running down my spine as she pumped me closer to orgasm.

Still, I used the duster to strike across Elandra's ass. Each time, she moaned for more, her own fingers now inside her, bringing her close.

Content that I was as rock hard and primed as could be, Sienna slipped her breasts from around my cock, her fingers curling around my shaft as she guided me into Elandra, a single finger running across Elandra's folds, her juices glistening on my girl's finger as she brought it away.

Elandra backed closer, encouraging me deeper as I pushed inside her, feeling her tighten around me as I slid more and more of me inside her, her groans increasing as I thrust. I could feel the walls of her pussy tense as I brought her on, her legs shaking beneath us as she lowered herself to her elbows, her ass high in the air.

My fingers pressed against her hips as I held her tight, pushing harder and deeper with every thrust, her cries increasing, her breath hitching.

Finally, her arms tensed as she came, and I joined her, the warmth of my release shooting inside her as she moaned in ecstasy.

Elandra panted, her cries softening as she slid herself forward, my shaft easing out of her. She turned on her knees, a huge grin on her face, her cheeks flushed.

Taking my cock with one hand, she slid me between her lips, her tongue flicking up and down and around, tasting, before she eased herself back, the smile never leaving her face.

She gestured behind me, toward the bed. "Hope you're ready for more?"

I turned in place, still rock hard, to see Sienna on tiptoes near the head of the beds that we'd pushed together, pretending to clean high on the walls.

"I'm ready," I growled, striding across the room and moving in behind Sienna as the hem of her dress rode high, exposing her pert ass cheeks.

I slid a hand behind her left knee, lifting her foot onto the bed beside her and exposing her glistening folds. Sienna dropped the duster to the floor and immediately braced herself against the wall, palms flat as she looked back at me over her shoulder.

"Mmm, my turn, Jadyn?"

"You bet it is."

I moved a hand between her legs, circling her pussy, juices already glistening on my fingertips as I teased entry. She eased herself back against me as she dropped her hand to her breast, massaging herself as I slipped the tip of my cock inside her.

She groaned, back arching, as I pushed deeper, holding her in place as I rocked back and forth.

She moaned with the rhythm, and I kept going, content to enjoy the feeling of her walls gripping me with each thrust until her breathing quickened. I upped the pace, thrusting harder, faster, as she shuddered against me.

"Yeah, Jadyn.... Fuck, yeah..."

I slipped both hands up the sides of her body, feeling her soft skin under a sheen of sweat as I ran my hands around the front and took her huge breasts in my hands. I tensed my fingers, kneading gently, then harder as I pumped deeper, Sienna crying out as she came, once, then again as I continued, relentless.

As she faltered in place, her leg buckling slightly with the euphoria, I shot ribbons of cum inside her, joining her in breathlessness as we fell to the bed, Elandra already beside us, that grin still present.

"Holy fuck..." Sienna whispered beside me, and I pulled her in close, dropping kisses across her neck and shoulders.

"We should clean more often," Elandra added, and I laughed.

As we lay together on the bed, all still short of breath, Elandra nudged me in the side. "You think there'll ever be a time we can go away somewhere?"

I smiled. "Just the three of us?"

"Yeah. You think it'll ever be quiet enough for us to just get away? Maybe visit somewhere new."

Sienna sat up beside me. "That would be wonderful."

"I've never even seen the sea," Elandra whispered, and my eyebrows must have flown up because she continued, "yeah, yeah, I know. A water mage who's never seen the sea is crazy, right?"

"We can do that," I told her, looking to Sienna to make sure she was on board.

"You mean it?"

"Sure. As soon as we can, the three of us will take our griffins and fly to the coast."

Elandra smiled, her brown eyes glistening as she pulled herself closer to me. "It's a date."

## Chapter Four

My eyes flew open, and I sat up, alert, overflowing with energy. You couldn't keep me away from the girls currently sleeping at my side if you tried, even if this mana surge didn't happen. The fact it did was just a nice addition.

Elandra groaned from my right-hand side. She'd also be feeling a boost in her mana, albeit on a smaller scale, but she wasn't much of a morning person. Sienna, on the other hand, pushed herself up, the cover dropping as she did so, her breasts falling free.

Damn...

"Eyes up here, Jadyn," she whispered with a chuckle, and I reluctantly did so. "We need to get sorted to meet the others."

"Suppose so." I nudged Elandra.

She groaned again before surprising me and pushing herself up and out of bed in one fluid motion. She padded across the room, her bare ass swaying as she peered back over her shoulder, grinning at me.

Hah. Maybe she was a morning person, after all.

She bent over at the wash basin, splashing water onto her face, and it took all my control to get ready without racing across the room and taking her right then and there.

Part of me sure wanted to. All of me really—who was I kidding?

A half-hour later we left the room together, all clean and dressed for the day ahead.

I sent the girls on ahead to the meeting room, making a small detour to the food hall. Finding both Enallo and Lana present, I gestured for them to join me for a moment.

The pair both agreed, taking a seat at a quiet table I'd found in the corner.

Enallo smiled. "What's up, Jadyn? Got some news?"

"I do, actually. Sars has discovered some mentions of an ancient language in his studies, and we also might have a lead on what lies beyond the door."

The Darlish Coaster leaned closer, keen to hear more, but Lana just rolled her eyes and barely stifled a yawn. "Hardly worth pulling me over, Jadyn. We have found similar."

Of course, you have, I thought. "And you didn't think to share it?"

"Not until we have concrete information. I am not about to run off with half the information needed."

I had to stifle a laugh as Enallo rolled his eyes next to the redhead.

"Right, so... as I was saying, Sars has discovered a few things, and we are going to spend the morning going over it all to see if we reveal anything more."

Lana sighed. "And?"

"And, I was wondering if you would both like to join us?"

Enallo shook his head, the disappointment obvious. "I would have loved to, Jadyn, but I can't miss our studies this morning."

Lana was much more dismissive in her response. "Hardly seems worth it. We'll likely solve it all before you all anyway." With that, the frustratingly attractive redhead pushed herself to her feet, spun, and strolled away.

I shrugged. I'd tried, at least.

Enallo rose, ready to rejoin his squad as they moved to depart the hall. "Fill me in later if you find anything."

I nodded. "Will do."

I waited a moment for Enallo's squad to leave and then I left the food hall and jogged across the gravel courtyard, passing through an empty main hall. I only slowed when a stern Beralda clocked me running and harrumphed me to a walk.

I smiled sheepishly and slowed, walking past the dean's office and on to a single wooden door next along the hallway before the infirmary. Turning the doorknob, I entered a room bustling with activity. Sars had already laid out all his information, in a much more Sars way than the previous evening—everything in its place—and those present had all taken a seat.

A quick glance around the table told me that the same six we'd left out last night were missing still. I didn't see any point in waking them. They wouldn't be good for much, and we had plenty of us here to get results.

"OK," I started, looking at Sars, "what do we look at first? Deciphering the doorway or finding out what it guards?"

"To me, it makes sense to work on the symbols," he answered. "For all we know, translating the door's message will tell us all about what lies beyond."

"Good point." I dropped into a chair and ran a hand through my blond hair. It was starting to get a little long at the front, and I found myself constantly pushing it aside.

"So, I have started to collate the translations for the symbols Tilo and Tadrur mentioned," Sars explained, "and I think I have got around a third of the door's message uncovered."

Sienna gasped. "Oh, wow. That fast?"

"It is not as good as it sounds," he admitted. "I think the top half of the door describes how to open it. It talks of a sequence. The bottom half speaks of a darkness, travel, and then, I think, something about keys." He pointed to a symbol. "This is the one Tilo rather tentatively refers to as a key."

"OK, so how do we help?" Mallen asked from across the table.

"I have made copies of symbols they talked of but had not completely defined their meanings. I would like us to try creating potential translations through trial and error to estimate their most likely meaning. I also found another couple of books in the library last night—"

"You went back, after the Molerat?" I interjected in disbelief.

"Of course, " Sars replied as if it was normal behavior to never really sleep. "Anyway, Jadyn, if you take this one"—he handed me a red leather-bound tome—"I will work through the other."

"Looking for more translated symbols?" I confirmed.

Sars nodded in response without looking up, already flicking through his book.

I spent the next couple of hours reading through the book Sars had handed me. It was another one written by Tilo and likely nearly as old as the academy building we sat in. I made notes when anything came up that might be of use. Once, I spotted a small section of symbols that Tilo had managed to translate from the ancient symbols into old Atanian, which I then translated into our current script with another book Sars handed to me.

Sars would every now and again scribble down notes of his own while the others worked at different patterns and sequences, making a couple of breakthroughs that had my Darkbrand friend almost euphoric.

As I was coming to the end of my book, Sars erupted from his seat. "I have the magical symbols! The elements!"

"What now?" Elandra asked, looking over.

"I have the individual symbols for the different branches of magic."

"So... we can work out the sequence?" I asked, checking the significance of this breakthrough.

"We can!" He scrambled around for the paper containing the symbols Brom and I had copied down from the stone door.

He waved the others over, and we crowded around. Sars ran his fingers across the symbols. "So, from what I learned yesterday, plus what you have found today, and then this latest development, the text suggests the following."

We waited with breath bated.

"So, the order seems to be Shadow, Earth, Water, Wind, Lightning, and then, finally, Fire.

"One after another?" Sienna asked.

"I think concurrently. As in each has to continue to run while the others are added. The spells need to be cast into their corresponding symbol."

Elandra looked to me. "Well, we can do that, right?"

"We absolutely can," I confirmed.

"If I am understanding it correctly," Sars interjected, "it was one mage doing all six."

My eyes went wide. "What?" That must mean that there had been others like me in the past.

"Hopefully, it will not matter, but it seems to be the case."

"Only one way to find out," Mallen said, rising to his feet.

"Do we not need to decipher the second half of the door first?" Elandra asked, and the half-elf paused and looked to me.

"Jadyn?"

"What do we have so far from that section?" I asked Sars.

He fumbled with a couple of sheets before clearing his throat. "Underground... keys... a vault of some sort... and mention of griffins, I think?"

"OK. So likely an underground system of sorts we can traverse with our griffins. Collect a key, and open a vault. That sort of thing?" I was dumbing it all down, and with time I was sure we could uncover more, but I just wanted to see if we could get the door open.

"That is a pretty basic understanding, but it is a fair enough starting point," Sars replied.

"OK. I'll alert the dean. Mallen, can you grab Enallo, and then... Sienna, can you grab Lana? It feels like something they should be present for. Then, Bernolir, can you see if Therbel is free? Everyone else, head straight for the arena."

I figured that Enallo and Lana, as fellow squad leaders, should witness the attempt despite their inability or reluctance to join us this morning. Therbel, the dwarven casting teacher, would likely be able to guide our efforts.

Everyone filed out of the room. I followed them out, made the short walk to the dean's door, and knocked. Sienna waved at me as the rest headed past and down the staircase at the end of the hallway.

"Enter," came from beyond the door, and I turned the knob and did just that.

"Dean Hallow," I greeted.

He looked up from his desk, a small half-eaten pastry in his hand. "Ah, Jadyn, how can I help?"

"We've had a breakthrough with translating the symbols on the door, sir."

He straightened up in his chair, placed the pastry down next to a book he had been reading, and gave me his full attention.

"Go on..."

"We were wondering if it would be OK for us to try now, and would you like to join us?"

"Absolutely, Jadyn. Of course." He rose from his chair, absently brushed a few crumbs off his shirt, and came to join me in the doorway. "Lead the way," he said, lifting a long jacket from the back of the door and slipping it on.

I nodded and turned back out into the hallway, the dean following close behind.

It was only a short walk down through the gardens to the arena, and we reached the large stone structure with Bernolir and Therbel already there. A few minutes later, Mallen and Sienna turned up with Enallo and Lana, the squad leaders showing two very different emotions on their faces.

Enallo was wiggling, giddy with excitement, whereas Lana kept shooting a variety of withering looks my way. Her squad had been working on this problem, too, and I could almost smell the jealousy on her.

Sars was already deep in conversation with Therbel. The short-haired dwarven teacher gesticulated as he responded to the water mage's questions. Sars caught my eye and waved me over, and Therbel looked across and smiled as I approached with the dean.

"Jadyn, good to see you."

"You, too, sir." He hadn't traveled north with us, so I hadn't spent a lot of time in his company these past few weeks.

"Sars here says you wanted my assistance with opening this godsforsaken door?"

"If that's OK?"

"Of course," he replied jovially, his waist-length beard swinging freely as shifted from foot to foot. I wasn't sure I'd ever grow used to how undwarfly chipper the man was, but I did like it.

"We'll require the six mages who'll be working the spell. Everyone else, except you, Dean Hallow, will need to stay to the side of the arena. Never really sure how these things are going to react," he explained, and Sars, the dean, and I nodded in understanding.

He paused, waiting on...

Ah, OK.

"Brom is Shadow, Fitmigar is Earth, Sars here is Water—"

Sars coughed, and I hesitated.

"I will be supervising the approach with Therbel," he explained.

"No problem. In that case, Elandra will be Water." She was likely a better choice anyway with her currently increased mana levels. "Sienna is Wind, Mallen Lightning, and I'll be Fire."

Therbel nodded, hand brushing through his beard. "Let's get this started then."

I got everyone together and passed on what was happening. Lana's glares intensified upon learning she wasn't picked as the earth mage, but I felt Fitmigar deserved the opportunity after the work we'd all put in.

"Does it matter what spells we use?" Brom asked as we walked over toward the uncovered section of the arena floor.

"From what Sars has told me, it shouldn't," Therbel replied, ambling along at our side. "But don't place yourself physically upon the stone door as we don't know the effect that could have."

Brom murmured agreement, his brows dropping in contemplation as he likely scanned through his options.

We reached the top of the hole, passing another two sullen guards in the process.

Therbel paused. "Ready?"

We all answered in the affirmative.

"I'll stay up here with Sars if you all want to go down. Spread yourselves around the doorway, one at each end, two down each side, positioning yourselves closest to your relevant symbol."

I joined the others in slowly descending, once again careful with my footing. I'd watched the way Ella had done this, and by mimicking her sliding approach somewhat, I found it easier this time around.

Reaching the bottom first, I walked to the far-most end and took my place, stepping a couple of yards back from the door's edge.

The others took their places in turn, and then we turned to look back to Therbel, waiting for the sign to begin.

The dwarven casting teacher nodded, and Brom's expression turned serious. He tensed a little, focused on the relevant symbol etched into the door, and released his spell. Normally, it would call forth [Shadow Blade], but now, it just illuminated the symbol for shadow.

As the symbol glowed softly, Fitmigar moved into action at his side.

With a grimace of concentration, the dwarven earth mage released a gentle [Earth Wall] spell. The earth symbol glowed in the stone door's surface, but no wall formed.

"You need to speed this up. Mana is already dissipating from the first symbol," Therbel called from above.

Elandra and then Sienna released their spells, followed by a toned-down [Lightning Bolt] from Mallen.

Right. Time to finish this off.

I took a deep breath, pulled on my mana, and surged it through my body. Crouching for a moment, I held my right hand out. A [Fire Elemental] formed, bent its knees, and dove into the fire symbol.

Each of the six glyphs glowed with the colors of their element.

We all held our breath, waiting, one... two... three...

Bright light splintered between the symbols, each one brightening until we had to squint to protect our eyes. Then, down the center of the door, a fine seam appeared in what had seemed like a solid slab of stone. Its halves fell inwards as though hinged.

The scent of ancient rock and dust wafted upwards as cool air rushed to fill the space around us.

Elandra gasped at my side as a stone ramp came into view, leading to a tunnel that led deep underground. A soft glow appeared a few hundred yards or so down, illuminating what appeared to be a chamber of sorts.

"Do we go in?" she asked, turning to me as if I'd have all the answers.

I looked to Therbel and Sars at the top of the hole. They conferred with the dean quickly, before edging their way down to join us.

"Hmm," Therbel started, gazing down to the underground chamber. "Seems to be safe enough. The fewer we risk the better, though."

Sars slid a notebook from his pocket and looked to me. "Can you six walk down with me?"

"Of course," I replied, looking at the others and seeing looks of affirmation. We didn't have all our weapons with us, but I had access to the most mana and the most branches of magic should we need to defend ourselves. A few of the others carried daggers and the like. There could still be spies around, after all.

"Let us go and look then," Sars said, and we took our first steps into the tunnel.

As with the stone floor we now walked on, the walls and ceiling of the tunnel were of solid stone. The gradient was low, but we walked slowly, eyes scanning for any sign of danger. I'd have to ask Therbel if this was dwarven- or magic-created as the surface was incredibly smooth to the touch.

Something on the wall caught my attention, and I stepped closer to inspect it. An ornamental bracket with no sign of wear had been attached to the stone. A sconce. I drew on my mana, formed a [Fireball], and tossed it onto it. As with previous experiences, multiple sconces burst into life, illuminating the entire tunnel down to the chamber below.

"That is better," Sars noted, balancing his notebook on his weaker acid-damaged arm and scribbling away. I thought of asking what he was detailing but decided to not interrupt his thought process. He could fill us all in later.

It didn't take long before we reached the bottom. Our earlier assumption had been correct, and we found ourselves in a chamber around forty feet or so in diameter. The curved stone ceiling rose around fifteen feet above our heads.

The far wall was covered in a large mural depicting scenes of mages fighting upon griffinback, single mages firing off spells that looked like nothing I'd ever seen before. I walked over, running my hands across the images, wondering what it would be like to wield this level of power.

As I scanned the image, I blinked as I saw the beasts of nightmare they fought, huge titans as large as cities.

Brom's voice came from my side. "Ah, man. Battling Geilazar in dragon form was fuckin' challenging enough."

I nodded in agreement. "You got that right."

"Good fuckin' job there aren't creatures like these in the world anymore, or we'd be wiped out."

He had a point. How could we hope to cope with this level of threat if it ever came to pass?

Sars coughed for my attention, and I turned and walked across to where he stood studying a map etched into the stone next to a huge solid oak door. There was no way wood should look as pristine as this did, considering the years it must have lain undiscovered beneath the arena floor, but it did. It must be magically protected.

The map detailed what appeared to be three levels of a vast tunnel system that lay beyond the door. The symbol we had discovered translated as 'key' shone in a golden outline, once on each level. It seemed our estimations had been pretty accurate.

"Any idea on scale?" I asked.

"Not that I can tell," Sars admitted, putting his notebook away for the moment and running his hand over the map. "Not until someone explores the other side."

"And the door?"

"Just a regular door, albeit large enough for griffins to pass through. No magic. At least, as far as I can tell."

"Are those the symbols I think they are?" I asked, noticing three different symbols, one on each level of the map. Unlike the key symbol, these were not outlined, so I hadn't noticed them at first glance.

"If you think they are the symbols for Water, Fire, and Wind, then yes."

"So, each level beyond the door is going to be focused on a different element."

"Seems that way," Sars agreed.

"Anything else of note?"

"I cannot make out much. Various settlements of some sort, particularly where these key symbols are. Monsters in water. Traps, here, on the second level. Winged beasts..."

*Okay. Plenty to look at then.*

Satisfied Sars knew little more, I lifted the metal latch on the door and heaved it open. The door creaked as I pulled it toward me.

Impenetrable darkness lay beyond. A sconce had been placed on the wall, and I formed another [Fireball], tossing it onto the fitting. The area around the doorway lit up, casting the stone tunnel into a dim gloom, but other than a couple of further sconces farther down the tunnel, what lay beyond remained shrouded in darkness.

"Huh?"

"What is it?" Sars asked, looking up from his notetaking.

"They didn't relay like the previous times."

"There might be a distance factor involved, or maybe they light up as we walk?"

"That seems most likely," I admitted. "Guess we'll find out when we go in. We are going to need to document all of this first, though, aren't we?"

Sars had resumed his notetaking. "I think that is best."

I got the others' attention from where they stood, looking over the huge mural, and they stayed with Sars while I headed back to the surface with Elandra to collect drawing supplies.

As I set about my errand, Elandra at my side, the others took it in turns to head down to the chamber, Enallo, and Lana included. For reasons known only to him, the dean declined.

Once we had everything taken down for our records, only then could we decide how to approach what lay in the tunnels beyond the chamber.

---

The dean placed his cup down on the table between us and picked up the drawing of the map again.

"So, we think this is what Rivers was after?" he asked. "Access to these tunnels, these keys?"

"It would appear so," Sars confirmed.

"So, now we have the door open, it is just a case of heading through these tunnels, collecting three keys, and opening a vault of some kind?"

"I'm sure it won't be that easy," I told the dean—nothing ever was—"but that's about the gist of it."

The dean rubbed both eyes. He looked like the stress of everything was catching up to him, so I decided to help where I could.

"We were thinking about sending down squads to map the area beyond the tunnels. There is not an immediate rush to complete this with Rivers imprisoned, so we can afford to do this properly while the entrance is guarded."

The dean nodded. "Yes, Jadyn. That seems sensible." He looked around the table, his gaze eventually resting on the Darlish Coast squad leader. "Enallo, please gather your squad."

"Sir?" Enallo appeared taken aback at the dean's request.

"Collect your squad. You will be the first group to go down." The dean turned to Lana. "And you will take the second group tomorrow."

Lana flicked her red hair from her eyes and glared at me smugly for reasons I couldn't currently fathom. She then nodded and graciously accepted the task from the dean.

"And my squad?" I asked the dean, wondering why we weren't going first. We'd got the door open, after all.

"I'd like you to spend today and tomorrow trying to further translate the lower half of the door. Then, the day after tomorrow, you can take your squad down with the information gathered by Enallo and Lana's squads.

"Understood." I'd wanted to be the first to explore, but I accepted the dean's decision with as much grace as I could muster.

# Chapter Five

A short, sharp tap against my door woke me, and I opened my eyes to darkness. It was late, and I had been pretty tired, having spent most of the day with the rest of the squad browsing through page after page until I started hallucinating letters.

Lessons had been dropped for the day, but I'd taken a few hours' break from research to help Ella catch up on some basic learning, with Sienna and Elandra's help, of course.

I'd also taken the opportunity to learn some of the ranger's hand signals. Ours were pretty complicated in comparison, and I wasn't confident in Ella picking them up quickly enough, not with everything else she had on her plate, so I tried to become something of a translator.

I padded across the room, careful not to wake the sleeping girls at my side. Elandra murmured but didn't open her eyes. Sienna remained fast asleep.

I eased the door open to find Enallo there, looking a little disheveled. He held a scroll in his hand, lifting it as he spoke. "Hi, Jadyn. Sorry to disturb you."

"Everything OK?" I whispered.

"Sure is," he replied. "We've just got back for the day. Thought you might want a catch-up?"

"Absolutely. Give me two minutes to throw some clothes on."

He nodded and stepped back from the door. I fetched my clothes and was soon back out in the hallway with my fellow squad leader.

"Where to?" I asked.

"The food hall will be empty. Will that do?"

"Sure," I agreed, following him outdoors. I grimaced as the chill air hit my arms. Blasted cold.

We headed left, entered the empty food hall, and quickly found a table. Enallo slipped a green ribbon off the rolled-up parchment, flattening what appeared to be a rough map out before me, and then took a seat.

The map detailed a series of hand-drawn tunnels alongside scribbled notes, which highlighted potential issues and points of importance, I assumed.

"So, how did it go?" I started.

"Yeah, pretty good. We spent the best part of the day mapping out the route. Luckily, there aren't many points where you can lose your way; any tunnels leading off the main track lead to dead ends pretty quickly. Most are just what appear to be empty storage spaces."

I nodded, gazing over the map. "Any hostiles?"

"Nothing that we couldn't manage." He pointed to what appeared to be a cavern. "Here, we ran across some creatures. Small, dark-dwelling things. Came at us without fear, even gifted a few of our squad some shallow but nasty bites. Slippery little things. We dispatched them efficiently once we got a handle on them."

"How did the griffins cope with the journey?" I asked. Heading underground with our bonded partners wasn't something I'd ever really considered before.

"Better than I expected. There weren't any real chances for them to spread their wings, but Lana should get farther tomorrow and will likely discover more opportunities."

"And did it turn out to be water-based?" I remembered the symbols on the map in the chamber.

"It was. There are plenty of places where water drips through the otherwise faultless ceiling. We looked, but we couldn't how it was getting through. There are also a few small streams, if you could even call them that, running across the cavern."

We spent another half-hour or so going over the map, with Enallo talking through gradients, temperatures, and more. Rather than try the water sources, they had collected samples and brought them back for Madame Summerstone to study.

Satisfied I'd learned all I could, I thanked Enallo for bringing me up to speed and then headed back to bed.

The morning arrived far too quickly, leaving me unusually sluggish. As the girls both flitted around the room, in various stages of undress, I did my best to wake up and fill them in on my late-night conversation with Enallo.

As we headed out for breakfast, we met Lana and her squad exiting the hall, all set to partake in their exploration of the tunnels. I wished her good luck as she passed, but she just murmured something intelligible in response and was soon gone. A couple of her squadmates were more polite, at least nodding as they passed.

Heading inside with the girls, I noticed how even Sars was already seated at our usual table.

Grabbing some hot food and a steaming mug, I dropped in next to Sienna, directly across from Sars.

"Everyone good?" I asked, scanning my friends' faces, noticing that Rammy had his usual double portion of food piled high on his plate.

I was greeted by a chorus of tired mumblings. Everyone was OK.

"More of the same today?" I asked Sars.

He shook his head. "I wanted to speak about that."

I sat up, alert. Anything to not spend another day nose-deep in musty books. What we were doing was important, I couldn't deny that, but it was far from exciting.

"I finished it off last night in the library."

Of course, you did...

"Want to hear what I have got? I have already passed it along to Lana."

And the redhead had still looked sullen. Then again, maybe that was determination.

"Yes, please, and then I'll fill you in on my late-night chat with Enallo."

Sars grimaced as he shifted his body. His weaker left arm swung to the side as he pulled a couple of sheets of parchment from his inner pocket. He lay them on the table, smoothed down the edges, and cleared his throat.

"OK. So, I have done all I can. Some gaps remain, but I am confident that they will remain that way regardless, so there is no point wasting more time on it."

"I wouldn't call it wasting time," Mallen said from his right.

The water mage shrugged. "You know what I mean. Anyway, the lower half of the door, when coupled with the map of the three floors in the chamber, grants the following."

We all leaned forward, elbows resting on the table, food and drink forgotten.

"There are three levels beyond the door. Each level contains a key, and all three keys are required to unlock a vault that can be accessed after the third level."

Brom huffed, shaking his head. "This sounds suspiciously like a fuckin' dungeon, bro."

Sars nodded, aware of the books the shadow mage typically read. "You could say that. There is no mention of what we might find in regard to potential hostiles guarding these keys, but I do believe it will not be easy."

"Sounds simple enough, though." I looked around to gauge others' opinions. "We work together, and there is no reason we can't complete this without having to rush our approach."

"Any talk of what the vault contains?" Sienna asked.

Sars shook his head. "Not really. But whatever it is, it is going to be ancient."

"What happens after we get the first key?" Rammy fidgeted in his seat, looking like he couldn't wait to get started.

"It is not clear. I do not yet know if we would be forced to carry on or if we could return here to send others for the second key. That is if we were the ones to find the first."

"OK. That seems relatively straightforward." I looked around at the faces of my squad, seeing both determination and an eagerness to begin. "Thanks for getting it all cleared up."

Sars smiled a forced smile. "Not much use for anything else." He glanced at his left arm.

I shook my head. "That's not true, buddy."

Mallen placed a hand on Sars' shoulder. "Seconded."

I changed the subject, talking everyone through the Enallo conversation and answering questions. Despite all odds, once I was done, we managed to have the time available to attend Therbel's class.

"Morning, everyone," the jovial dwarven casting teacher greeted us as we filed in. Enallo's squad was already present, and I took a moment to thank him again for the previous night's catch-up.

Therbel waited for me to finish before speaking again. "Didn't expect your squad to be present today, Jadyn."

"All finished on the door translation," I explained and spent the next few minutes filling in the others who had not been present at breakfast.

Satisfied that everyone was up to speed with developments, Therbel proceeded with the day's lesson.

"So, today, we're going to be looking at different uses for spells. We all know how difficult locking in a [Spell] is for most of you."

I sighed in relief, glad that Lana wasn't here to boast about her twelve functioning [Spell]s and the ease with which she had done it.

"To begin, how about we run through a scenario. Mallen, can you join me for a moment?"

The half-elf nodded and strolled over the dwarf's side, towering over our teacher.

Therbel addressed the rest of us. "So, you're in battle, and an orc, brandishing a mighty cleaver, has just gone and removed young Mallen's arm from his body. Blood be pouring from the wound. What can we do?"

Brom shrugged at my side. Clearly, he didn't fancy using a shadow-based spell to save his friend. To be honest, I wasn't sure how that would work either. Might be worth thinking on. Wasn't that what Therbel had us doing right now?

Therbel gestured for us to think faster. "Quickly now. Young Mallen doesn't have long left."

I raced through my spells, mulling over his question. Needed to stop the blood loss and seal the wound. So... fire. I didn't think he'd appreciate a [Fire Wall*] coming at him, likewise [Fire Burst]. [Fire Elemental] was a little slow to form still, so [Fireball] it was.

"I'd use [Fireball]," I told Therbel, and Mallen's eyes went wide.

The dwarf rested a hand on his chin, deep in thought. "How so?"

"It doesn't burn me as I form it, and there is nothing that says I have to launch it at a target."

A smile appeared on the casting teacher's face. "Go on."

"So, I'd just approach Mallen and hold a sufficiently sized ball of fire against the wound to cauterize it."

"That would fuckin' hurt," Brom mumbled beside me.

Therbel smiled and shook his head slightly. "Yes, young Brom, it would most certainly do that. Would also succeed in stemming the flow of blood, saving Mallen's life. Good job, Jadyn."

I nodded as Mallen came back over to join us, giving me a look that suggested I'd better not try it for real anytime soon.

Therbel waited for Mallen to turn back to face him before he continued. "I'd like you ta work together, as a squad, and come up with five unique ways ta utilize your current spells an' achieve something new. Something you may not have considered before."

Satisfied we knew what was expected of us. Therbel turned and headed across the room to take a seat.

Breaking up into our respective squads, I placed a hand on Sars' shoulder. "You okay to jot down a full list of all the [Spells] we have between us?"

He immediately twisted slightly to move his left arm so that his right could retrieve his notebook again. "Sure, Jadyn."

I wanted to keep him involved and feeling needed.

The next couple of minutes involved each of us approaching my Darkbrand friend and listing off their learned [Spells]. I noticed Bernolir shaking his head as he walked away after speaking with Sars. I knew he was making progress on adding to [Rock Fall], but he had nothing as of yet.

With the list complete, Sars passed it to Mallen on his right, and the half-elf read it and then passed it on. Soon, we were all up to speed on all the options we had available.

I looked around my squad.

"So, who wants to start us off? It doesn't need to be your own spell."

For as learned as he was, I was still surprised when Sars spoke up first. "I have given this some previous thought. Though, I must admit, only so far as with my own spells."

Maybe not so much of a surprise. "OK. What do you have for us?"

"Well, as you all know, I have [Ice Blast]. Normally, I would use it to fire ice at an attacker, though I have used it, with Jadyn and Elandra, to create ice large enough to transfer people across a river."

We nodded, all having been present for the River Yorn crossing.

"However, I have also been thinking on a smaller, more precise level. Given a lock we cannot open, I believe I could perhaps ease water into said lock and then use [Ice Blast] to freeze the water rapidly, expanding it within the lock and breaking it open."

"That sounds reasonable. Have you had the chance to practice?"

Sars shook his head. "Not yet."

"Okay. Well, that's one. Anyone else got anything?" I scanned my squad's faces.

Syl lifted a hand. "I believe I might have one, sir."

I gestured for him to speak, used to the honorifics now.

"I'm not sure how possible it is, but could we use [Wind Wall] to move a person, perhaps even a group of people, faster?"

I paused to think on it. "How so? Is the wall pushing them along? Seems unlikely."

"I was thinking more on the top of the wall, sir."

I looked to Sienna. I'd only just come into my wind magic, but Sienna should be able to better judge the likelihood of success.

"What do you think?"

She shrugged. "Honestly, I'm not sure. You'd have to look into how we would move with the wall, rather than the spell just moving under us and on without us. Could work, though. Needs more thought."

I noticed Sars writing it down, so I figured we could move on.

"Thanks, Syl. Nice thinking."

The tall, black-haired wind mage nodded and stepped back.

The next five minutes were spent banding ideas around, each seemingly more outlandish than the previous. When Brom suggested using a new form of [Ballad Boost] to lull enemies to sleep, I knew it was time to rein them back in.

"Can we focus? We only have two ideas so far."

Brom snickered. "Mr. Handsome putting his foot down, hey."

"I like it when he's forceful," Elandra added, and I struggled not to laugh as Brom's face fell.

A gruff, feminine voice spoke up, and I turned to face Fitmigar.

"I been thinking a ways to adapt me [Earth Splinter]."

Okay. That was more like it. Fitmigar's spell was a good one. Useful for fracturing the ground under our enemy's feet. It covered a pretty large area when she unleashed it to its full potential.

"Okay. So, what do you think?"

"I be thinking I could use it in smaller, more focused bursts, you see. It could focus on one assailant. Make them lose their footing. Send their spell wide a the mark."

I smiled, a broad grin crossing my face. "I like it. Great work."

Sars mumbled in agreement as he jotted the details down, carefully continuing to balance the book on his thigh. He was still scribbling away when Elandra spoke up.

"I could use [Dehydrate] to help preserve meats for our travels."

"You can do that?" Rammy would no doubt be thinking of the benefits of access to more food on the road. I was still to meet anyone who could consume the levels of food that the redhead did.

"Already been working on it."

"Sweet!" Rammy was bouncing from foot to foot now. "Happy to sample the results. Just give me a shout."

Elandra laughed. "Consider it done, Rammy."

Happy that Sars had finished noting the latest idea down, I addressed the entire squad again. "OK, just one more then. Anyone?"

"I've got one," Brom said, and I must have raised my eyebrows in shock because he rolled his eyes and sighed. "Seriously?"

"Sorry, man. Go on."

He puffed his chest out a little as he spoke. "I think I can possibly adapt [Shadow Cloak] to cover other things, not just myself."

When no one interrupted to refute his claim, my friend continued, "Say, if we need darkness, I could wrap shadows around the sconces, cutting off the light."

I nodded. "Which would work well as you could then utilize [Night Vision].

"Exactly!"

Sars looked up from his notebook. "That is a great idea, Brom. Really good."

My stocky friend smiled in response. "Not just a pretty face, am I?"

---

With class over, and a few new ideas on how to utilize our available spells, we headed for a quick lunch before the entire squad walked to the stables together. We'd barely had a moment to spend with our bonded animals since returning, and the opportunity to assist in cleaning out their stalls was a good chance to both help out and relax.

Upon arriving in the mud-slicked stable yard, Master Froom informed me that they had stabled Kelia next to Hestia, as I'd requested. It would allow me to help Ella with something she'd never done before.

The afternoon passed pleasantly as I moved between brushing Hestia down, cleaning out her stall, and talking Ella through the necessities of looking after Kelia. A few times I overheard the blonde elf talking to the griffin in elvish, and each time I heard a more confident chirp in response. She was making progress.

I poked my head around Kelia's stall door as the afternoon came to an end. "Hey, Ella, we're going to finish up now."

She turned and smiled. It was the first time I'd seen a hair out of place, a few strands of hay sticking haphazardly from her ponytail. I laughed softly.

Pinkness rose in her cheeks. "What is it?"

"Nothing, just a bit of the stalls trying to come with you."

"Can you grab it?" she asked, approaching and turning her back to me.

"Uh... sure." I pulled the few strands free, wondering how she could still smell so good after all that mucking out. "All done."

She turned, leaned in close, enough that her chest pushed against mine, and pressed her lips softly against my cheek. "Thank you, Jadyn."

I stifled a grin as she pulled away. Didn't see that coming. "Anytime." I then turned away, part of my anatomy seeing more in the kiss than perhaps was meant. Perhaps not...

I decided to wait up that evening for Lana's squad to return, not wanting to be pulled from sleep by the competitive redhead who was impatient at the best of times.

The sound of soft footsteps approaching caught my attention. "Jadyn."

I looked up from the table where I'd waited for her arrival. Her long red hair had been pulled back tightly in a ponytail. As I lowered my gaze and tilted my head to the side, noticing how perfectly her bodice pushed up—

"Are you finished?" She pulled my gaze back up to her narrowed emerald-green eyes. "I've got better things to do than stand here and be ogled by you."

I smiled despite the reprimand and gestured to the seat opposite. She remained standing.

"My apologies, Lana," I said wryly.

She scoffed. "I don't want to have to tell you this twice, so listen up."

*Ouch.*

"When you're ready," I said.

She shook her head and rolled out the parchment Enallo had shown me the previous evening. It now contained a lot more detail. Despite everything, Lana was more than competent.

She leaned forward, and I immediately dropped my gaze to the map. There was no way she was going to catch me checking her out again. No way at all.

"So, we re-covered the areas Enallo traveled," she started, businesslike. "Of course, we added more detail to it."

*Of course, you did, Lana...*

"There were no new threats in the cavern."

I nodded. That was good to know and would likely mean we could pass through quickly.

"Once we moved on past there, we found an increase in the number of side tunnels."

I nodded again, following along.

"Each of them has been mapped out the best time allowed. All concluded in either dead ends or what we assumed to be empty storage areas." She coughed. "Are you following?"

"Yes." I glanced up at her eyes, barely noticing the way her breasts threatened to tumble from her shirt as she leaned forward.

"Hmm. Well, we have managed to map all the way up to a substantial body of water. An underground lake. From what we have seen, it is very dangerous to attempt to cross."

That got my attention. "How so?"

"There are a series of islands. A creature slipped on one, and a huge beast appeared from the water. Swallowed it whole. It's all down in the comments here." She pointed out a detailed section.

"OK."

"Everything else you need to know is noted down. I've had a long day, and you've taken up enough of my precious time. Don't mess up tomorrow, Jadyn."

"I had no intention of doing that, so you're all good, Lana," I replied, matching her hostile tone.

She laughed without humor and turned to strut away.

"Thanks, Lana," I said to her retreating form, but she was already half out the door. If she heard me, she showed no sign.

I shrugged and sat there for a while longer, reading through the copious notes. It paid to be prepared. Tomorrow, it would be our turn to check the underground tunnels out. I smiled, realizing I was actually looking forward to it.

Bring it on.

## Chapter Six

Urgent thumping against the door jerked me awake. I sat up in bed, rubbing my eyes. Sienna and Elandra groaned as they woke with me, pulling the cover up. I hopped out of bed, pulled on some pants that lay discarded on the floor, and yanked the door open.

"Tad?" I said in surprise, noting the smithy was breathing heavily, hands resting on his knees. "What is it?"

"The guards are dead."

"What?"

"The guards. All eight. Dead."

"What's going on?" Sienna called from the bed.

"The guards are all dead."

She let out a gasp.

"Thom discovered them this morning," Tad explained, referring to Galen's young red-haired combat teaching assistant. "Two in the arena, then six in their beds, throats slit."

"Fuck..." I muttered, shaking my head in disbelief.

"Dean Hallow wants to see you all. In the hall. Now."

"Understood," I told him, closing the door and striding across to the room to source some clothes.

Slipping out of the girls' room, we met Ella in the hallway and headed toward the hall, jogging across the courtyard and forcing open the large double doors.

The main hall was already abuzz with activity. Fourth-year students chatted in groups, anxiety and disbelief evident in their voices and expressions.

Brom, Fitmigar, Sars, and Mallen were already present, so we headed across, finding them deep in conversation.

Brom looked up as we reached his side. "Any idea what the fuck's going on?"

I shook my head. "Nothing, man. As much in the dark as you are I'd imagine."

"Got that right," Fitmigar said, a grim expression on the dwarven earth mage's face.

People continued to file in while we talked. Before long, the entire fourth year stood waiting on the dean, hushed conversation filling the room.

The short, balding man coughed once and then addressed us as a whole.

"First, what you already know. The guards sent by King Aarlan have all been murdered. By whom we do not know, though do rest assured your safety is paramount, so extensive investigation is already underway."

Students gasped, and more than one sniffle could be heard as everyone took in the severity of the situation.

The dean waited a brief moment for the noise to calm before continuing. "What you may not yet have heard is that persons unknown have accessed the tunnels below the arena and are likely somewhere on their way to accessing the first key.

"Fuck," Brom mumbled beside me, and his cussing brought me out of my temporarily shocked state.

"On that note"—the dean raised his voice to drown out the chatter—"we must send some of you after them. We don't know numbers, but we have no time to delay. We must catch and apprehend these murderers. We cannot afford to wait for days before more men from the capital arrive."

I glanced around to see how everyone was processing the news. I wasn't sure if it was due to our personal experiences at Brickblade Fort, but my squad all looked resolute. Determined. They might not know what awaited them, but they were ready.

"Jadyn," the dean called, drawing my attention, "you'll be taking your squad down without delay."

I nodded. "On it, sir."

"The other two squads will remain on high alert on the academy grounds, rotating shifts until we are sure this danger has passed. More attackers could be on their way."

Lana huffed to my left, and I glanced her way to see her staring daggers at me. She was never happy.

"Jadyn, can your squad stay for a moment? The rest of you can depart. Lana and Enallo, sort out between you who will be on shift first."

As the two other squads departed, Enallo nodded at me. "Good luck, Jadyn."

I clasped wrists with the Darlish Coaster. "You, too."

The dark-skinned squad leader smiled, turned, and headed out. Others followed after him. Lana didn't even grace me with a glance as she pushed her way past the others.

Once we were alone with the dean, he beckoned us closer.

"Jadyn, we are putting our full trust in you and your squad here. I said we don't know anything about these attackers, and that was pretty accurate. We don't know how many of them there are. At this point, we do not even know if they are magic wielders."

I nodded slowly, absorbing the news. We'd faced uneven numbers before, but they'd been orcs. These could be anyone. Anything. And, if we were unlucky, we might not be the ones with the advantage of quality over quantity this time.

"You can count on us, sir." I forced as much confidence as I could into my words.

"That's good. Because we are. Counting on you, that is. I trust you have the mapped sections?"

"Lana dropped them off with me yesterday evening," I confirmed.

"Good, good." He nodded, lost in thought.

I paused a moment, waiting for him to continue. When he remained silent, I coughed and brought him back to the present.

"Right. Master Froom and his team have been preparing your griffins. I want you to grab supplies and weapons, then collect your bonded griffins from the stables. I expect you to be departing within the hour."

"Understood, sir."

"Go on then. Go find these fucking bastards and make them pay for what they've done."

My eyebrows rose. I'd never heard him so much as cuss before.

Nodding a goodbye, I turned and led my squad back out into the courtyard.

"OK. You heard the dean," I said, "let's get our shit together and meet at the stables as quickly as we can."

My squad burst into action. Some hurried for the weapons stores, others to the dormitories.

I beelined to Madame Summerstone's laboratory to collect as many health potions as we could carry and afford to take. Madame Summerstone wasn't present when I arrived, but Elmar had clearly been briefed. A cart laden with small glass vials had been pushed to the doorway.

"Thank you, Elmar," I said to the flighty assistant, quietly glad that he wouldn't have to join us this time around. He wasn't built for war.

"You're welcome, Jadyn. Hope you get them."

"Me, too." I pushed the cart across the courtyard to the dormitories, the wheels bumping and jolting over the gravel. I left it outside next to one containing food and water. My squad could grab any they needed as they exited.

I headed inside, grabbed a bag from my worn, oak wardrobe, and tossed in a couple sets of clothes.

Satisfied I had what I needed, I returned outside, grabbing a handful of health potions and some food and water as I passed the cart before heading over to the combat halls.

Galen was already inside, assisting my squad with arming up with their melee and ranged weapons and armor, Thom racing around collecting our lances.

"Ah, Jadyn," Galen said, catching me coming in. "I've got these ready for you."

He handed me Orcgrinder and Dragonkiller, and I shook my head ruefully at Tad having had me name my scimitars. Truth was, they'd both earned their names since, so it had to stick now. Damn smithy…

The weapons were both sheathed, only the griffinbill pommels visible. Luckily, we'd all gone straight to Tad on our return from the northern border, and he had sharpened all edged weapons after we'd dulled them somewhat on orc and draconic bones alike.

"Thank you," I told the elven combat master.

"Only thanks I need is you all coming back safely," he replied, and I forced a smile.

"That's the only aim I have," I agreed. "Well, that and making these fuckers pay."

With that, I joined Mallen, Ella, and Syl and headed up to the stables, lances resting on shoulders. Truthfully, I wasn't sure what was going to happen with Ella on this journey. She'd spent a little time with Kelia since arriving, including that decent period yesterday, but if the griffin refused to bear her now, she'd likely have to remain at the academy. She couldn't hold animal form long enough otherwise to keep up with us as we'd likely have to keep a relatively rapid pace.

After passing the smithy, Tad nowhere to be seen, we reached the stables to find the others already there, Froom leading the griffins out one by one, their tension evident in the sheer number of claws and talons kicking up the stable yard ground and heads tossing in unease.

I weaved between the others, heading over to Hestia's stable door. Unlatching it, I pulled it back to be immediately nudged by her beak, her thick neck feathers brushing against my cheek.

"Hey, girl," I greeted as she wrapped her huge wing around me and pulled me in. "You ready for more adventure?"

She chirped in the affirmative, and I led her out into the stable yard, lifting her straps off the wall as I passed. Froom and his team had enough to do without me standing around and waiting on them.

Master Froom must have noticed because he patted me on the back in passing. "Cheers, lad."

"Anything I can do to help," I told him, tapping Hestia so she lowered slightly, enabling me to effortlessly loop the straps over her body, tying them off underneath, her chest straining against the leather.

Before long, the griffins were all prepared, and I felt a tap on my shoulder and turned to see Ella, a shy, nervous look on the elf's face.

"Can you help me with Kelia?"

I smiled, trying to put her at ease. "Of course."

Master Froom's team had already fitted her straps, and now Froom himself led the light-brown griffin across the yard. It was impossible to miss how skittish she appeared.

Ella approached, and just as she had both after the battle at the northern border and yesterday during mucking out, she got in close and spoke in the elven tongue, the griffin visibly calming before my eyes.

She then turned back to me, her blue eyes wide, pleading. "Can you show me how to mount her?"

Of course. Ella had spent time with Kelia, but she had never ridden a griffin before. Luckily, she'd spent plenty of time on horseback in the forest, so I hoped this would be a simple transference of skills.

I joined her at her side, showing how to place her foot in the strap, highlighting where on Kelia's neck to take hold to pull herself up.

Her first attempt, considering how surefooted she normally was, left a little to be desired. She slipped, and only me catching her by the ass saved her from hitting the muddy ground at our feet.

I resisted the urge to squeeze, but even that didn't prevent a soft blush from appearing on her cheeks. "Um... thanks," she told me, and I smiled at how flustered she'd become.

I lowered her to her feet and stood back. "Ready to try again?"

The elf nodded, slipped a foot in, pulled herself up, and effortlessly maneuvered herself onto Kelia's back like she'd done it a hundred times before.

Huh? That was more like I'd expected the first time around. Did she lose her grip on purpose? I had no actual way of knowing, so once I was sure that she was settled and Kelia wasn't going to object, I turned and headed back to mount Hestia, not failing to miss Brom's exaggerated eyebrow wiggle as I passed him by.

"Again, the handsomeness knows no bounds," he whispered, and I returned a hand gesture that would make a dwarf blush.

Hestia saved me the trouble of climbing up, lowering herself enough that I could leap up and on in one jump. Froom then passed me my lance and scimitars in turn, and I turned my bonded griffin around to face the others, my bag interwoven through her straps.

"Okay. We all ready?" I asked, scanning their faces as the stable hands stepped back, the weapons already handed out, only Ella riding without a lance, her much-needed lessons still to take place.

Satisfied that we all were, thirteen griffins padded their way down the path to the central courtyard, heading across the gravel and down the winding path to the arena.

Leading from the front, I inhaled deeply, puffing out my chest, trying to get a full grip on my emotions. This was rushed and manic, but we had no choice. We'd been woken at dawn, and the light was only now brightening sufficiently to make out the arena below, but we hadn't paused for a moment.

"We're going to be okay," I told Sienna as she guided Dawnquill alongside Hestia, a hint of unease on her face.

"I'm sure we will be," she said, "I just wish we had more time to prepare. We don't know what we're going to be facing.

"Time is not a luxury we have," I replied. "We'll have to discover everything we need as we go."

We had each other, and the thirteen of us would be all we needed to track down these murderous fuckers and make them pay.

We entered the arena in single file before spreading out around the hole. Enallo and his squad guarded it currently.

"All ready, Jadyn?" the Darlish Coaster asked.

"As ready as we'll ever be." I looked around the arena. We didn't know the next time we'd be above ground. Now, I wished I could feel the rain on my face one last time before we left.

Enallo and Harlee, his Darlish Coast native second-in-command, stepped aside, and I led our squad past them. Dirt flicked up under our griffins' claws as we approached the hole, Hestia's steps as surefooted as Ella's had been.

At some point in the night, the sconces had flickered out, or maybe the intruders had extinguished them. The tunnel down to the chamber below was dim, lit only by the early morning sun.

I lit a [Fireball] on my palm. Eyeballing the distance, I threw the ball of flame toward a bracket on the tunnel wall. The flames engulfed the nearest sconce, and the rest lit up with a cascade of bursts.

"Very cool!" Elandra sat on Veo, a broad grin on her perfect face. "You're showing off again."

Hah. "Not really. I just seem to gage distance well."

"Well, I saw Het try something similar recently, and I'm pretty sure she was closer to setting her foot on fire."

Elandra was talking about the bespeckled, ruddy-faced fire mage in one of the other squads. She did seem to struggle at times, but I'd always tried to help her.

"She'll get there," I said.

"Sure..." Elandra laughed.

I returned her smile. We were heading into unknown danger, possible death, but we'd always try to keep each other's spirits up.

We arrived at the chamber, and I turned to Sars. "Got the maps ready?"

"Of course." He grimaced as he maneuvered his damaged arm out of the way to pull out the latest map. I'd stopped by his room the night before after speaking with Lana to drop them off.

"No time to waste," I reminded him, trying to ignore his discomfort as I slid from Hestia's back and pulled the huge door open. Sars wouldn't be able to overcome his condition if we kept bringing it up. He was mentally strong. He'd deal with it in his own time, of that I was sure.

Sars scanned the first sheet. "Right. Follow me."

I was already back on Hestia before he passed my position, so we fell in behind him. I repeated my sconce trick from before, and as with my previous experience, only the first three sconces burst into life. As we reached the first, the fourth lit, and we found ourselves traveling in roughly a hundred and fifty feet of light.

I'd expected the tunnels to show signs of age—sections crumbling away, cobwebs covering the ceiling at least—but the smooth surfaces had an almost pristine shine to them. The floor was a different story, with odd fungi and moss sprouting here and there, some trampled by those that had recently gone before us.

Sars remained at the front, holding the sketch in his hand, muttering every now and again as we continued on. I'd moved alongside him at one point in case he needed someone to bounce thoughts and ideas off, but he remained enclosed, focused within, so I moved back behind him.

The stone-walled tunnel descended almost imperceptibly over the first couple hours. We were heading deeper, the temperature rising slightly.

I took a quick drink and nudged Hestia's flank. She picked up speed, pulling up on Sars' right-hand side again.

"How do you keep track of where we are?" I asked the water mage as he folded the sheet and placed it back in his pocket.

Sars gestured toward the tunnel walls. "Enallo's squad did a great job of marking the tunnel walls. Hardly perceptible marks under every tenth sconce."

I hadn't spotted them. But then I hadn't been looking. So far, we'd been traveling exclusively along the main tunnel, yet to reach any of the tunnels or storage spaces that Enallo had discovered branching off from this one.

"How soon until we reach the first cavern?"

"Another hour, maybe less," he replied.

I nodded and dropped back into the column.

Both previous squads had traveled through the cavern I spoke of, the various smaller tunnels and storage spaces branching off the main route mostly occurring after that point. Enallo's squad had removed those few low-level threats that had made the cavern their home, allowing Lana's squad to run through them without issue. I assumed it would remain the same for us.

As we traveled, we passed the first of the short, dead-ending tunnels. The temperature inside them seemed warmer still, the walls narrower, and we took it in turns to check them out, confirming they were empty of possible assailants before continuing on. The mysterious attackers had entered the tunnel hours before we had, and although they could be long gone, we couldn't rule out the chance that some had remained behind to slow us down.

As resolute as we all were, there were clearly nerves and tiredness at play. At one point, Charn began to hum, low, barely reaching our ears, but a warmth suffused our bodies. I noticed a few of my squad sit up a little straighter on their griffins, any lingering tiredness at our early start gradually ebbing away.

Mallen rode alongside Ella, Kelia appearing to have bonded successfully with the elf, and I hoped any friendly conversation between them helped Mallen come to terms with his elven heritage.

Sars lifted his right hand, catching my eye, and I guided Hestia alongside him.

"Everything OK?"

He gestured at the map on his lap. "Around the next bend. It should be the cavern."

"Understood." I passed the message on to Sienna, who relayed it to the others.

Sars looked wary, eyebrows raised. "It should be clear, right?"

I paused before answering, considering the likelihood that the situation had changed. "It should be. But that doesn't mean it is. It's likely the first real spot for any kind of ambush. That's only if any of these bastards have stayed behind to delay us, of course."

"Well, there are two exits from the cavern," Sars explained, awkwardly folding the map and tossing it across to me. "The one at the far end leads to a dead end a few hundred feet farther on. We don't want to end up stuck in there if we do encounter trouble."

"And the other?" I asked, scanning the map and doing my best to memorize the layout. I'd studied it when Lana had shoved it at me the previous night, but it never hurt to remind oneself.

"If you take the far wall as north, think of it as being west-northwest of the entrance."

"OK. So left of the tunnel we want to avoid. Anything else we should know?"

"The cavern is only about thirty feet high in some areas, and you do not get much warning in places where it is low. There are columns rising from the floor in a few locations, the ground can be slippery as there seems to be a trickle of water running through, and the far wall is a few hundred yards away. The light is pretty bad, too—even with all sconces lit."

"OK." It seemed relatively straightforward. With any luck, we'd just pass through and be on our way.

I tossed the map back, smiling as Sars caught it. We decided to head in as a single file, following the route mapped out by Enallo, but we'd move Sars back into the middle of the column.

"You two OK heading up to the front?" I asked Rammy. "We're not expecting trouble, but you never know."

A broad grin crossed Rammy's face. "Of course, Jadyn." The large red-haired boy shifted on his griffin as though itching for some action.

Helstrom mumbled something beside him, rubbed his eyes, and let out a stifled belch. I guessed Charn's

[Ballad Boost] could only do so much to help with a hangover.

Anyone else and I would have been worried, but Helstrom did some of his best work hungover.

Rammy led us around the bend in the tunnel and into the cavern beyond. The pair were fire mages like myself, but I was glad when Rammy was the one to throw out a [Fireball] at the nearest sconce. I didn't want to think how accurate Helstrom's aim might have been.

The cavern burst into light, though due to the towering stone columns dotted across the glistening stone floor, shadows perpetuated throughout. The still-dim light illuminated only around half of the expanse, the rest remaining in shadow.

As Sars had mentioned, the cavern was of varying height, some sections high enough that we could have potentially flown across, but then other sections looked barely tall enough for Hestia to walk through standing tall.

As we slowly progressed into the cavern, weaving around the thick stone columns that rose toward the ceiling like giant stalagmites, I noticed Hestia start to tense up. I wasn't sure if it was down to the dark, ominous surroundings, the slightly damp footing, or if she sensed danger, so I pulled on my core, easing mana into my body in case I needed to cast quickly.

We continued to move farther into the cavern, weaving around columns, single file, heading toward the exit Sars had pointed out.

A noise to my right caused me to turn, and a spark caught my eye.

Lightning arced across the cavern, striking a column near Rammy at the front of the line and sending shattered stone skittering across the floor.

"Cover!" I shouted, pulling Hestia to retreat behind the closest column.

# Chapter Seven

Another arc of lightning flew across the cavern, and I threw up a [Wind Wall] to buffer it away. Helstrom covered his eyes from the bright light.

"Ella!" I caught the elf's attention and signaled her to scout.

She nodded, transformed into a falcon, and took flight.

Another lightning strike flew out at us, crackling into a column of stone.

"Back up!" I shouted and repeated in handsign. "To the entrance."

The attacks stopped when we rounded the corner and put a solid wall between us and the cavern. Ella circled back soon after, landing on Kelia's back and shifting back into her natural elven form, not a pristine hair out of place.

She threw up a series of gestures that I had to translate into academy signs amid the clamor of the squad. The enemy consisted of two assailants: one in the right corner, one in the left. Both were lightning mages.

We really need to teach Ella our signs.

"Okay, so, here's how this goes."

Catching the squad's attention and getting them to quieten down, I moved to explain our approach once we went back inside the cavern.

"Charn, I'd like you to stay in the tunnel here, joined by Mallen, our only lightning mage. Mallen, you'll be less effective fighting against your own element."

The pair nodded and moved to the rear, ready to stay put.

"Bernolir, I'd like you to stay, too."

The dwarf didn't ask why, just nodding and moving to join the other two. I knew that he'd be ready to help at a moment's notice regardless. They all would.

I nodded to show my thanks before continuing. "Sienna and Syl, I need you to move to the eastern wall. There's a spot highlighted on the map that should be useful to set up at for ranged weapons. You can hopefully pick off one of the assailants from there if we can manage to flush them out."

The pair nodded and immediately moved to the front of our column, ready to track the edge of the cavern around to the right.

"Brom, I need you to also head right. You'll be responsible for drawing out that target in the far-right corner of the cavern.

My friend nodded and immediately disappeared from my view as [Shadow Cloak] activated.

"The rest of us are going to head left, around the western wall to try and ambush the first mage in the left-hand corner of the cavern, near to the exit we need to take. Take them alive if you can. We need answers, but we use lethal force if we need to."

I noticed Fitmigar pause, a look of concern crossing her dwarven features.

"What is it?" I whispered.

"Brom. Too much danger for him alone."

"Trust him," I assured her. "Brom can do this. If you join him, you'll just alert them to his presence, putting you both at risk."

She grumbled, eyes flicking worried glances Brom's way.

"Trust him, he's competent."

"Ah, aye, I know. It's just…"

I clapped her shoulder, nodding. "I know. Now move, I need you here."

She clapped her face hard enough to knock a lesser woman out, cursed in dwarfish, and pushed on back out into the cavern.

No sooner had we moved back out, Sienna, Syl, and a [Shadow Cloak]ed Brom heading right, the attacks started up again.

A [Fireball] arced across the space, coming from the very spot we were heading toward. Fitmigar cursed and threw up an [Earth Wall], blocking the attack.

I looked across to Ella, seeing a confused look cross her face.

"There was only one there before! The lightning mage! I'm sure of it!"

There had to be a third mage.

"They're funneling us toward the rear wall and the dead-end tunnel," Elandra called.

She was right. Attacks from both corners were pushing us straight toward the rear wall of the cavern.

*Yeah, that's not happening.*

I signaled the others closer and quickly passed on the plan.

Sensing we couldn't afford to delay, Fitmigar nodded toward me and immediately pushed Gren forward, hand held out in front of her determined expression.

Her gaze flickered east once, but then she continued, throwing out [Earth Splinter] as close to the point Ella had noted the original attacker had placed themselves as possible without coming into their line of sight.

The ground shook, cracks spiderwebbing around the particularly large column that, according to Ella's intel, hid our attacker, and a thin, shadowy figure darted to the left to avoid being caught in the attack.

Sars and Elandra threw out [Water Burst]s, the forceful jets of water speeding across the cavern and forcing the shadowy figure to retreat toward the rear wall.

Even as they were forced back, dodging the attacks, they threw out one last haphazard attack before one of Elandra's attacks struck home. Our enemy's attack went wide of the mark, but much more of that would threaten to damage the structure of the cavern. We needed to get this finished before the ceiling came down on us all.

The soaking wet, cloaked figure lifted their hands. Lightning crackled briefly between their palms, but it fizzled out, unable to form.

I threw a [Wind Wall] at the figure, slamming them against the rock wall. Their head made a painful-sounding crack, and the figure struggled to rise to one knee.

They fell, and my mouth dropped open in surprise as I looked to see Fitmigar charge in, Gren nowhere to be seen, her mace lifted high above her head, fury etched across her face.

The cloaked figure grimaced, lifted a hand, and a [Fireball] formed in their palm.

*What the hells? Another dual-wielder?*

As they drew back their arm to release the spell, I launched [Ice Blast]. Razor-sharp ice projectiles crossed the divide in a blink before puncturing the darkened figure, their body dead before it crumpled to the ground.

"What the hells was that?" I shouted to Fitmigar, but she'd already turned, charging off toward the eastern wall and the second assailant.

*Fuck!*

"Everyone else, hold here!" I shouted. "Elandra, Sars, check the corpse for anything that might help!"

I nudged Hestia's flank, and she raced after the beserking dwarf. A hundred feet passed by slower than I'd have liked as we evaded the columns, some damage from our assailants' initial assaults making pathways impassible for the griffin, and then Hestia skidded to a stop.

I caught a gasp in my throat. The dwarven earth mage was crushing the second assailant's head to a pulp with her mace, screaming in blind fury.

Judging by the nine or ten arrows protruding from the cloaked body, they'd been dead before she arrived, but she didn't seem to care.

Hestia must have sensed my unease as she reached forward and plucked the dwarf clear into the air with her beak. Fitmigar's screams continued until she ran short of breath.

Brom and Shadowtail materialized at our side, his [Shadow Cloak] dispelled. I didn't fail to notice the look on his face. Was that fear or pride?

"Fitmigar, what the hells was that?" I repeated.

"Keeping people safe," she replied, her glare threatening to send a shiver down my spine.

"You could have been killed back there," I told her. "It was beyond reckless."

"Brom needed me," she replied, sullen, arms now folded across her chest as she swung in the air.

"We can't lose our shape, forget our plans, charge off like that," I stressed, shaking my head.

"Brom needed me..." she repeated, softer this time.

I backed off. She was struggling, really struggling, with having someone to care about, someone to protect. She had always looked after all of us, but this was different. Was it that serious with Brom? Was that why this was happening?

"Ahh, whatever... No one got hurt, so no damage was done," I said, sighing. I had bigger things to worry about, but we'd need to address this before long.

I'd have preferred to capture a prisoner for interrogation, and to find out more about the mage able to cast two elements, but making it out safely was the most important thing. I slid from Hestia's back and walked over to inspect the one with the crushed skull. Looking down on the grizzly mess of bone and pulp, I found myself kind of thankful we'd skipped breakfast.

Pulling the figure's cloak away, I revealed a thin, almost skeletal body beneath, clad in a darkened leather. They appeared half-starved. Without the head it was hard to tell, but I didn't think they were human. Nor any other race I could think of. In the dim light of the cavern, their skin gave off a faint, purplish hue.

After patting down the body and finding it devoid of any convenient clues, I returned to the first body. Hestia followed behind me, still proudly carrying Fitmigar in her beak. The dwarf calmed a little as she swung from side to side.

Sars and Elandra were still crouched around the corpse.

Sars looked up as I approached.

"You are going to want to see this."

"It's proper messed up, Jadyn." Elandra shook her head, running her hand through her dark-brown hair.

I dropped down next to them. Sars pulled the hood back, revealing a deathly pale face, with the same hint of purple in the skin, and white hair. The eyes remained open in death, red irises staring blankly ahead. What drew my attention, however, were the long, pointed ears.

"Dark elf." Ella frowned at the body.

"A dark what now?" I asked.

"A dark elf. There is mention of them in some of the darker children's stories we have back in Birchvale."

"You're telling me that this is something from a children's story?"

"There is some truth in a lot of stories," Ella continued. "Most thought they never existed, but others said they were apparently driven from this land centuries ago. Some thought over the seas, others that they'd been forced underground."

"Which do we think it is?" I asked.

Ella shrugged.

Sars hummed softly beside me, balancing his notebook on his knee, scribbling away, jotting down all that Ella had revealed.

"Can you head over to check out the other body for me?" I asked Ella. "See if they were also one of these dark elves?"

"Of course," she replied, smiling. "Elandra, you want to head over with me?"

"You got it." Elandra leapt over and dropped a deep kiss hard against my lips before springing up and following the blonde-haired elf on foot.

I turned to Rammy. "Can you go and let the others back at the entrance know that it's safe to come across now?"

"Sure, Jadyn." He climbed onto his griffin, Chiron, and took off.

Ella and Elandra returned soon together with Sienna and Syl who'd retrieved their arrows.

"Good shooting," I told them.

The pair beamed with pride.

"Looks like you didn't do too badly here either," Sienna said, noting the body at my feet.

I glanced at Fitmigar. Hestia had placed her down, and she was deep in conversation with her shadow mage partner, Brom appearing to be calming her. "We managed..."

Sienna's gaze told me she wanted to know more, so I made a note to fill her in as we traveled, out of earshot of our dwarven friend. She'd likely seen what Fitmigar had done to the other assailant's head, so she'd pick it up pretty quickly, no doubt.

"So, was it another dark elf?" I asked Ella.

The elf nodded. "It was."

It seemed we were going to have to learn on the fly about the dangers we faced.

"If we're all done, we need to get moving again," I said, noticing Rammy approach, Charn, Mallen, and Bernolir following closely behind.

"Not much now by way of potential ambush points until we reach the lake Lana's squad managed to reach yesterday. There things will get interesting if their notes are anything to go by. After that, we are on our own until we find this key or more of these cloaked ones, " Sars explained.

"OK. So, without delaying any longer, let's get moving. Rammy, can you and Helstrom lead the way again. Sars, can you sit in behind them, giving them direction. After just now, I'll feel better if you've got a little buffer."

"Sure thing, Jadyn," Rammy said, chipper likely due to the recent combat.

"Aye, brother, " Helstrom added. Fighting seemed to have helped him shed the last of last night's grogginess.

Sars nodded. "OK. Off we go then."

Rammy and Helstrom led us out of the cavern and back into the tunnels beyond.

I noticed a barely perceptible descent again as the tunnel weaved lazily like a slow-moving river. There were more signs of recent passage—discarded small animal bones, the signs of a fire—but we didn't run into further trouble.

I found myself surprisingly alright with traveling underground. Other than the cold, it was kind of comfortable. There was no sense of feeling trapped, the weight of the world threatening to crush us at any moment.

I spent the journey at Sienna's side. I'd meant to fill her in on the situation with Fitmigar, but I never found a chance as the earth mage and Brom had dropped in behind us. Instead, we discussed the next obstacle that would slow our journey: the lake.

"What do we know about it?" Sienna asked when I broached the subject.

"Only what little Lana and her squad managed to deduce before they had to return to the academy yesterday evening."

"And…" she nudged, giggling gently at my non-answer.

"Ha. So… apparently, the tunnel reaches a body of water that covers around a hundred yards. There is a relatively narrow stone walkway across the first part of it, wide enough for a griffin to traverse at a push, and then there are a series of islands between gaps in the path offering multiple potential routes across."

"Sounds simple enough." She shrugged. "Where's the catch?"

"Yeah, well, it turns out it's not so simple. While they were noting things down, ready to report back, a small creature darted across the walkway, slipping and sending a trailing leg into the still waters."

Sienna gestured for me to continue.

"Something huge shot out of the water, clamped the animal in its maw, and disappeared back under, dragging the screaming creature with it."

Her eyes went wide. "Uh-oh, I see what you're saying now." Sienna went silent for a while, face wrinkled in intense thought. When she spoke again, it was to ask: "We have any plans yet to avoid it?"

"Sars?" I asked, and he turned on Ralartis's back.

He'd clearly overheard because he dove straight in. "The map Lana provided, and the detail I can make out from the illustration I copied down in the chamber, shows a winding path to the right-hand side of the underground lake. It avoids whatever dwells within, but it would add hours, perhaps even so much as a day, to any journey time."

"And we are playing catch-up..." Sienna whispered, the realization setting in. "We're going to have to cross, aren't we?"

"We are, but we'll do it as safely as we can."

Sienna gave a single nod of acceptance. "I trust you to guide us through it."

"We'll do it together," I told her, and she smiled.

As we continued along the dark tunnels, we found ourselves having to spend more and more time confirming side tunnels were empty of potential attackers. Having been assaulted once, we couldn't afford to relax. Most were empty and ended in dead ends, but a few held equipment of sorts, empty boxes, old chains, and even rusted water containers.

As the squad performed the checks, I spent the time cycling through my spells for a way to combine them into something we might need. The creature, or creatures, in the lake seemed to respond to either sound or movement. Could I freeze the water, trapping whatever lurked there within? We had three mages who could use ice, after all.

Maybe I could create something that would push the waters to the side, allowing us to walk across unhindered, or was that a little more than I could currently do?

I likely wouldn't know until we arrived and settled on a plan, so I just continued to flick between possibilities until Elandra moved alongside me.

"Bet you haven't done it underground before, have you?" she whispered, and I stifled a laugh as I looked across.

"Ha. Bit focused on other things right now, but it's on my list of things to do," I replied, throwing in an exaggerated wink.

"Just you wait until I find somewhere perfect."

"I'm holding you to that," I told her, happy for the distraction.

"I'd let you hold me anytime…"

I smiled. I needed this. There was so much pressure on us now to track down these shadowy figures, these dark elves, and to succeed in getting these keys before they did.

I was about to continue our conversation when Mallen spun around in front of us.

"Rammy said he can make out something glistening ahead, a dull green glow."

I exhaled. So much for a moment to forget about it all.

"OK. Let's do this, but let Rammy know to hold at least thirty feet from the water's edge while we finalize our approach.

As we pulled up, I slid from Hestia's back and approached the lake. The sconces around the water's edge didn't penetrate the soft green surface, and the footing was treacherous, even without a threat lurking in the water.

Something caught my eye, perched precariously on the edge of the stone walkway. My eyes widened when I realized it was an arm.

I slid from Hestia's back, edging along the walkway to lift it from the floor while keeping mana prepared in case I needed to give some jumpy underwater monster a surprise breathing hole.

I returned to the others with the appendage. "This one of these dark elves again, Ella?"

She slipped down from Kelia's back to inspect it. "Doesn't appear to be. Same clothing style, but this appears human, muscular, more of a pink hue to the skin."

So, it wasn't just dark elves we were hunting. They had human allies. The dean needed to know. And the king. This could have huge implications for the safety of the kingdom. But, still, we needed to know more before we could report back with any degree of certainty.

Something had clearly got to this one, and either there was a human ahead missing a limb or the group we were chasing had one member less now.

This might have been enough to send them around the lake, but I couldn't rule out them having crossed regardless.

Taking a deep breath, I signaled for everyone to dismount and gather around. We needed to work out how we would cross.

It was time to dodge another underwater beast. I just prayed it wouldn't end up in a repeat of the sea drake episode...

## Chapter Eight

"Can we just fly across?" Brom asked, and I shook my head.

"Check the ceiling in the middle section," I said, gesturing toward the lake.

It hung low enough you'd need to watch your head if you were riding a boat. No way for a griffin to fly through that.

"Maybe we could lure the beast out and kill it," Rammy suggested. "Like take out the threat and then cross?"

"What makes you think there is only one?" Sars asked, glancing up from his notebook.

"Shit. Good point." Rammy's mouth tightened with concern.

We stared at the softly glowing pool of murky green.

"Do we think it's the lake surface being disturbed that draws the monster out, or could it be pressure on the ground sections?" asked Sienna.

"Good question. Let's find out."

I turned to Fitmigar. She looked focused, and all signs of her earlier craze were gone.

"Can you use [Earth Splinter] on that island there?" I pointed about a third of the way across toward the first island after the initial walkway. Each island was only a relatively short jump from the previous.

"Aye." She focused for a moment before gesturing toward the landmass.

We all waited, breath held.

A soft rumble broke the silence, and the island fractured slightly.

We waited.

Nothing happened.

Okay... what next?

I looked down by my feet, noticing a small, flattened pebble. Momentarily, I was taken back to my youth, skimming stones over the white-tipped waves that crashed against Atania's southernmost shores.

I slipped it into my hand, bent my knees, and threw the stone. It bounced once and was snatched out of the air by huge jaws breaking through the surface of the previously tranquil lake and plunging back under the rippling surface.

There were a few yelps.

"Well, shit..."

"Okay," Sars started from beside me, "it seems to be anything that disturbs the water's surface."

"That was huge."

"Griffin-sized."

"Griffin-eating-monster-sized! Holy crap."

"Calm down, we've got this," I said to my companions, despite sharing their nerves.

"No fuckin' pressure then," Brom mumbled.

I patted him on the back. "We've got this, buddy."

"If you say so, Jadyn." He didn't sound convinced.

I gazed around the party. "So, who wants to go first?"

A moment passed.

Syl lifted his hand. " I will, sir."

I smiled at the wind mage. "You sure?"

"Absolutely, sir. Palae and I will go first." He gestured toward his griffin who stood motionless, no sign of anxiety present.

"OK. And you understand the risks, right? If you disturb the water, you get the hells out of there, you understand? Blast it with a [Wind Burst] if you can and hope Palae can carry you across without striking the ceiling."

Syl nodded. "Understood." He was putting a brave face on it, but I could tell he was apprehensive.

With that taken care of, Syl pulled himself up onto Palae, edging forward.

"You sure it's best to ride the griffins across?" Sienna asked from my side.

"Honestly," I admitted, "this is just an educated guess. I figure if something goes wrong, it's the best chance of keeping us safe."

Sienna didn't respond. Her attention followed Syl and Palae as they took the walkway toward the first island.

"This is fuckin' tense, man," Brom muttered from behind me.

"Yeah." I had to keep a confident front as the leader, but my nerves were tight, too.

We watched as Palae bent her legs, wings tucked, and then leapt to the first island. Once she landed and nothing happened, twelve breaths were released in unison.

So far, so good...

Over the course of the next couple of minutes or so, Syl and his griffin repeated the jump seven more times until they reached the far bank. The tall, dark-haired wind mage then slipped from her back, kissed the ground, and stood waving at us with an expression of relief.

Rammy offered to go next, and we spent the minutes that followed watching the giant red-haired boy guide Chiron across, no paw out of place.

Maybe this wouldn't be so bad.

Helstrom crossed next, followed by Bernolir and then Charn.

We relaxed a little.

Then Charn's griffin, Glawtus, lost her footing, and a claw broke the surface of the lake. Luckily, Syl was alert, immediately launching a [Wind Wall] that he'd been holding since the beginning.

An unnervingly wide jaw broke the surface, only for the wind to blast into it. Glawtus screeched as she fled from the dark waves and splashing appendages.

The griffin landed on the far shore, spinning and rearing up in case the beast chased her on land. Charn clung on, knees clenched, the fear in his eyes evident from where we still stood.

Then water returned to its previously calm state.

That'd been close. Way too close. Maybe it really would be better to remove the threat before anyone else crossed. But how?

"Elandra?"

The light-brown-skinned girl immediately turned to face me.

"How does [Dehydrate] work?" I asked. "Do you need to see the target of your spell?"

She nodded. "At least part of it."

Not great. "Like a fleeting glimpse or for the duration?"

"For the duration. Until I've pulled all liquid from its body."

I sighed. That wouldn't work. We might be able to get it to briefly come above the surface, but there was no way we could keep it there. Unless...

"Sars, I need to run something by you. You ready?"

He nodded, pulling his notebook out again.

"So, I'm thinking we might be able to tempt the beast out of the water. Do you think you and I together have enough strength to freeze the water around it, locking it in place long enough for Elandra to [Dehydrate] it?"

"Possibly. But before we try, do we have any idea of the size of the beast and the depth of the lake?"

I looked around, seeing a whole host of blank faces. "Er... no, and no," I confirmed.

Sars snapped the notebook closed and dropped it back into his pocket. "OK." He smoothed down his hair and then rubbed both eyes, exhaling as he did so. "I have no idea."

"So..."

"In my opinion, it would be too dangerous. Firstly, there is no guarantee we could hold it long enough. If it broke free, that likely would not cost us, but it might. We would also need Elandra to guess at the size of the beast, making sure she pushed just enough mana into her spell to kill it. Not enough and it would remain a danger to us all. Too much and she could put herself out of action for days at the very least."

"You could have just said no," Brom grumbled.

"That's off the table then." There was an idea there, pulling on the corner of my mind. I clicked my fingers, trying to speed up my thoughts.

"The chains!" I shouted, a grin spreading across my face.

Brom looked confused, brows creased. "What now?"

"The chains we discovered back in the storage tunnels."

His brows had lifted slightly, but I was going to need to run the whole idea by him it seemed.

"You ever been fishing, buddy?"

Realization dawned, and the shadow mage laughed. "Oh, this is gonna be fuckin' awesome."

It would have been nice to have the strength of Rammy on this shore right about now, but Brom and Fitmigar disappeared off to get the chain, leaving us waiting on their return.

Sienna sidled up to me as I stood at Hestia's side, running a hand through her feathers. "You think this will work?"

I shrugged. "Don't see why not. As long as we have the combined strength to get it onto the land, we should be fine."

"How do we know it can't attack us on land?"

"We don't. So, we need to be prepared. Once we start pulling, we'll need you nocked and ready to fire. The griffins will do most of the work, so we'll likely all be ready to act if needed."

Elandra joined us, running a semi-discrete hand across my ass. "All I need to do is [Dehydrate] the monster, right?"

"You sure you can manage a beast of this size? I can help if you like?"

Elandra shook her head. "I can do it. And no offense, but you've only just come into the spell. We'd likely need to start you on something smaller first."

That was fair enough. "Well, I'm here if you need me."

"And I appreciate that." She leaned over and pulled me into a deep kiss.

The clanking of metal chains broke the momentary silence, and Brom and Fitmigar appeared on griffin-back, pulling a huge section of wrought iron chains behind them.

Brom's laugh followed. "Enough of that, brother. We've got a fish to catch!"

I reluctantly pulled away from Elandra's perfect lips and sighed. "That we do, buddy."

Shadowtail and Gren released the chain, and I walked over to check it out.

[Fire Elemental] made short work of turning the end of the long chain into a hook, the figure effortlessly breaking links and welding sections together. I was really starting to master my control over the spell to the point that I preferred it over many others.

"How far out should we toss the hook?" Mallen asked.

Sars pondered for a moment, chin resting on his right hand. "Being as we shall be pulling it from the water, I would say as close to the shore here as possible."

Mallen laughed. "That's logical."

I smiled and addressed the squad, keen to now get our plan rolling. "Fitmigar, I need you ready to release an [Earth Wall]. We'll use it to hold the chain in place once the beast bites. That should stop it pulling away from us."

The dwarf nodded, moving into position, still seated on Gren.

"Everyone else, we'll split, half this side of the tunnel entrance, half the other. The griffins can then move into position next to the chain to pull."

We had about thirty feet of space before the lake to work with, and without the need for words, we all moved into position.

Satisfied we were ready to go, I pushed a [Wind Boost] directly behind the hook and shoved it out into the lake, the metal immediately dropping below the surface.

I was expecting the chain to tense, the beast likely taking the bait immediately, but what I wasn't ready for was the shrill, pained roar that accompanied it. Luckily, Fitmigar was swift in her reaction, and the dwarven earth mage threw up an [Earth Wall] that locked the chain in place.

"Pull!" I roared, and the griffins let out a shrill of acknowledgment as they forcefully pulled on the chain, their talons finding secure purchase on a slick ground that had almost sent me tumbling more than once already.

Slowly, the disturbance in the water grew, the beast thrashing below the surface, waves lapping, then crashing up against the shoreline.

It was working. "Keep going!"

The griffins strained, muscles tensed, and they heaved the monster toward the land, a maw filled with razor-sharp teeth breaking the surface, the pained roar growing ever more defiant as it thrashed against its captors.

Soon, the entire beast's head was above the surface, its emerald-green scaled skin reflecting the dim light of the lake. Its head flopped onto the stone shoreline, and it shook itself again, pulling the griffins back toward the water.

Sars looked up from his notebook where he'd be scribbling down what I'd assumed to be a calculation of sorts. "We need more!"

I wasn't sure I had anything I could do to make it easier, so I called on the griffins again. "Keep pulling! We're almost there!"

Screeches sounded out again as the huge creatures strained and pulled, the lake-dwelling monster now flopping against the stone shore, the first ten feet of its body slithering over the ground.

It had no legs, best resembling a huge eel of sorts, so now it struggled to pull back against the chain.

Sars shouted again. "That's far enough!"

I lifted a hand of acknowledgment. "Fitmigar, another wall!"

The dwarf sprang into action, throwing up a second wall and locking the beast on land.

"Elandra, are you ready?" I called.

My girl appeared at my side, resolute and ready for action. "You bet I am."

I watched as her brows lowered, concentration evident as she launched [Dehydrate] at the floundering murder eel.

Its cries heightened as it shriveled, pained roars causing more than one of the squad to discreetly raise their hands over their ears as Elandra pulled with all her magical self.

"Pull again," Sars called, and the griffins effortlessly eased the beast farther from the water, still no sign of the beast's end visible above the surface. Dry patches were appearing on the beast's scaled skin, its emerald skin dulling and cracking, its gums receding from its teeth.

Elandra grunted from my side, knuckles white as she pulled deep. She had extra mana reserves due to our relationship, but would it be enough?

The beast made another attempt to force itself free, but it no longer had the energy as Elandra continued to suck the moisture from its huge body. Its thrashing slowed, its surges becoming nothing more than pitiful attempts to stay alive.

As the eel slowed, I noticed Elandra falter slightly, her leg buckling. I moved to assist her, but she stayed me with a hand.

She had this.

She dropped to a knee as one final, pained whimper left the beast, and then it stopped moving, its skin now thin, hard, and cracked beyond recovery.

Elandra had killed the monster.

---

The squad exchanged weary high fives and cheers of relief. We'd all made it across, saving up to a day's travel in the process by not taking the long way around.

Walking over to Syl, I placed a hand on his shoulder and smiled. "Great work before, Syl. You reacted swiftly and averted disaster."

Charn was still flushed, even after all that had gone on since. "Aye, thanks, Syl. Saved me no doubt."

Syl stood proudly, chest pushed out. "Glad I could assist."

"How about a song to get mana levels shooting up again?" Charn said, trying to distract himself most likely. "Any suggestions?"

Brom opened his mouth to speak, but Mallen cut him off, "Not a chance, Brom!"

My stocky friend closed his mouth, a mock frown on his face.

"You decide," Mallen told the still-shaken wind mage.

Charn immediately [Ballad Boost]ed a folksy number that had everyone relaxing again as warmth suffused our bodies.

Rested enough to move on, I nodded to Rammy and Helstrom, our semi-permanent vanguard pair, to prepare to lead us again.

We had Sars' copy of the drawing from the chamber to guide us, but the map drawn by Enallo and Lana's squads stopped here. We were on our own, with the dark unknown ahead of us.

"What's next?" I asked Sars as he scanned his notes.

"If the scale of the diagram is to be believed, we have still got a march of around a day before we reach an underground settlement of sorts. It is there where we'll find the first key."

"So, we are going to have to find somewhere to rest."

"From my best guess, we have another hour or two before night falls above ground," Sars said.

"Anywhere ahead that would be defensible?" I asked, choosing to refrain from asking how Sars knew what time it was.

"Most of it is. At least, it appears so. Another two hours or so ahead we will pass the point where the route that bypassed the lake reconnects with the main tunnel."

I nodded, seeing where Sars was going with this. "So, if those murdering bastards went that way, we'll know if they try to get back in front of us."

He nodded in confirmation. "Exactly."

"That works for me. Let's say another three hours, and then we'll find somewhere to make camp."

"Agreed." Sars stowed away his notebook, brushed down his shirt, and climbed back onto Ralartis.

I signaled for Rammy and Helstrom to lead us on and pulled myself up on Hestia, patting her neck. "Let's go, girl." She followed on after the others, moving us alongside Sienna and Dawnquill.

"Hey," she greeted, and I smiled.

"We going to be able to get any alone time soon?" she asked, leaning forward. Her breasts pushed against the fabric of her shirt, threatening to fall out at any moment.

"I'm not sure," I admitted. "It's going to be pretty full-on for a while."

"I'd be fine with you just using me for the mana boost," she said. I chuckled, but I wasn't sure if she was joking or not. I would have expected that from Elandra, not so much Sienna.

"We find the time soon, I promise."

She nodded with a fake pout but accepted it. We were underground chasing and evading an enemy we knew hardly anything about. This wasn't the best place for sex.

"Did I overhear Sars saying we'll need to camp in a few hours?" she asked.

"Yeah, it's not going to be possible to reach the key's location without taking a few hours, at least, to get some rest, grab a bite to eat."

"How can you even tell what time it is?"

I laughed. "I can't, but Sars seems to have some way of knowing. Not sure how he does it, but it's good enough for me."

The next couple of hours passed by quickly. I spent most of the time checking on everyone in the column, making sure everyone was good. I noticed Ella and Mallen deep in conversation again. It was good to see him chatting away with an elf. Maybe a friendship would blossom.

I hadn't noticed us going deeper since the lake, the tunnel leveling out. If the illustration in the chamber was accurate, there were two more levels below this one. How deep would we end up going?

A shout from Rammy caught my ear, and I nudged Hestia up the column, soon finding myself at the redhead's side.

"What is it?" I asked.

"Thinking this might be the point where the other tunnel joins back up with ours?"

"Sars?" I called over my shoulder. "This the point where the paths merge?"

"That would seem likely," he replied, scanning the map. "Any sign anyone has used it lately?"

I slid from Hestia's back and approached the tunnel, tossing a [Fireball] into the first sconce I saw. Flickering light illuminated the first hundred feet or so of a tunnel with floor and walls covered in a mattress of fungi. Some stood over a foot in height. None were broken or trampled.

"Doesn't look like it," I called back.

Helstrom spoke up from my side. "So, we move on, find somewhere to get our heads down?"

"In a moment. Actually, if you and Rammy lead everyone else on, I'm just going to grab Bernolir, see if we can't slow these fuckers down a bit."

"Understood," the dwarf replied, heading on, Rammy at his side, Sars and Syl behind.

I got a few looks as the column passed me by, but I decided I could explain all a little later. As Bernolir approached on Mahtava, I held up a hand and gestured for him to join me.

The brown-haired dwarf immediately moved to the side, Brom and Fitmigar the last to pass us by.

"Everything OK?" Brom called, and I nodded.

"All good, buddy. Just leaving a present."

"Hah! Nice! Let me know how it goes in a bit."

"Will do," I returned as they ventured down the main tunnel.

"How are you doing?" I asked Bernolir. I wanted his help, that much was true, but it didn't mean I couldn't check in on him first.

"Bit better," he admitted. "Distraction definitely helps with guilt. With grief."

"Distraction I can definitely help with."

He waited on me to continue.

"Can I ask a question. One that relates to your spell?"

"Am an open book," he replied.

I smiled. I'd seen enough books to last me a year lately. "Does your ability allow you to know the structural integrity of something?"

"Assume you're referring to the tunnels?"

I nodded. "I am."

He considered the tunnel before us. The one that would lead back to the lake. His body tensed as he pulled forth his mana, his grey eyes glazing over slightly as he tilted his head, first one way, then the other.

"How big a section do we want to bring down?"

"Enough to slow them down sufficiently without bringing down the main tunnel, too." I didn't really fancy being trapped underground should we need to head back for any reason.

"Can pull down a fifteen-foot-thick section," he started, rubbing his beard, "but any more would seriously risk integrity of entire section."

"Whereabouts is best?" I asked.

"Thirty-two feet in."

"OK. Let's do it then."

We left Hestia and Mahtava at the point where the tunnels joined and headed down the smaller one. Bernolir counted out his paces as he went. Once he was satisfied, his eyes glazed over again, and I stepped back to make sure he could focus on what he needed to do.

"Right. Good." He turned to me. "Need to back up to the main tunnel. Will do from there. Keep us both safe."

I backed up the tunnel, keeping watch the entire time should we be interrupted, but all was silent.

"When you're ready, Bernolir."

The tunnel floor vibrated when he pulled on his core, his eyes glowing bright grey as his mana suffused his body.

Lifting a solitary hand, he called forth [Rock Fall] for the first time since the battle at the fort. With a huge crash, the roof of the smaller tunnel collapsed, blocking off anyone hoping to join back up with our current position.

Of course, those multi-wielding dark elves and humans might have a way to reverse the damage, but it would at least slow them for a while. Fixing a collapse would be harder than making one.

"Good job." I patted Bernolir on the back.

"Glad could help," he replied and pulled himself back up onto Mahtava's back.

It would take time for the Bernolir we knew to return to us, but I was confident he was still in there somewhere. He just needed easing out. Hopefully, using his skills helped with his confidence.

Rather than rush to catch up to the others, I fell in alongside Bernolir. We rode in companionable silence for the next hour until we caught up with the others. They were setting up a perimeter in the tunnel, guards at either side, allowing the others to rest and eat.

"I'll take over here for a bit," I told Helstrom as we reached the group, relieving him of his sentry duties. "You've done enough already."

The dwarf spun around to join the others, hand already pulling out a few pieces of bread. I hoped he hadn't snuck along any ale to wash it down.

Bernolir followed behind, his back seemingly a little straighter, his shoulders back. Helping out back there might have been just what he needed.

I passed the next hour at Hestia's side, absently running a hand through her feathers, rubbing her neck while we watched for any sign of trouble. I wasn't expecting our enemy to reach us just yet, but we couldn't know what other creatures lurked in these tunnels.

"Your turn to eat, Cap!"

I turned to see Mallen, the half-elf looking pretty content. "Thanks, man," I said. "How are things going? Saw you chatting with Ella quite a lot."

"Good, thanks. She's helping me to see that I could potentially have a close friendship with an elf. Starting to feel like the sister I never had."

The last part had filled me with relief, and I wasn't sure why. Actually, that wasn't true. I was sure why. I was jealous. I felt the beginnings of a connection with the shapeshifting elf, and I hoped, maybe, that I'd get the chance to explore it further someday.

"That's good," I told Mallen. "I'm glad to see you smiling."

Relieved of my post, I joined the others. Sienna and Elandra sat a little away from the others and beckoned me over.

I dropped down between them, kissing Sienna, then Elandra, and pulled them in for a hug. "I've missed you both," I told them, feeling like we'd been apart most of the day.

"We've missed you, too," Sienna said, running a hand down my cheek.

"All of you," Elandra added, discreetly feeling my cock through my pants and giving a little squeeze. After the way she'd been forced to drain her mana to kill the eel, I was amazed Elandra could even think like that right now.

"Not sure everyone would appreciate that here," I said, laughing, but I didn't move her hand.

"What's it going to be like when you have three of us to satisfy?" Elandra asked, and my mouth dropped open.

"Three?"

"It won't be just us forever," Sienna added, joining in. "If you want to get more powerful, you'll need to keep adding other magics. Other girls."

Elandra looked shocked. "He's not a power-hungry manwhore, Sienna. Our Jadyn only wants girls he feels for."

"Why not? I wouldn't blame him. Mmm, it kinda makes me hot to think I'm only used for power."

Elandra gasped in mock shock and turned to me. "Jadyn? Would you do that?"

I shook my head. What was going on? They weren't bickering, but they certainly had opposing views on how we might add to this harem of ours.

"I couldn't do that," I explained to Sienna. "You say you feel a connection with me, right?"

She nodded, her raven-black hair shaking free.

"Well, how fair would it be for me to force those feelings onto someone if I didn't truly care about them?"

"You're too good, Jadyn. Others wouldn't think twice."

"I'm not them." I squeezed her thigh in what I hoped she realized was an affectionate manner and not just lustfully.

She pressed her thigh against my touch.

"Got your eye on anyone?" Elandra asked, lifting her eyebrows in that way that Brom did so often, just slower, reflecting her tired state.

"Anyone tall, blonde, sexy as hells... elvish?" Sienna added, and both girls giggled.

"Maybe..." I started, looking around to make sure we were out of earshot of the others.

"We'd like that," Elandra said, and I realized they'd already been talking about it.

"Guess we'll see what happens," I said, leaning back against the tunnel and closing my eyes, ignoring any attempts on the girls part to grill me further.

# Chapter Nine

"Jadyn."

A foot nudged my side gently.

I forced my eyes open and saw Sars loom above me. "Yeah?"

"It is time to move."

"How long was I asleep?" I rubbed the sleep from my eyes and sat up. Sienna and Elandra were both already up and ready to move.

"Just a couple of hours. Thought you might want to get moving."

Sars was right. I did. It must have been the small hours of the morning above ground. We'd cut off the enemy by taking a shortcut across the lake and needed to use that advantage to get to the key first and then set up an ambush to dish out some bloody punishment.

"How far to the settlement?" I asked, still getting my senses.

"A few hours. Best guess four, maybe five."

"No time to waste then," I noted, forcing myself to my feet and wobbling over to Hestia. I pulled some meat from my bag and passed it across, wishing I'd thought to do it before I rested. "Sorry, girl, that shouldn't have happened."

Hestia nudged me and chirped, wrapping a wing around me and pulling me in. Apology accepted, it seemed.

Once we were all mounted and ready, Rammy and Helstrom led the way once again. Today they moved with lances out, mana gently easing out of their cores, preparing them for any potential ambush.

It paid to be prepared.

The tunnel sloped downward again at a much steeper angle than before. I noticed a steady thin rivulet of water flowing down, and I marveled again at how surefooted the griffins were on wet stone.

As we traveled, we came across an increasing number of small creatures. Toads, frogs, and more than one variety of crab appeared from small offshoots from the main tunnel that we still had to check out as we passed. There was nothing substantial enough in number to slow us down or cause us undue worry until a few snakes appeared.

I was cycling through my spells, once again mulling over potential new merged multi-branch spells I could create, when Rammy called out to alert us to their presence. Our whole column paused as a group of six-foot-long snakes slithered their way toward us. I pondered using a spell to take them out, perhaps roasting them all alive in a large [Fire Wall*], but there were other simpler options available to us.

One of the benefits of being griffin riders was that griffins were fairly badass. Rammy and Helstrom never even needed to use a single spell or weapon. Their mounts tore the snakes into pieces and snacked on their flesh.

It was around this time that I also noticed the thin rivulet of water at our feet had become more pronounced, almost a full-on stream now running down the center of the tunnel. It still wasn't clear where it was all coming from, but I thought I had a handle on where it would all ultimately end up.

I imagined an underwater settlement being the sight that greeted us at the end of this level, but that wasn't what we found at all.

It was Rammy's voice that alerted the rest of us to the upcoming underground city. I nudged Hestia to pick up speed and join the redhead and his dwarven partner at the front. As I passed Sars, he pulled out on Ralartis and joined us.

My mouth dropped open as the tunnel opened up, and I took in the sight of the first-level city.

A city of ruins.

The city must've been a couple of thousand yards across. The cave around it was truly titanic, big enough to feel like we were outdoors at night and not hundreds, possibly thousands, of feet underground.

The ruins were dark, likely black granite or some such material. Long, expansive stone walkways connected them, barely above the water level. Vines snaked up the sides, twisting tightly around the structures as though to stop them from crumbling into the water below.

Lower sections of the buildings were submerged under semi-clear water that afforded us a view of around eight to ten feet below the surface. Gauging the layout and size of this cave, I had no doubt that sections went much, much deeper. I found myself hoping that the key, wherever it was, was somewhere above the surface.

Yeah, Jadyn, and how likely is that...

All manner of waterborne creatures swam below the surface, from turtles and fish to what appeared to be eels, some over twelve feet in length. I hoped that was all that resided there, and none of the eels resembled the lake-dwelling murder eel we'd killed earlier.

"If there are any fuckin' sea drakes in there I'm going home." I didn't need to turn to know that Brom had joined us.

"You and me both," Rammy added.

Sienna moved alongside us on Dawnquill. "Who do you think used to live here?"

I glanced at Sars. This was one for my learned friend.

The water mage shifted awkwardly, his left arm swinging free as he retrieved his notebook. He flicked through the pages for a while, humming as he did so.

"Honestly? I have nothing. Hopefully, exploring will provide an answer."

At least the ceiling was high enough to let us fly around the city. Most of the smaller buildings were topped by narrow spires, but we could land on the larger roofs.

A luminous golden sparkle lit the ceiling and reflected in the water below, which I put down to the likely presence of microorganisms that called this huge underground cave system their home.

"So, where be the key?" Helstrom asked, scanning the city before us.

I turned to Sars, hoping he'd have the answer or, at least, an idea about where we could start.

"Based on the map in the chamber, best I can tell, it is most likely in one of the four largest towers. That is about all I have as they are the only ones depicted."

"Do we even know what it looks like?" Rammy asked.

Sars shook his head. "No, but it would have to stand out from the ordinary. The images of the key on each level have a golden outline, so I figure maybe look for a golden key? If that does not work, we will have to get together and try something else."

"That works," I agreed, looking around at the others. "So, we divide into four groups, fly to each of the buildings, and then search them for any sign of this key."

For a moment, I thought I might need to divide the squad up, but I need not have worried.

Brom turned to Fitmigar and Mallen. "Shall we take the one farthest away?"

The pair both nodded in acceptance and waited for Brom to mount Shadowtail before edging toward the city.

"Couple of hours should suffice. Leave your griffins on the roofs, and have one of them screech if you discover anything," I explained.

They nodded.

"Oh, and stay safe. No stupid risks."

Brom winked and pushed his knee into Shadowtail's side. The griffin raced forward and took to the air. Fitmigar and Mallen swiftly followed.

We watched as they flew across the huge cavern before landing on the farthest building from our current position. Satisfied they had alighted without issue, I nodded to Syl, Charn, and Bernolir. "Ready?"

"Yes, sir," Syl replied.

I gestured for them to head right, taking the shortest of the four stone buildings. Charn began to sing, low at first, but it would reach us all within the city, boosting our mana levels as we searched.

Once they'd taken to the skies, heading across the giant underground city, I turned to my side.

"Sars, if you take Rammy and Helstrom and check out the closest tower, I'll head over to the left and check out the tallest structure with Sienna, Elandra, and Ella."

The tallest structure was also the only one of the four with a spire on the top, making our task that much more difficult. I had no doubt that the griffins could manage such a landing, but we would need to be careful dismounting. I didn't really fancy falling eighty feet into the waters below.

It made more sense, in our case, for our griffins to fly us across, drop us on the building, and then fly back to this point. That way they could watch over the entrance to the city should our pursuers arrive while we were indisposed. One screech from Hestia would immediately alert the others to any impending danger.

Sars nodded and pushed Ralartis forward, the light-brown griffin soon pushing into the air and leading Rammy and Helstrom out over the water.

Time for us to begin our search. "We good?"

Sienna nodded. "Ready when you are, Jadyn."

"Okay. We land on the spire, carefully dismount, and send our griffins back to guard the entrance."

The girls readily agreed, and we pushed off into the air, Hestia taking the lead.

As we flew toward the largest tower, I marveled at Hestia's reflection, the huge griffin's wingspan reminding me again of the power of my bonded partner, her talons' image sparkling in the water below.

I looked back up as Hestia's wings spread, and she glided onto the spire that crested the tower, her talons finding purchase long enough for me to slide from her back, careful to take my scimitars with me. There was no telling what dangers resided within the tower or below the surface.

The bottom of the spire had a stone lip that meant I could slowly slide down without the risk of disappearing over the edge. Heights I was okay with. Falling not so much.

I paused as my feet pushed against the lip, waiting on the girls to join me. As a pair of feet appeared next to mine, accompanied by a soft sigh, I noticed Elandra still looking weary. I couldn't afford to forget that she had single-handedly killed the murder eel. I made a note to keep a close eye on her. Particularly if we ran into danger. Her mana levels would still be low.

Sienna slid down to my left. "How do we get inside?"

"There's a door around here," Ella said, walking effortlessly around the spire.

"That's—"

Ella cut me off. "But it's locked from the inside."

"We could smash it open."

I raised an eyebrow at Elandra and received a tired smile in return as we shuffled around the side of the spire to view Ella and the door in question.

"Any other options?" I asked, scanning the dark wooden door that snugly fit into the stone-tiled spire. There was no lock visible, so it was either magic or a simple latch on the other side.

"One, yes." Ella didn't elaborate, instead transforming into a mouse before my eyes. I wasn't entirely sure of the etiquette involved, but I averted my gaze for a moment.

A soft squeak sounded, and then Ella disappeared under the door. Barely a moment passed before the sound of a latch being lifted on the other side of the door greeted us, and then the door swung up and open, the elf, as perfectly formed as ever, greeting us with a smile.

"That's a handy skill to have," Elandra commented from my side, lifting an eyebrow as she looked to the elf and then back at me.

Seriously? Had Brom been teaching her that look?

I smiled, winked, and then headed inside, Elandra and Sienna following behind.

As I expected, the inside of the tower was dark, with only narrow windows allowing any of the subtle cavern glow to reach inside. A dark staircase wound down before us, and I paused to scan the walls.

"Looking for this?"

Ella was pointing at a small sconce on the wall.

I stifled a laugh. "I was, yes. Not too keen on falling inside the tower, either."

I tossed a [Fireball] onto the small metal fitting, and light immediately grew to a decent level, casting light over the spiraling steps that would take us down the levels.

I slid Orcgrinder from its sheath, prepared to cast a defensive spell if needed, and took the lead, descending into the tower on the lookout for a golden key that could be just about anywhere.

Sienna walked behind me, Ella and Elandra conversing in a low tone behind her, out of my earshot.

"You think we'll find it in time?" Sienna asked.

"We have a lead on them. If it's just a case of searching, I'd rather be first here than second."

"I can't believe there's no clue, no sign to help search."

That had struck me as odd, too. It was like searching blind. "Maybe we've missed something?"

"You think?"

"We'll find out soon enough, I guess."

I paused at that point, a door appearing on my left for the first time in our descent. Our first room to search.

I lifted the dark metal latch on the outside of the wooden door and pushed it inwards, a low groan coming from the hinge as it opened. Stepping inside, scimitar raised, I found myself in an office of sorts.

I immediately noticed how despite its unique appearance, everything was where I would expect it to be located. I hadn't been in a room where all the furniture was made of dark stone before, but it looked orderly.

A desk was in the left-hand corner, a chair of sorts pushed up behind it, a tall shelving unit on the opposite wall. A low table had been placed in the center of the room, four more stone seats surrounding it. This could have been Dean Hallow's office in another world.

One fact stood it apart. The room was barren. No books, no color, no soft furnishings. No sign of life.

Sienna appeared at my side. "Should be an easy search, at least."

"Seems that way." It should have been relief I felt, but the room seemed so... grim.

"If you and Sienna want to keep going down, Elandra and I will search this one if you like."

I smiled at Ella. "Sure. Just shout if you find anything."

The elf nodded, took Elandra's hand, and led her into the room as we continued our descent without them.

The next room was only a couple dozen steps below, the room almost identical in its layout and design. Once again I was struck by how empty it was.

We were halfway through our search of the room when Ella and Elandra passed the doorway, heading for the next room below. I barely looked up to acknowledge their passing before diving back into our search, peering behind furniture and running my hand over shelves devoid of clutter.

We continued searching in this manner for the hour that followed until we reached the first room with anything different of note.

A soft chuckle passed Sienna's lips. "Well, you did say it'd likely be underwater."

I shook my head, my feet already soaked by the half foot of water that coated the floor. "Let's just search this room and then work out how best to continue."

Ella and Elandra soon joined us, helping to clear the room before we considered how best to approach the next section.

Satisfied no golden key lay hidden in the room, we moved back out to the staircase, the steps below now all under the water level. With no method of holding my breath underwater for more than a couple of minutes at best, I debated asking Ella if she could shapeshift into something waterborne.

I wasn't about to put her in danger, though. Not without checking it out myself first. I was the leader here; I'd lead.

I placed my scimitars down, removed my upper armor and shirt, eased my boots off, and prepared to head lower.

"That's distracting," Elandra said, eyeing my chest, a grin brightening her tired face.

"My apologies, ladies," I replied with a chuckle, happy to see Ella's gaze as much locked on my body as the others. "Now, I'm just going to swim down a few levels and see what I can discover. I'll report back within a couple of minutes."

Sienna stepped closer and kissed my cheek. "Be safe."

I smiled. "I'll try."

Elandra huffed, but I could tell it was mostly in jest, despite the nerves. "You'd better do more than just try. Don't make me come after you, Jadyn!"

"Understood," I told her before taking a deep breath, dropping under the water, and swimming down the spiraling staircase, keeping an eye out for anything of note. None of the larger creatures from outside the tower had breached the inside. Something I was increasingly glad about.

The first three levels consisted of much of the same, and I forced the doors open to see rooms devoid of clutter or anything of note. I swam through each, giving a cursory glance behind fittings and on upper shelves.

Everything changed when I pushed open the fourth door, a golden glow coming from the room at the same time as my lungs began to strain for air, my chest constricting, pain blossoming within my body.

Annoyed that I couldn't stay longer, I pushed myself back toward the others, circling the stairway as I went.

"Well?" Elandra's voice greeted me as I broke the surface.

"I think... I might.... have... found it," I panted, straining to refill my lungs.

"Might?"

"Fourth level down.... pushed the door open... saw a golden glow."

"Any dangers?" Ella asked.

I shook my head. "Nothing. Other than a distinct lack of air."

"Well, that's not a problem," the elf replied as I pulled myself out of the water, "I'll grab it."

My mouth dropped open in surprise as she jumped into the air, transforming into an octopus that started a deep brown color before shifting into a dark blue that better blended with the tower water.

Her legs, all eight of them, forcefully pushed away, and she raced down below the surface, soon out of sight.

Sienna whistled beside me. "Well... that was impressive."

"Wasn't it just," Elandra agreed.

I nodded. Ella was impressing more and more. Coming into our squad she could have been nervous, quiet, reserved, but she was far from it. Quick to assist. Easy to be around. It was even more impressive that she could shift into a sea creature having been raised in the forest.

The surface of the water soon broke, and Ella transformed as she lifted herself from the water, her shirt sticking to her in all the places I tried not to stare at.

"How'd it go?" I asked.

Ella looked a little sheepish. "I went where you said. Fourth level down. But I couldn't see any golden glow. I looked around the room, but... nothing."

That didn't make any sense.

"You sure it was the fourth level?"

The elf nodded. "I even went as far as the sixth, checking them all over, but no golden glow. No sign at all."

I was about to head back down again to check I hadn't imagined it when a splash alerted me to Sienna's retreating form disappearing under the water.

Hopefully, Sienna could confirm I wasn't losing my mind.

When the raven-haired beauty pulled herself out of the water a couple of minutes later, shaking her head, I sighed, rubbing my hands over my face. "This makes no sense."

"You want me to look?" Elandra asked.

I couldn't let her go. Not with how weary and mana-dry she looked. "It's okay. I'm going to go again."

Not waiting in case she pushed back, I inhaled deeply and dropped back into the water. This time, I headed straight down to the fourth level below the surface, once again finding a golden glow illuminating the room.

Having nothing delaying my descent, I found I had enough air to search the room, homing in on the glow that seemed to resonate from below the table in the center of the room. I attempted to push the table to the side, but I found it unwilling to budge. Typical.

Not one to be denied, I forced a [Wind Burst] against the obstacle, and it slid a small distance across the floor, partially uncovering a small trapdoor beneath. I repeated the spell, fully uncovering the door beneath. With my lungs starting to ache, I pulled on the door, finding it locked.

Shaking my head and clearing my thoughts, I remembered our recent class on magic uses and forced [Ice Blast] into the lock, shattering both the lock and half the door in the process. Small splinters of wood drifted through the water in front of my face. Pushing a hand out, I cleared them away, my lungs aching as I moved.

A smile formed on my face as I then dropped my hand into the uncovered space and clasped a golden key. Gripping it tightly in my hand, tight enough to pinch my skin, I kicked back for the surface, the golden glow lighting my way as I sought the air above.

I panted as I broke the surface, inhaling as deeply as I could, my lungs screaming for air.

Arms grabbed mine, and I felt myself pulled from the water and onto my back. I opened my eyes to see Sienna and Ella peering down at me, concern on their faces.

"Well, how is the idiot?" Elandra called from nearby, and I wheezed a laugh.

"I'm... good..." I forced, feeling anything but.

I took a moment to get my breath back, but then the girls couldn't wait any longer. Sienna leaned closer. "Well?"

"Can't you tell?" I asked as the golden glow seeped between my fingers and reflected off her flawless skin.

"How would I know?" she asked, eyes narrowed in confusion.

"You're practically golden."

Ella peered into my eyes. "Jadyn, you didn't happen to bang your head at all, did you?"

"What? No!" *What is going on?*

I pushed myself up to a sitting position and opened my fist, revealing a golden metal key. I hadn't had the chance to examine it under the water, so only now could I gasp in awe at its ornate design.

The key was around four inches in length from the bow to the tip. The bit was reinforced, a series of notches and grooves confirming it would be destined for a unique lock. The shaft then led up to a collar, my mouth dropping open as I noticed the griffin design of the bow beyond.

However, that wasn't what stood out the most. The key still glowed.

"Nice griffin design on the key," Sienna said.

"What happened to the glow you spoke of?" Ella asked, peering closer.

"You can't see it?"

Ella shook her head. "It's still glowing for you?"

"It is. I can't believe you can't see it."

The elf shrugged. "Must be something special about you that means it shows for you."

Elandra spoke up again. "I'm just glad it does. We could have been here for days."

She was right. If I hadn't noticed the glow coming from under the table, who knows how long it would have taken us.

Feeling fully rested, or at least sufficiently full of breath, I pushed myself to my feet and pulled my shirt and armor back on, choosing to only briefly acknowledge Elandra's sigh as I did so.

"We best alert the others," I said, reattaching my scimitars.

The walk back to the top of the tower was not a short one, and my exertion still left me a little winded, but I pushed on regardless.

Pushing open the door to the top of the tower, my eyes widened as I stepped out and looked upon complete chaos.

# Chapter Ten

My gaze swept the cave before me, rapidly flicking left and right, counting nine griffins and their riders sweeping across the expanse, diving and twisting to avoid huge sections of the roof as they fell, crashing to the waters below.

What the hells?

The taller buildings were all swaying, section after section crumbling or coming loose and falling free. The far tower I'd sent Brom, Fitmigar, and Mallen to explore staggered, the entire mid-section collapsing, sending the top crashing into the churning waters below, waves rolling across the surface.

We needed our griffins.

Was this the key's doing? Were we under attack?

Another tower teetered and swayed, rocks falling free before the entire structure fell, taking out a whole series of the low, stone walkways below as it hit the water.

I lifted my hand to my mouth, preparing to whistle for Hestia when I noticed our griffins were already airborne, winging their way toward our precarious position. This tower could go any second.

The stone beneath us groaned. They're not going to make it in time.

"Ella, transform. Fly!" I shouted amid the noise.

The blonde elf shook her head, eyes wide. "I'm not leaving you all."

"Go!" I repeated. "Before it's too late. We need to keep the key safe."

Ella reluctantly nodded, transforming into a falcon and grasping the key in her talons before pushing into the air, sparing a look over her shoulder as she flew away.

Elandra grasped my arm, fingers digging in weakly. "Fuck!"

I pressed my lips against her forehead, kissing her and then pulling back. "We're going to be OK. Just a little more time..."

The tower swayed again, a section below falling free as it tilted drastically and began to fall.

I grabbed both girls by the arm and shouted, "Hold on!" as I cast [Wind Boost], powering us away from the falling tower and toward our approaching griffins.

For a brief moment I thought we weren't going to make it, but then Hestia, Dawnquill, and Veo powered closer before tucking their wings and surging under us, lifting us away from the churning waters below not a moment too soon.

I held tight with my knees as Hestia whirled away from the destruction, lifting us higher into the cave, mindful of the glowing sections of the ceiling that were still falling free.

We need to get out of here.

I scanned the cave, trying to locate the entrance again. I didn't want to head back the way we came, but there was likely no choice. That thought was soon thrown free, the entrance now nothing more than a pile of rubble, blocking any chance of us escaping that way.

There must be somewhere else…

I scanned the churning waters below, hoping against all hope that our chance of escape didn't lie beneath the surface.

Seeing nothing, I pushed Hestia left, circling the huge cavern in the ever-decreasing light as section after section of building or ceiling dropped into the depths below. As more and more stone hit the surface, the water level rose, giving us less space to maneuver through the air.

Desperation was setting in as a section of the ceiling came free, almost clipping Dawnquill in the process, only a flailing [Wind Burst] from Sienna keeping her safe.

A glint of gold caught my eye, and at first, I assumed it to be Ella carrying the key, but it was high in the walls of the cave, past the farthest tower that Brom, Fitmigar, and Mallen had searched. A tower that now resided under the surface.

I nudged Hestia with my knee, sending her up and across the huge expanse, weaving up and around the falling rock. As we got closer, I realized the golden glow was coming from a tunnel entrance hidden high in the wall.

A way out.

I turned Hestia in the air, whistling loudly and throwing out handsigns to any riders close enough to witness. Word spread through the chaos as the squad passed the message along, griffin after griffin soon powering past my position and into the tunnel beyond as Hestia hovered in place, allowing me to count off the riders as they sped by.

Only when I was satisfied that everyone was safely out of the cave did I tap Hestia on the side of the neck. She immediately followed the others, taking us into the golden light of the newly discovered tunnel. I hoped this was the haven we needed.

We immediately slowed and dropped into a walk, Hestia tucking her wings in tightly as we padded along, following the others deeper into the tunnel. I breathed a long, deep sigh of relief and leaned forward, running my hand through Hestia's feathers.

"Good job, girl," I whispered.

Everyone was crowded around ahead of us where the tunnel had widened out into a chamber. The space was a good thirty yards across and over twice that in depth, so the griffins were afforded the space to be able to move around and catch their breath. The ceiling was low enough that we couldn't fly in here, but Hestia wouldn't have to duck down either.

The walls of the chamber were the same dark stone as the cave and the tunnels before, but the golden glow provided a much-needed boost to the visibility within, reflecting off the stone.

I noted several of the squad were sporting minor injuries, presumably from falling debris, Helstrom the most serious-looking with a small stream of blood running down the left-hand side of his face.

I needed to check to make sure the others were all doing okay.

I was stopped in my tracks as a rumbling, grinding noise turned me around. A huge stone disc eased across the entranceway, running across metal tracks that I'd missed on entry and blocking all light from the collapsing cave system beyond.

Brom groaned from somewhere up ahead. "Fuckin' great."

"What's the problem?" I called back. "Just keep going toward the golden light."

"What? It's fuckin' pitch-black, man."

What was with this golden light? If none of them could see it, I'd need to sort something out.

Then again... "Brom, brother, you've got a spell called [Night Vision]. You might want to use it."

The stocky shadow mage's laughter echoed off the walls. "Ha. Good idea."

Satisfied my stocky friend could now see me, I gestured for him to check the right-hand side of the chamber while I slid from Hestia's back and skirted around the left, looking for a way to light up the space.

With nothing immediately apparent, I considered taking one of the two archways at the back of the chamber to further explore, but a shout from Brom stopped me in my tracks.

"Got something!"

I jogged over, evading the squad who still sat in darkness, the more alert amongst them tracking my footsteps as I passed. It didn't escape my attention that Helstrom was drinking from something that looked suspiciously like a hip flask.

"What've you got?" I asked, reaching the shadow mage's side.

"There's a narrow ledge of sorts, up high." He gestured toward the cavern's ceiling. "Thought it might be worth checking out?"

"Good spot." I'd need to be higher up to gain access. I gestured back toward Hestia, but she remained motionless, not picking up my movement. I assumed she must also be struggling to see.

I whistled softly instead, and Hestia's head immediately turned to the sound. With careful precision, she padded across the cavern floor, evading the other griffins and riders alike until she reached my side. She lowered her head and nuzzled my neck.

I placed a hand on her right flank, and she lowered herself to the ground, allowing me to effortlessly pull myself up onto her back, tucking my knees in against her side.

A ruffle of the feathers on her neck was all it took for her to rise, and I found myself now only a few short feet from the ledge. I'd still need to stand on Hestia's back and jump if I was going to reach it.

As though sensing my plan, Hestia tensed her body, and I pushed myself to my feet, wobbling slightly before catching my balance. Bending my knees, I pushed off, fingers outstretched, flying up and grasping the edge of the ledge. My arms strained as I pulled myself up to inspect the feature.

I was expecting a flat ledge or lip. A decorative feature, nothing more. Instead, I found a small trough, my fingers grasping the edge. An odorless liquid sat in the channel, no more than a couple of inches deep.

"Well, what is it?" Brom called up.

"It's a trough. Contains a liquid of sorts."

Sars rose to his feet in the center of the chamber and blindly made his way across, stumbling more than once over trailing limbs. "That could be our means of lighting up this space."

"And if it's not?" I called back, arms straining as I tried to keep myself at face-level with the ledge.

"Then I guess it will not light up."

If it was possible to shrug while hanging almost twenty feet up in the air I would have done so. Instead, I sighed, rolled my eyes, and released my right hand from the ledge. Hanging one-handed, fingers immediately starting to slip, I formed a [Fireball] and tossed it into the trough as I let go, falling to the ground below, bending my knees as I landed.

A whoosh sounded, and flame immediately spread around the top of the chamber wall, circling the room and casting us all in a flickering light. The trough must have continued out through both exits at the rear of the cavern as light burst into life there, too. The golden glow was now gone, lost in the new light we had produced.

"Whoa, that's fuckin' awesome," Brom said from my side, and I couldn't disagree.

The squad immediately burst into life, some more active than others. Sienna was already handing Helstrom a couple of health positions, so I walked across to check on his condition, scanning the others as I passed.

"How are you?" I asked the dwarven fire mage, noticing how he'd managed to stem the flow of blood.

"I'll be fine, Jadyn, lad. Just took a bit of a bang."

"You sure?"

"Aye. 'Tis but a scratch."

I nodded and moved on. Minutes ago, we'd been dashing through the cave, trying to just stay alive, and now we were trapped here. I needed to explore, but I also needed to look at the golden key in more detail.

Satisfied Ella had the key still safely tucked away, I chose to check out our current predicament, Sars coming across to join me.

I looked at the two exits. "Left or right?"

Sars shrugged. "Left?"

"Okay. Left it is." I headed through the large archway that led into the space beyond, immediately finding myself in a relatively short tunnel with three openings down the left-hand side of the stone corridor, the first two smaller than the third.

Poking my head through the first opening, I discovered what appeared to be sleeping quarters. So, this must be a safe area of sorts upon completion of the first level. The predominance of stone meant it didn't appear the most luxurious of settings, but I was sure the squad would accept anything if it meant they got the chance to rest.

While I'd been perusing the first opening, Sars had already moved onto the second. "It appears to be a series of bathing areas."

"Oh, right." I moved alongside him and peered in, the flaming light around the top of the room reflecting back in the waters of a circular pool easily large enough for five or six of us. Steam rose from the water, heat buffeted my face, and I found myself tempted to dive right in. Another archway was placed beyond the pool, and I could easily make out a second, then a third pool in the distance.

I smiled, and for a moment, the weight of our current situation seemed to ease slightly. "This is amazing."

"It will certainly help with morale."

I hadn't noticed it being all that low, but it certainly couldn't do any harm. "What do we think for the third area?"

Sars was already walking toward the opening. "Based on this griffin carving"—he peered through the enlarged opening—"and this huge expanse beyond, I do not think you need to worry."

I joined my friend's side, and my mouth dropped open. A huge cavern lay before us, the flat, moss and fern-covered ground perfect for our griffins to roam and rest. As with the cave before, a natural green glow came from the ceiling, accompanied by the light of the burning trough that circled the huge area. Small creatures skittered across the ground, and I knew we wouldn't need to worry about our bonded griffins' sustenance.

"That's our rest sorted. Makes me wonder what the second arch leads to."

Sars nodded, turning on the spot and immediately heading back toward the main chamber.

Before we headed through the right-hand arch, I called out to Sienna.

She walked over, a gentle sway to her hips as she approached. "Anything of note?"

"Spaces to rest, bathe, and for the griffins to roam."

"Shall I lead everyone through?"

I paused, thinking about it. What was to say that the stone disc wouldn't just roll right back any minute. This area felt safe, but we still needed to be on our guard. "Ask Rammy and Syl to watch over this central chamber, and then the rest of you can head on through. We'll join you shortly."

Sienna leaned forward and brushed a kiss across my cheek. "On it. Stay safe, okay?"

"Will do."

With Sienna departing to pass the news on to the others, I followed Sars through the right-hand arch, and we immediately found ourselves before two huge stone doors, several carvings prominent on each.

Sars pulled his notebook out and immediately flipped to his desired section.

"What can you tell me?" I asked as he took a seat on the ground, resting the notepad on his thigh.

"Well, Jadyn, the arrows seem rather self-explanatory. This door on the left leads up. Presumably back to the surface."

"I guess a way for us to exit after the first level if we wish to."

"That seems likely. The second leads down."

"The second level?"

"Based on the fire symbol next to it, I think that is a pretty safe bet."

"And we get them open how?" I rubbed both hands over my face, my eyes tired. I'd used a lot of mana today, and I could do with a rest. But not until I knew what we faced.

"The door to the surface opens with a simple sequence spell again: fire, wind, then water."

"OK. So, we could open that now. Head back to the academy with the key." I'd need to check to see if anyone wanted to do just that. I knew they wouldn't, but I felt the need to at least offer.

Sars nodded. "Quite. The second door, however, shows as opening after a certain amount of time has passed." He pointed to an image vaguely reminiscent of the hourglasses several of the academy teachers used.

"How long?" I asked as a click sounded, followed by the sound of something tumbling into place behind the stone door.

Sars flipped a page in his notebook, running a finger over earlier notes that I assumed related to understanding time. "Best guess? Eight hours? Could be slightly more. Could be slightly less."

Eight hours was enough time to eat and catch up on some much-needed rest. My mind then slipped to thoughts of Sienna and Elandra. Maybe something else, too...

"You okay to remain here for the first two hours?" I asked. "We'll swap out every two hours. Two in the main chamber and one in here. Just in case the door opens sooner."

Sars didn't even look up from his notes as he responded. "Sure, Jadyn."

I passed on the details to Rammy and Syl in the main chamber, both happy to take the first watch, and then I headed to join the others. The griffins were all absent, so I relaxed, knowing they were freely roaming the third room.

Several of the squad had already gone through to clean up. The tunnels were pretty damp, and a thin layer of grime had found its way to most after the collapse of the cave and the buildings below.

Sienna had already cleaned up and returned, and I held back a sigh of disappointment. It would have been nice to join her. My raven-haired wind mage must have read my mind because she came over to whisper in my ear.

"Elandra needs you more than I do right now."

Sienna tilted her head, and I noticed Elandra lying on a stone bench, eyes closed, the signs of mana depletion pronounced in her paler-looking skin.

"She did [Dehydrate] that murder eel alone. No wonder she's so tired." I started to remove my armor, placing it down beside where Sienna had placed her own and Elandra's.

"If only we knew of a way to boost her back to safe levels..."

"You sure she could stay awake long enough?" I asked, lifting a single eyebrow in doubt.

"You bet your perfect ass I could!" came from across the room, and I laughed, seeing Elandra sat up, eyes wide, leaning forward, her breasts threatening to tumble free before my eyes.

"I think the others might object to watching." I shook my head, stifling a laugh.

Sienna giggled softly. "Actually, Jadyn, I've already explored the pools. There are a couple of private ones after the first three. Doors you can latch and everything.

"Yeah!" Elandra pushed herself to her feet.

A broad grin broke out across my face, and I took my beautiful water mage by the hand and led her out of the room, winking at Sienna as we passed.

# Chapter Eleven

I led the Elandra past the first of the pools. Brom and Fitmigar were already splashing around and laughing. My friend paused long enough to wiggle his eyebrows at me before going back to frolicking with his dwarven partner.

Bernolir and Helstrom were relaxing in the second pool, and I nodded in passing, glad to see that Helstrom wasn't alone so soon after a head injury.

The third pool was empty, and of the two private pools beyond, one was vacant, the other in use.

As Elandra pulled me into the vacant one, the door to the other opened, and Ella slipped out, blonde hair dripping wet, shirt held against her body, glued to her nubile figure, covering the best bits but baring a stunning amount of slender nakedness.

Damn...

She smiled shyly as we passed, a faint blush appearing on her porcelain cheeks.

Elandra called, "You'll have to join us soon, Ella!" and the elf mumbled something too low for me to make out in response, a grin teasing the corners of her mouth as she turned away and headed out, a blush appearing on her cheeks.

I pulled the door closed behind us, and I immediately felt Elandra's hands hungrily pulling at my shirt, yanking it free over my head. Immediately, her hands flew to my waist, fingers pulling at my waistband.

Where was all this energy before?

I pushed the thought away and pulled Elandra close, hungrily kissing her, forcing my tongue beyond her full lips. Her fingers slid up and around and dug into my back, threatening to tear my skin. I growled and pulled her tighter.

She moaned against me. "Fuck yeah, Jadyn."

My fingers flew to her shirt, and I slid the top buttons apart before lifting it over her head, her breasts falling free. Instantly, I felt her nipples harden against my chest.

She dropped her hands, slid herself out of the rest of her clothes, and stepped back, giggling, landing with a splash in the steaming waters.

Her eyes widened, and she pouted. "Well, you going to get in here and fuck me or not?"

I grinned, shoved my pants to the floor, and jumped in beside her, immediately pulling her against me, her skin soft against mine.

She kissed me hard, urgent, and I realized she didn't have the energy for much. As though confirming my thoughts, she urged, "Fuck me, Jadyn. Now."

I moved her across the pool, her hands running through my hair, her kisses deep and hungry. I pushed her up against the side of the pool, easing her legs apart, and sliding my hand down, feeling the ease with which she got ready to receive me.

I teased at her lips beneath the water, running first one finger around, then a second before sliding them in, feeling her heat contract around them. She moaned and nibbled my ear, arching her back against me as I plunged my fingers inside her.

Elandra twisted closer, nibbling at my neck as I curled my fingers, pushing against the walls of her pussy, bringing her on.

She dropped her hands beneath the water, pulling on my cock, finding it already alert and ready. "Now, Jadyn."

I smiled, slid my fingers free, and guided myself inside her. I was unable to see through the steam, but I could feel her warmth against my shaft as I pushed deep, forcefully, giving in to her urgent needs.

She bit into her bottom lip, stifling the screams of ecstasy that threatened to burst free. I continued to thrust into her, faster, harder, deeper until she couldn't contain herself any longer, and she screamed out, "Oh, fuck yeah! That's it!"

I didn't slow, powering into her, feeling every twitch, every shake as I pushed her toward release.

Her hands snaked around me again, her nails digging in, breaking the surface, and I could sense thin rivulets of blood snaking down my back as I released into her, thick jets of cum filling her completely as she sagged against me, breathless but with that fire back behind her eyes.

We stayed locked together, the water lapping against us until I felt hands on my back, softly washing away the blood.

"That felt so good," Elandra murmured. "Just what I needed."

"Me, too," I told her and meaning it. I already felt so much better than before, my mana levels flooding back toward full.

Aware that Elandra still needed to rest, we reluctantly pulled ourselves from the pool and dried off before redressing.

The pools were all empty as we passed them by, the others seemingly done or choosing to wait for later.

Maybe they were still trying to offer us a modicum of privacy.

Elandra smiled and leaned closer as we walked. "So, lover, what are you going to do now? Will you rest with us?"

"I'll join you shortly, "I promised, "I just want to sit with the griffins for a while. This mana burst stops me feeling tired enough to sleep."

"Don't be too long. You do need at least some rest, too."

"Promise. We've got the last watch, you, me, Sienna, and Ella. Actually, I need to let the others know the watch schedule. Go and get some rest, and I'll join you later."

Elandra kissed me. She looked far more alert now than before, but I think she still appreciated the chance to close her eyes for a few hours.

After filling everyone in on the watch schedule, I wandered through to the third room and took a seat on the dirt-packed ground, gazing over the expanse before me.

I'd come here to be able to think over our situation. We still had no idea why the guards were murdered, other than to allow these dark elves access to the tunnels. We had no idea who had sent them or what they were after. If we couldn't keep one alive to question, I doubted we'd ever know.

Movement across the cavern caught my eye, and I realized there was more to the griffins' actions than simple roaming. Back at the academy, if they weren't with us, the griffins were in their stables or out in the paddock. Here, alone, they were acting differently than I'd noticed before.

It was easy to forget each of the griffins had their own personality. Seeing Shadowtail playfully nudge Gren into a small body of water, I considered if we'd bonded with griffins that matched our own. Rammy's bonded griffin, Chiron, sat nearby, consuming the largest pile of animal corpses I'd ever seen and further strengthening that theory.

Hestia was around halfway across the space, close enough to nod in greeting to me when I looked across but too far for us to properly interact.

I watched as she appeared to be guiding some of the other griffins through their paces, chirping out commands as two-on-two matchups took to the air, attempting to best each other in aerial combat, talons retracted.

Hestia never took her gaze from the action, chirping agitatedly when a griffin appeared to err in their challenge.

It was easy to forget with all that we'd seen that the griffins were also adolescents, still learning, having to grow stronger in unique surroundings. I'd worried how they'd all react to being underground, but the relatively frequent chance to spread their wings had made it more comfortable than I'd imagined.

However, who could say how long that would last?

The next floor was supposedly fire-based. That likely meant increased temperatures and possibly more cramped conditions. I made a note to make sure all water containers were filled to the brim before departure. We'd have to add some of those pills Madame Summerstone had passed on to ensure it was safe to drink. You never knew.

Footsteps to my right broke my concentration, and I turned to see Bernolir approach, a serious expression on his face.

"Everything OK?"

The dwarven earth mage nodded once and dropped down next to me. "Aye, Jadyn. Actually arranged to meet someone here."

I lifted an eyebrow. "Yeah?"

"Not like that." He laughed, shaking his head. "I been struggling since the fort. As you well know."

I smiled softly but didn't interrupt.

"Figured it was way past due that I added at least one more spell to me arsenal, maybe two."

"And who better to practice with than me," came from the room's doorway, and I smiled to see Charn wandering in.

Our two single-spell mages were practicing together, looking to improve.

"I'm tired of being guarded," Charn admitted, the wind mage running a hand through his sandy hair. "Figure it's time I can better assist you all."

I understood. "You do plenty to help. Your [Ballad Boost] has already helped us beyond measure, but I can see your reasoning. And, Bernolir, without you at the fort, taking out a shaman, we might very well have lost more. But, again, I commend you for looking to improve."

Bernolir clapped me on the shoulder. " We knew you'd understand, Jadyn."

"Of course. We are all always looking at ways to grow stronger. You want me to stay and help at all?"

Charn shook his head. "We've got this. Don't worry. Today could be the day one of us adds a second spell."

"Well, good luck, both of you. Keep me abreast of your progress."

"Will do," Charn called over his shoulder, the pair already heading for a quieter corner of the chamber.

I sat there for a while longer, watching the griffins interact, appreciating their intelligence, their camaraderie, and even their wit. With time, we would become truly formidable.

---

"Jadyn."

A hand shook me awake, and my eyes flew open. I felt fully rested in what couldn't have been more than a couple of hours since I lay down.

Helstrom leaned over me. "Time for ya watch. Nothing to report."

"Thanks, Helstrom. Appreciate it." I nudged the girls at my side as the dwarf turned and headed off to get his head down.

Elandra looked fresh and well-rested as she rose beside me, her shirt creased where she'd been pressed up against me in slumber. "Wow. Now that's how I like to feel."

I lifted a finger to my lips to signify the fact we needed to be quiet, and then I slid off the bed, softly walking across the room and kneeling next to Ella.

Her blonde hair lay loose across her face, and I felt my breath catch as she exhaled, her chest falling before rising again. I could have stared for hours, but we had work to do.

I placed a hand softly on her shoulder and shook her gently. "Ella?"

"Mmm?"

"Time for our watch."

Her eyes flickered open, and a sweet smile spread across her face when she saw me next to her. "Best way to wake," she whispered, gazing into my eyes, and I couldn't fail to miss the meaning behind her words.

I stood and offered her my hand, pulling her to her feet. She leaned against me momentarily, steadying herself, and I felt the warmth of her breath against my neck. Before something started stirring out of control, I eased away.

We joined Sienna and Elandra, and the four of us headed out into the main chamber, relieving Bernolir and Mallen who had remained behind after Helstrom came to wake us. I nodded at Bernolir. He couldn't have slept at all yet.

"How come you didn't do the watch with Brom and Fitmigar?" I then asked my elven friend.

Mallen stifled a grin. "Brom asked if Charn could swap. I saw no reason why not. He made out that he wanted Charn to teach him some romantic tunes to sing to Fitmigar, but I'm sure it was more like Brom teaching Charn some new songs."

"Aye, pulled him from our practice for that." Bernolir shook his head, though he didn't appear too cross. Maybe they'd made some progress.

I shook my head, a laugh rolling free. "And we all know what kind of songs those would be."

Mallen nodded. "That's my fear."

Still smiling, I sent the pair to bed and turned to the girls. "Sienna, are you and Elandra OK here? I'd like to be around the stone door when it's due to open, and if Ella joins me, I can go over the key again."

"That works." Sienna pulled me into a kiss. Elandra repeated the goodbye, adding in a grab of my ass for good measure.

If I expected Ella to look awkward at the displays of affection before her... well, that wasn't what I got. If anything, she leaned closer, only a fraction, barely perceptible, and I found I had to stop myself from pulling her in, too.

Instead, I cleared my throat and gestured to the right-hand archway. "Got the key?"

Ella patted her pocket. "Right here, Jadyn."

"OK." I headed through the archway and took a seat in front of the pair of stone doors.

Ella dropped down next to me, and I realized this would be the longest I had spent alone with the beautiful elf since we met.

Keep it professional, Jadyn.

"How are you feeling after before?" I asked. "Did all the shapeshifting lower your mana levels much?"

"I hear you have a way to boost them if they did..."

I spurted and coughed at the same time, turning to see Ella laughing, a soft feminine giggle escaping her lips.

"Sorry. I couldn't resist."

That was the first time she'd joked in my presence. She continued to open up. It was nice.

"To answer your question, though, it was nothing a rest couldn't replenish. Birds, sea life, and small rodents don't drain me the way the jaguar does."

I nodded. "That makes sense. When do you think you'll be able to move past the jaguar?"

She shrugged. "Not any time soon. One of the drawbacks to joining the academy is the sheer amount of stuff I need to learn that takes away from the time I need to push and learn a larger form."

"That's understandable. I'm sure this latest challenge doesn't help either."

A wry smile appeared. "It's not ideal, no. But I'm still learning a lot as we go." She slid a hand into her pocket. "So, what can you tell me about this key we found?"

I took the golden key from her hand, turning it over in my palm, the glow present again, lighting up my hand.

"Well, not much really. The griffin depicted in the bow of the key confirms we have the right thing, I suppose."

"It was glowing when you found it. Is it still doing so?"

I nodded. "It is, yes."

"No point asking why you can see something no one else can, I suppose?"

"Not sure there's anything I can tell you. I thought I was unique with the multi-wielding, but then at least one of these dark elves seems to be able to do the same."

Ella paused in thought for a moment. "Do you think we'll run into them again?"

I shrugged. I'd given it plenty of thought, but the truth was, I didn't know. "Part of me hopes not," I admitted. "We've completed the first level, and I'm not sure how they could also reach the second level if not through here. Doesn't feel like a dungeon, as Brom calls it, designed for more than one party at a time, but what do I know?"

"If they can't get through, they'd have to go back, right?"

"That's my other worry. If the cave is destroyed, impassible, they'll have to head back to the academy. We have Enallo and Lana's squads there, but that puts them in danger from a direction they may not expect."

Ella smiled. "From the little I've seen of them both, they are plenty competent to deal with the threat."

"I agree. I'm doing them a disservice. I'd just rather face the danger than have someone else do it."

"You might still get that wish."

She was right. We'd started off as the hunters, but the roles were now reversed. We'd become the prey. If they could, I knew they come after us. I just wish we had even a vague idea of the numbers we faced.

I found I'd tightened my fist, the metal of the key digging into my palm. The pain broke me from my thoughts, bringing me back to my initial purpose.

From what Sars had said, we needed to collect the three keys and then they could be used to unlock a vault after the third level. Something that would give us access to untold... well, untold something.

I turned the key over and around, running my fingers across the metal, looking for anything I might have missed in my initial inspection, but there was nothing. It was just a key.

I slid it into my pocket, sighing as I did so.

Ella offered a smile. "I'm sure it'll all become clear in the end.

"I hope so."

I had no way of following the time as it passed, but Sars had left a page of his notebook with the others in the main chamber, and they had been tallying the hours as best as they could approximate. Helstrom had passed it to Sienna, and she appeared in the archway to let us know the end of the eight hours was in all likelihood approaching fairly soon.

The clicking and tumbling sounds from behind the right door had been fairly consistent while I sat in conversation with Ella, but when one was immediately followed by the sound of heavy chains creaking and shifting, I sprang to my feet.

"Incoming," I called through to the chamber, and Elandra appeared, Sienna choosing to stay and guard the entrance. The enchanting water mage slid her sword from its sheath and dropped into a pose beside me.

Ella looked from me to Elandra and then back again. "Are we expecting trouble?"

I lifted a shoulder. "Can never be too sure. Pays to be prepared."

The elf nodded and seamlessly shifted into her jaguar form, tensing her back legs, ready to pounce.

The grinding noises grew louder, the shifting of gears more pronounced until the huge stone door slid to the right on screeching metal rails, exposing a temporary stone floor beyond that would presumably transport us to the level below.

As the door shifted across the final couple of feet, a short, hairless, grey-skinned creature staggered forward, coming to a stop halfway to our position and falling to a knee. A trickle of dark grey liquid ran from what appeared to be a cut on their head, and a section had been sliced from one of their two large ears. Broken spectacles rested haphazardly across their slightly elongated snout.

I gazed past the creature, beyond the door, seeing two more small grey figures, both prone, dark pools of grey liquid around their crumpled forms.

Slowly, the figure raised their small, dark eyes to meet our gaze. It gave a single nod of greeting and then rose gingerly to its feet, standing no more than three feet tall, dressed only in ragged, blood-soaked shorts, a small, leather bag hanging on one hip.

I looked to Ella and Elandra, then back to the creature as it twitched, struggling to maintain its composure.

"Parden my intrusion, Great Ones. I am Maxillenitaneous. I beg that you follow me now. Only you can save my people."

My eyes widened in shock as the creature swayed before collapsing to the floor at our feet.

What the hells?

## Chapter Twelve

Sienna pressed the health potion against Maxillenitaneous's lips, and slowly, he came back around, his eyes widening as the cut to his head stitched itself together.

"The others?" He wheezed, trying to twist his neck to look back toward the platform.

I shook my head, and he looked away. "I'm sorry. It was too late."

He sighed and pushed himself to a sitting position, his arms almost buckling under the strain. "We must return them to the stone before we leave."

"I'm sorry," I admitted, "but I'm not sure how to do that."

He shook his head, his eyes downcast in sorrow. "Help me up, please. I can perform the ritual. But we mustn't delay."

I leaned closer and offered my hand. He grasped my wrist, small fingers digging in as I lifted him to his feet.

"Maxillenitaneous, how can we help?"

He shook his head. "Just Max is fine. I understand you surface dwellers have simpler names. Not like we kwells."

I made sure to hide my relief. "So, Max, what can we do?"

"If you can carry their bodies to me here, I will take care of the rest."

Max stood where he had fallen, only now facing away from the stone doors. I passed him by, Ella back in elven form at my side, and we entered the stone platform, bending and gently lifting the two broken bodies into our arms. They weighed barely anything.

As we returned, the kwell gently shook his head before closing his hand into a tight fist and beating it twice against his chest, the sound echoing softly off the walls.

"Please, here." He gestured to the ground at his feet, and we placed the bodies down before taking a few steps back, joining Elandra once again and Sienna who had just walked through to join us from the main chamber.

We watched on silently as Max knelt beside each figure, carefully removing the bag each carried on their hip and placing it on their chest before folding their arms across the top.

The kwell then placed his palms against the stone floor. A humming sounded, surprisingly deep for the tiny figure before us, and the stone beneath his palms rippled as the temperature of the air became warm, then hot, almost unbearable.

The cadence of his humming changed, speeding up, and the ground eased aside to allow the bodies to sink into the floor, the stone pulling them into its embrace before covering them over and solidifying once again.

Once they disappeared from view, the humming stopped, and Max pushed himself to his feet, shaking slightly.

"Do you wish to say any words?" I asked.

The kwell shook his head. "No need for words. The stone knows all, Great One. Now, we must get moving."

"Can you tell us more about the danger?" Sienna asked.

"With a few quick alterations to the mechanics, the platform will take fewer than two hours to reach the floor below. If it is okay with the Great Ones, we shall talk as we descend."

Sienna looked to me, and I shrugged as Max pulled a series of small tools from the bag at his waist and moved toward the platform's visible mechanisms. "Let's get everyone together. Prepare to head for the second floor."

---

We stood gathered at the platform as Max finished making changes to the metal pulley system that would lower us to the second floor. I'd passed on what little we already knew, even mentioning the left-hand door where a platform would instead return them to the surface, but no one was keen to depart that way.

I had to admit I'd been a bit skeptical after Max's appearance, but Bernolir, Helstrom, and Fitmigar all had tales of the kwell—a grey-skinned, underground-dwelling race of peaceful, hardworking creatures—though, none of the three had heard talk of them being seen in centuries.

One by one, we led our griffins onto the platform, and I found myself glad the walls enclosed us on all sides. We didn't want any accidents on the way down. Sconces had been positioned in the four corners of the large stone platform. I tossed a [Fireball] into the closest one, and the other three simultaneously burst into life.

With the griffins content, we settled down in a circle, Max joining us, prepared to fill us in on the details behind his desperate plea as we descended. A groan sounded as the stone door slid back into place, and then a cranking of metal followed as the stone floor slowly moved down.

The conversation hadn't even begun before Sars pulled out his notebook, ready to note down the kwell's words.

Max looked around, taking the time to look us all in the eye. "Am I okay to start?"

I nodded and patted him gently on the shoulder. "When you're ready."

He sighed and pushed his broken spectacles higher. "No point delaying things."

If his entire race was at risk, this wasn't going to be an easy listen. I slipped my hand into Sienna's at my side, giving it a squeeze.

He softly cleared his throat and lifted a tiny hand to rub his forehead. He looked worn down but defiant. I wouldn't make the mistake of assuming him to be weak due to his size. He had just buried two of his own, and now, he had to talk us through the danger that currently threatened his people.

He pulled in a deep breath and began. "I assume only the dwarves amongst you even know of our existence?"

I nodded.

"As they likely told you, we kwell are a peaceful underground race, originally tasked with assisting the Great Ones."

I looked to Sars, but he just shrugged. "Great Ones?"

Max's eyes narrowed in confusion. "The Griffin Knights of Old. Are you not the same?"

"Well, we're definitely griffin knights," I confirmed, not sure how close to these Great Ones we really were.

"Then Great Ones, you are." Max gave a single nod, and that was that. There was clearly more to it, but the main thing was to find out why his people were in peril.

Sars looked up from his writing. "What threatens you and your people?"

The kwell took a deep breath, physically trying to straighten his back and find the fortitude to speak. What came out was more of a whisper. "Dark elves."

"Fucking bastards!"

I looked to Brom and shook my head. He needed to keep it together.

"How long have they plagued you?" I asked.

"A mere day. They came from the floor above, sweeping through our smaller settlements, showing no mercy."

Sienna gasped and gripped my hand harder.

"We evacuated as best we could. Sent all healthy enough toward Yrill, our city, but we are not a race blessed with speed. I can only hope they made it in time."

Sars pulled the map from his pocket and opened it up, making some notes in Atanian script as Max mentioned place names and locations.

Something needed clearing up. "And you came the other way? To us? Why?"

"We were alerted when the door to the surface was opened and have been preparing ourselves for your arrival. Ready to assist. When the attack started, several of us were immediately sent to the platform. We hoped you would be able to provide help in our time of need."

Sienna leaned across me to look at Max with sorrow in her eyes. "How many of you were sent?"

"Twenty. I am all that remain to pass on the message."

"Fuck..." This time Brom didn't need admonishing. Twenty kwells had been sent. One remained.

"I'm sorry for your loss," I told him, placing a hand on his shoulder again, noticing his bones pressing through his thin skin.

"It is nothing compared to the loss below. That is why we need your help. Those in the city will have barricaded themselves inside. But our stone magic and metalwork won't hold out forever. The shield door is not impenetrable. If the dark elves enter the city, our race is doomed. It will be a slaughter."

I released Sienna's hand and ran my hand through my hair before rubbing my eyes. This was a lot of pressure. At least, we were prepared for it. Griffin knights protected the kingdom, and I'd make damn sure we did just that now.

"How many dark elves?" Rammy asked.

"Hard to tell in all the panic," Max admitted. "Some humans, too. A couple of hundred maybe? Maybe fewer, maybe more?"

I shot a look at Brom, and he caught his latest outburst in time.

"And they came from above?"

"They did. Through a hole created in the ceiling of a tunnel slightly off our main thoroughfare. Another few feet to the side and they would have landed in one of our lava lakes."

Ah, so it is the fire floor. The symbol had suggested such on the map before we headed underground; no wonder the temperature was rising steadily as we descended.

We'd blocked the tunnel on the first floor, delaying our enemies behind it. We'd expected them to break through or head back and go around. Worst case, they would head back to the surface. Instead, they'd gone down, through the floor, giving up on the first key and taking the kwells by surprise. Brom was right: Bastards.

Now, they had a head start on us again, and we had an entire race to try and protect at the same time as locating the second key.

"Be the key in your city?" Bernolir asked as tactfully as he could from across the circle.

The kwell shook his head. "It is not, though I fear these dark elves are unaware. It is hidden past the city walls."

If we could somehow catch up to the dark elves, perhaps we could lead them away from the city. It was a big if, though. We were behind them, and I wasn't sure how we'd manage to catch them up.

"Can we fly at all on your level?" I asked.

"In some sections, yes. Others, not so much."

That was better than nothing. "And will we have a welcoming party shortly?"

The kwell nodded. "I think you can count on that with absolute certainty, Great One."

"How long?" I asked Sars, gesturing down.

"Less than an hour."

It was time to plan. The door at the bottom of this shaft would open to unknown numbers of attackers, and there was no way that we wouldn't be ready for them.

"Charn, can you [Ballad Boost] us?"

The sandy-haired wind mage nodded. "On it, Jadyn."

I then gestured everyone closer. "Okay. Here's what we're going to do."

---

The platform came to a stop, gently rocking before a click secured it in place. As it did so, I pulled the light from the sconces, plunging us into total darkness. Metal ground against metal, and slowly, the huge stone door slid to the right, opening up to darkness beyond.

The door had barely moved an inch before a [Shadow Cloak]ed Brom whispered from my side. "Ten. Cloaked. Can't tell if human or elven."

We'd expected the darkness. They just hadn't counted on Brom's [Night Vision] counteracting their plan.

"Spread or together?"

"Spread out."

"Plan C," I called over my shoulder, and I received calls of acknowledgment in return before Charn's voice rose, giving us one last mana boost.

I pulled air into my lungs, one final deep breath before chaos ensued.

The door was barely wide enough for Hestia when I pushed forward. As soon as her taloned feet hit the tunnel beyond, I launched [Fire Wall*], forcing the multi-elemental spell forward with all the power I could muster.

Screams and burning flesh assaulted my senses as the wall of flame surged forward, illuminating the space before us, flailing limbs confirming some level of immediate success.

Helstrom followed, weaving from behind me and throwing a [Fireball] high toward the ceiling, catching the lip Max had told us of and sending a surge of flame around the trough, bathing the area in lasting light like our safe area on the floor above. With a quick nod, the dwarf dropped back behind me to protect Charn and Max.

Three of our assailants had perished to my initial assault. Others had stayed behind shields of wind and earth, only now emerging, spells yet to form in the chaos.

Fitmigar surged to my side astride Gren, pushing an [Earth Wall] hot on the trail of my casting, Syl and Sienna adding [Wind Burst]s to force it forward, sending our attackers scrambling to either side before the towering earthen structure crashed into the far wall, a single scream confirming one more had perished.

We couldn't give them time to settle.

Rammy and Mallen flowed past, pre-prepared [Fireball]s and [Lightning Blast]s hitting another couple of our enemy, sending one crumpling to the ground, another to a knee.

Lightning flew back toward us, and I threw out a [Wind Wall] that sent it wide of its intended target: me. Before they could form a second attack, [Ice Burst]s flew from my right, the huge stone door now fully open. Razor-sharp four-foot-long icicles pierced my attacker's head and chest, throwing them back and pinning their body to the rear wall.

I looked back over my shoulder, nodding at Sars and Elandra.

Six down. Four to go.

A cloaked figure charged, sword drawn, no sign of magic, and I pushed my knees in tight as Hestia reared up and effortlessly batted the figure aside, claws tearing through their chest, blood spurting across the ground at our feet.

Three...

No... hang on...

One?

I scanned left and right. Two figures darted for the tunnels, making their escape. Content to leave the final attacker to the squad, I urged Hestia after the fleeing figures, a jaguar now bounding alongside us as we moved.

They had a head start, but I was confident we could run them down.

A hundred feet in, the tunnel split into two, and as I headed left, hunting down the first runner, Ella stayed on the main branch, already only a handful of steps from bringing her target down.

The tunnel's walls were covered with thin, glowing veins of what appeared to be molten lava. The heat was oppressive, the sweat already pouring down the back of my shirt, my armor doing nothing to allow my body to breathe.

As we sped on, I noticed grey, crumpled forms dotting the ground. Max's compatriots, motionless in death.

Despite Hestia's size and speed, we remained unable to catch up to our target, the figure zig-zagging to successfully avoid my attempts to use [Fireball]s to bring them down while always remaining in sight, the tunnel narrow but fairly straight.

Always in sight...

I smiled, eyes wide, and cast [Dehydrate], instantly locking onto the figure, an immediate misstep confirming I had them under my spell. They continued on for a moment, weaving slower and missing their footing as I drew the liquid from their body.

Smoke soon billowed from their cloak as they bounced off the lava trails that covered the walls, unable to keep themselves steady as they futilely attempted to evade capture.

Hestia slowed, my bonded griffin needing no sign from me to realize our target was done for. It was just a matter of time.

The figure stumbled one final time and then crashed to the ground, wheezing as I slipped off Hestia's back and approached, the low light from the trough above confirming my fears: a dark elf.

I dropped to a knee, intent on getting information from them, but I'd overdone the casting, not having practiced enough, and the dark elf expired before my eyes, a grimace etched on their purple-hued face.

Fuck... Nice one, Jadyn. Elandra won't let me hear the end of this.

Following my gesture, Hestia leaned down and lifted the corpse into her beak, her muscles barely tensing, the body devoid of moisture. Turning within the tunnel, I walked alongside her, and we headed back to join the others.

Rejoining the main tunnel, I smiled as a jaguar sidled up alongside me, an arm clenched in its jaws, a figure dragged along behind. I couldn't be sure if they were dead or just unconscious; I needed to wait for Ella to release them for me to know for sure. If the amount of blood was any indicator, this attacker was as long gone as mine.

Maybe the others had managed to contain the last attacker without killing them.

We approached the main party, and I sighed. We wouldn't be getting anything from the headless body that lay at Brom's feet.

As I raised an eyebrow, he grinned. "Never saw me coming, man."

Fuck.

We'd avoided any major injuries, a couple of the squad sporting nicks and some singed clothing, but it would have been good to keep one alive.

I dropped the elven corpse alongside the body, and Ella released her capture, his death now easy to confirm. As she shifted back into her beautiful elven form, Max came striding off the platform where he'd remained with Charn and Helstrom.

The kwell walked over to the loose head, drew back his foot, and booted it across the room.

Turning, he caught my gaze and gasped. "I really shouldn't have done that. My apologies."

Were our situations reversed, kicking an enemy's head was likely the least I'd want to do. "No apology needed. Now, let's get to saving your people, shall we?"

The kwell nodded, repeatedly.

# Chapter Thirteen

Time was of the essence. The immediate threat had been dealt with, but the kwell were currently trapped within their city, and if we didn't get there soon... well, it didn't bear thinking about.

Max had originally been more than a little reluctant to join me on the back of Hestia, but as soon as he realized we could travel faster and converse at the same time if he did, he pulled himself up and settled in before me. I'd expected him to have trouble staying in place, but he gripped Hestia's neck feathers with strong, bony fingers, and on we went.

We had the map, but it made sense for Max to lead us, so Sars pulled alongside us, and with Rammy and Helstrom, our usual vanguard, dropping in just behind, we headed off down the glowing tunnels of the second floor.

I noticed my Darkbrand friend twisting to retrieve his notebook as we moved out. "Sars, what do we have down by way of challenges on this floor?"

"Not a lot. Obviously, fire plays a huge role here, and if our translations are correct, there are a multitude of hidden traps closer to Yrill."

"Anything more you can give us, Max?"

"Well, you won't need to worry about the traps, for one."

Some good news at last. "How so?"

"The kwell are an industrious people. Once we get past the lava lake, I can guide us all to a hidden doorway, leading to our rail system. The carriages, normally used for the retrieval of stones and metals for us to work, are plenty big enough to transport us all to the city under cover.

This was getting better and better. "So, all we need to do is cross a lake?" Well, that sounded simple enough.

The kwell laughed without mirth. "Not just any lake. As you might expect with where we are, the contents are molten lava."

The tunnels we traversed were still crisscrossed with thin lines of lava, so it had already occurred to me that this might be the case. "Can we fly over it?"

"Of sorts."

I waited on Max to continue, and after taking a deep breath, the kwell did just that.

"The ceiling is forty feet or so above the surface, but this ceiling holds a plethora of stalactites. They drop almost to the surface, meaning there is no way to fly under them. They are magically formed, creating a maze of sorts. There is only one known route that can take you across, but it is far from easy, and without prior knowledge, it could take hours for you to clear."

Sars coughed to get the kwell's attention. "If you do not mind me asking... how did you get across?"

"We have a way around when we travel by foot. Tunnels so small and confined that not even your dwarves would fit. For anything larger, we use boats. Boats that the dark elves destroyed after crossing."

I nodded. Resolute. "So, we fly across. I assume you can guide us?"

"It would be my honor, Great One," Max replied.

The temperature continued to rise as we traveled the tunnels, the lava streams that lined the walls increasing in size and number as we went. Having remembered to fill the water containers, we kept ourselves fully hydrated, glad to hear from Max that fresh water was plentiful within the city of Yrill.

Small, hardy creatures scurried around the glowing tunnels, providing a plentiful supply of fresh meat for our griffins as they consumed kill after kill without breaking stride, our pace as fast as we could push ourselves.

A few hours in, we passed the section where the dark elves had dug through, stone and dirt covering the floor, a hole above leading back to the first floor. Aware that this was another potential ambush point, we slowed as we passed, checking for any sign of trouble.

With the lake approaching, we paused for a brief moment in a wider section of the latest tunnel to discuss the route over the lake. It wouldn't pay to take any longer than necessary to cross the field of lava. Lives depended on our speed.

---

"Fuck…"

Hestia moved up alongside Shadowtail, and I immediately saw what had caused Brom's outburst. We had reached the lava lake.

I'd always thought magma would come in bright, fiery colors, but instead, the surface was predominantly a deep black. Orange fissures spiderwebbed across the black, and thick smoke billowed from the cracks, rising toward the ceiling some forty feet or so above us.

The fact that we weren't choking in smoke told me that there was a way for the fumes to escape, somehow, up to the surface.

The huge stalactites Max had mentioned were dark black and imposing, hanging like obsidian sentinels above the lake. We would need to fly around them, following the path that the kwell had talked us through at our recent stop. We couldn't make out the far shore, far from it, but Max was absolute in being able to safely navigate us to it.

Due to the risk of something going wrong, I'd volunteered to travel at the rear. If anyone was going to get left behind, having to find their own way out of the maze, I'd rather it was me over anyone else.

A boom shook the cavern walls, breaking my contemplation. A ball of fiery lava burst from the lake's surface, crashed into a nearby stalactite, and sent fragments falling. A huge plume of smoke erupted when they plunged into the lake below.

I looked to Brom. "Aye, brother. Fuck..."

Sienna's voice came from my right. "Max, can I ask you something?"

The kwell shifted in his position before me on Hestia's back, bobbing his head, his spectacles almost falling free. "Of course, Great One."

"How is it that the kwell are able to traverse this lake in boats? It seems far too volatile."

The kwell's head continued to bob as he listened and considered his answer. "We kwell have the ability to be able to temper the ferocity of the lava. With enough of us present, we can tame it for a sufficient amount of time to reach the other side."

"I'm guessing you alone are not sufficient?"

I hadn't even heard Mallen join us, but here he was, determination etched on his face as he pulled his ponytail tight.

Max shook his head, his small eyes downcast. "Unfortunately, not. However, if you give me a moment, I can probably calm it somewhat."

Brom laughed. "Anything's better than this."

Max slid from Hestia's back and dropped to a knee. Placing one skeletal grey hand on the stone shoreline, he began to hum.

I studied the lake's surface. Nothing happened, and for a moment, I feared the change wouldn't be enough. Then several deep red pools darkened in color until they matched the pitch-black sections, and the smoke died down a little.

It was odd that Sars wasn't eagerly documenting this, but then again, maybe the fire reminded him of the acid attack on his arm. Maybe he was just in conversation about something else. Mallen could always pass on his observances.

"I assume this is a temporary hold?" I asked.

Max pushed himself wearily to his feet and nodded. "I'm afraid so."

"Then let's get moving. Rammy?"

The huge red-haired fire mage approached on Chiron, and Max pulled himself up onto the griffin to join him.

"As per the plan, Max will ride with you. He'll guide us. We'll all fly behind, single file, and we'll cross this lake before it becomes volatile again." I turned to face those gathered behind me. "We all good?"

Murmurs of acquiesce greeted me, and I nodded to Rammy.

Chiron lifted his head, chirped loudly, and pushed into the air. Wind buffeted beneath her wing strokes, forcing me back in my seat. With two beats of her powerful wings, she was airborne and gliding toward the first dark, hanging monolith. The start of the fiery maze.

"OK, let's go!" I gestured for the others to quickly follow.

One by one, the squad headed after the fire mage and the kwell, and by the time Hestia squawked defiantly and lifted us into the air, Rammy and Max were long gone. Only Sars, Mallen, and Ella were still visible to me.

As we pushed off from the shoreline, I noticed the surface start to break up. Molten lava had begun to force itself through again. The calming ritual wouldn't hold for long. I could only hope that Hestia was up to the challenge if our visibility decreased.

Ahead of us, Ella and Kelia banked to the left, then immediately right as they swerved around the first of the huge stone pillars. Max had mentioned it would likely take a few minutes to cross the lava lake, the slow speed down to the multitude of twists and turns rather than the distance we needed to cover.

Another boom from behind drew my eye to a burst of lava spewing from the lake. Smoke surged behind us, obscuring the shore. The heat was almost unbearable. My shirt was drenched with sweat, my face hot red, and my mouth parched.

Even Hestia was panting, sharp tongue lolling from her beak. "Faster, girl. The sooner we're through, the sooner it gets better."

She responded with a suffering but determined chirp, and then her wings beat faster.

We continued to weave around the maze of obsidian pillars, stalagmites, fallen stones, and sheer walls of collapsed rock. Hestia had lowered her left wing and was circling around a stone pillar when a shout came from up ahead.

"Ambush!"

That had to have been either Helstrom or Bernolir, I couldn't be sure. It was followed swiftly by the sound of shouts, steel, and faint flashes of light reflected by the pillars of black glass.

I cursed, noticing the kwell's temporary hold on the lake's surface was coming apart right as chaos broke out. Smoke was starting to choke my breath, and water streamed from my eyes. I spurred Hestia on, twisting and turning with her weight as pillars became walls of sheer black rock. Magically created, I now realized.

Damnit, the fuckers laid an ambush for us!

Smoke was starting to blur Kelia's retreating form ahead of me, so I threw out a [Wind Burst] to clear our path, momentarily easing our flight.

Booms, crashes, and flashes came from ahead, somewhere farther toward the shore, toward the end of the maze.

My eyes flew wide as a [Fireball] streaked toward me. I threw out a [Wind Wall], buffeting the attack harmlessly away. It had come from above.

High up in the ceiling, a cloaked figure clung to the wall. Another spell was already forming in his hands. I gambled on being the faster caster, so instead of another defensive spell, I threw out a [Fire Burst], concentrating it down to a thin stream of fire as I pushed everything into the force behind it.

Flame shot out at a speed that would have put Ella's falcon form to shame, crossing the space and burning a line through my attacker. Their body fell to the surface below in two scorched halves, consumed by the lava.

Smoke billowed across my vision again, and I threw out another [Wind Burst] to clear our path forward as we barreled on. Intermittent bursts of light and sounds of struggle penetrated the haze.

How many of these fuckers had lain in wait for us here, hanging from above?

Lightning shot across my vision, striking the stone wall ahead of me. A creaking sound echoed around us as a stalagmite fell, narrowly missing Mallen and Svendale but trapping Ella and me within the maze.

What now?

I cycled through my spells while staring at the rubble. Did I have anything that could blast a path through? Or did we have to turn back?

Kelia turned hard to the left to face me, Ella on her back. The elf handsignaled that all was not lost.

She knew another way across. The former ranger must have memorized the maze from Max's description and worked out another route.

I signaled relief and gave her the go-ahead to lead us.

Kelia dove right into the smoke. Hestia followed without command as I tossed out [Wind Burst] after [Wind Burst] to try and maintain a line of sight to our friends.

But try as I might, the smoke continued to thicken, our visibility faltering. Just as I feared we'd lose our way again, Kelia's feathers seemed to lighten, her fur whitening and glowing, making it easier to follow her through the smoke-filled air. I didn't know how Ella was doing it, but it helped.

No further attacks followed. Our assailants had likely stuck to the main route we'd planned on taking. I prayed that the others could hold on until we joined them.

Several far-too-long moments of being baked in a lava oven later, the obstacles cleared, and Ella brought Kelia down onto the dark stone shoreline, falling from her griffin's back and gasping in deep lungfuls of cleaner air.

Hestia landed soon after. I slid from her back and raced over to the blonde elf, pulling her into a hug. "Thank you."

"Glad I could help," she replied before pulling back and then pressing her lips softly against mine.

My eyes shot wide, but I tried to keep my composure. "How far are we from the others?"

"Not far. This way." The elf pulled herself back onto Kelia, the griffin no longer glowing.

We followed the shoreline for a couple of minutes, the heat from the lava oppressive. It soon bent around to the right, and a scene of pandemonium greeted us.

Syl's griffin, Palae, lay on the stone, one of her wings almost fully burned away. Several griffins paced around her, bowing their heads as her chest gently rose and fell.

The squad had dismounted, and those that weren't dealing with wounds — all non-life-threatening, thankfully — were grouped up around a figure lying prone on the floor, a glow highlighting their faces.

I slid from Hestia's back, racing over to join them, Ella at my side.

"What's happened?" I could only make out Syl's head as he lay prostrate on the ground, eyes fluttering, barely open.

The glow dimmed, and Sienna spun to face me. "A [Lightning Blast] took them by surprise. Palae took the brunt of the attack, sacrificed her safety for her rider, but Syl's bad..."

Sienna shifted her position, revealing Syl's broken body, his arm twisted unnaturally, his left leg missing completely below the knee. Now, I understood the glow. Sienna had used [Fireball] to cauterize the wound, keeping the tall wind mage from bleeding out.

Is he going to make it? I signed to Sienna, and a soft, wheezy laugh slid from Syl's lips.

"I'm not blind yet, sir."

I lifted a hand in apology. "How are you doing, Syl?"

"It hurts, despite the health potions, but I'll make it, sir."

Sienna leaned over the fallen wind mage. "We're going to need to do your arm next, Syl. Are you ready? The sooner, the better."

He nodded and allowed Sienna to place a strip of leather she'd detached from her bag back between his lips before she looked to Sars for guidance.

"No broken skin, so we can perform a closed reduction." The water mage then talked Sienna through the fracture distraction before increasing and then decreasing the deformity.

Syl, to his credit, barely made a sound under the increased pressure as Sienna maneuvered his arm back into a more natural position.

"We can't stay here," Mallen whispered from my side, and I nodded. There could be more attackers any minute.

I scanned our surroundings, eventually spotting Max in conversation with Brom and Fitmigar. The dwarf favored her left side, a clear dent in the greave above her right foot. I jogged over.

"How soon can we be at the tunnel and on this train of yours?" I asked the kwell.

He bobbed his head, barely meeting my gaze. Was this reverence or something else? "Barely five minutes away, Great One."

"Okay. We're going to need a few minutes to get Syl ready to be moved, and then we'll be on our way."

The kwell looked like he had more to say, so I gestured for him to speak.

"I am sorry that I did not warn you of potential ambush…"

I waved him away. "Not your fault, Max. We all should have been ready."

Not wanting to dwell on the matter, I headed back to Syl's side. I bent down, placing a hand gently on his shoulder. Sienna had done a fine job of splinting his arm. "We're going to quickly put a sled of sorts together, and then we'll have you on that train before you know it."

"Appreciate that, sir. Happy to hop if needed."

I shook my head. "No need for that, Syl. Give us a moment."

I cursed the fact that we'd not really brought anything with us by way of material, but we did have our lances.

"Sars, does anyone have any rope?"

The wind mage awkwardly retrieved and then flipped open his notebook, checking our inventory. "Helstrom and Bernolir are carrying some."

I thanked him and jogged across to the dwarves, passing on my plan to the pair. Though both looked a little the worse for wear, they sprang into action, collecting lances from six of the riders and then assisting me in lashing them together. It wouldn't be comfortable, but it would carry Syl to the carriages.

The heat of the nearby lava lake remained oppressive as we worked. Soon, we were easing Syl onto the makeshift stretcher. With Rammy's assistance, we took a corner each and prepared to move out.

Palae was now up and limping toward her rider. She would not take to the air again anytime soon with that wing, if ever. Pushing aside thoughts of Syl's future as a griffin rider, I addressed the squad.

"I know many of you are nursing injuries, but we need to reach relative safety before we can lower our guard. Max will guide us to the hidden railroad, but I need everyone alert. If we are to be attacked again, it could be around the next corner. Prepare yourselves."

A whisper of conversation reached my ears, but everyone did as requested. Sars took the lead on Ralartis, Max riding with him, guiding the water mage away from the lake. Sienna pulled up alongside them for a moment and lit the way with a [Fireball], flames soon surging along the ceiling trough.

The stifling temperature eased with each step we put between us and the lake. Ribbons of lava still marked the tunnel walls, but they were nothing compared to the oppressive heat we'd just experienced.

We kept Syl as steady as possible as we moved. Realizing that corners didn't work with our height differences, Rammy took one end, I took the other, and then Helstrom and Bernolir traveled beneath the stretcher, arms raised, taking some of the weight. Truth be told, Rammy and I could likely have managed alone, but I still felt the urge to keep Bernolir, in particular, involved.

The tunnel narrowed suddenly, and I realized that Max had guided us away from the main tunnel. Part of me was thankful we wouldn't be bypassing the settlements that the dark elves had destroyed.

A few turns later, our column came to a stop at a dead end. For a moment, I worried that Max had tricked us, but a call from the front had me gently placing the stretcher down and moving to join Sars and the kwell.

"Everything OK?" I asked, seeing them waiting at Ralartis's side.

Sars nodded. "Max just wanted you to witness the process of opening the door. I am going to make notes, but he thought it might be useful for you to watch, too."

The kwell spoke over his shoulder as he knelt before the wall. "It is a skill the Great Ones had. It may be one that you, too, in time, will have need of."

I shrugged. Might as well watch and learn.

# Chapter Fourteen

Max crouched against the smooth stone wall, humming softly. While watching him, I took the chance to take on more water. The temperature had eased, but the air was still hotter than a midnoon summer day. My mind went to summer days as a small child on the southernmost shores of Atania.

A grinding sound pulled me from my thoughts, and the wall slid back and to the side, revealing a set of glistening metal rails beyond. Several large bucket-type carriages rested on the tracks, each large enough to carry three griffins and their riders. The door in the side of each looked like they would revert to an access ramp when lowered.

Max pushed himself to his feet, wavered slightly, and gestured for everyone to move on past the opening. I'd allowed my attention to slip when I should have been paying closer attention to the skill or spell he used, but Sars would have notes that I could go over shortly.

As the first of our squad moved on through, the kwell stepped to the side and clicked a metal switch. The area burst into light as flames ran around another trough set high in the walls.

Made sense, since the kwell weren't able to throw [Fireball]s.

Beside me, Syl lay with his eyes closed, resting on the makeshift sled, wheezing a little. The sheer number of health potions he'd consumed would likely make him pretty sleepy. Hopefully, he'd be out of it until we reached the city and could find him somewhere to rest. Providing the city still stood, of course.

I continued to stand to the side as Syl and Palae were carefully loaded onto a carriage, Sienna still watching over him. Brom joined me, and our gazes went to the rear of our party. It wouldn't pay to be caught unawares again.

Once everyone was loaded in safely, I nudged Hestia on, and she moved through the entranceway at Shadowtail's side. Once we were past, Max pulled a lever I hadn't noticed before, and the doorway slid back into place.

We took off, with a gentle rocking motion the only sign that we moved along tracks.

"How long until we reach Yrill?" I asked the kwell sitting with us.

He struggled to lift his head. The effort of opening the hidden door on his own had really worn him down. "I've had to best approximate weights and such, fixing the top speed we can travel at accordingly... so, roughly two hours."

Impressive—both the speed and the kwell's ability to calculate the weight of our party on the fly.

With nothing to do while we traveled, and unable to view the others through the solid metal sides of the carriage, I fell into conversation with Brom. Max curled up and fell asleep in the corner, seemingly content that the carriages would deposit us as intended.

"What happened back at the lake?"

He shook his head and frowned as he met my gaze. "Fuckin' dark elves."

"How many?"

"Fuck knows. Five? Ten?"

"Hate to say it, but it sounds like we were lucky only Syl seems to have taken any lasting damage."

"You'd have been proud, man. They might have caught us unawares, but all of us, as one, reacted swiftly."

"In that visibility, that's impressive."

"Yeah, Charn was straight into a new ballad, really boosted us more than ever before. I can't say for everything that the others did, didn't have time to spectate, but I pulled straight on my [Shadow Cloak], [Shadow Blade], and [Night Vision]. It sucked on my mana like crazy, but I took out two of the fuckers before they knew what hit them. Sliced them up real good."

I lifted a single eyebrow. "Battle lust rubbing off on you from a certain young dwarven lady?"

"Hah. Might be." Brom laughed, perhaps considering the possibility for the first time.

"How goes everything with Fitmigar anyway?"

He smiled, the broad grin lighting up his face. "Good, man. Thanks. She's more than enough woman for me. Don't know how you do it."

"Do what?"

"Don't play stupid with me, Mr. Handsome. Sienna... Elandra... and soon Ella, too?"

I smiled, hoping I was coming across how I felt. Grateful for the women at my side. "Sienna and Elandra have been all I could ever ask for. Not sure what's happening with Ella, to be honest." It didn't feel right to tell him about the kiss.

"Pah. She's fallen for you already. There's no hiding that look they get when they fall under your charms."

I found myself hoping he was right. After that chat with Sienna and Elandra about love or power, I'd found myself going over my attraction to Ella multiple times. I was convinced I wasn't after the magical boost of it all, but was that true? Maybe a small part of me wanted that power, but I hoped that was just down to me wanting to keep those around me safe.

Right?

I shrugged. "Guess we'll find out soon enough."

Brom laughed. "I guess we will. Keep a track of the details for me, will ya?"

"You've got no chance."

The shadow mage feigned offense for a moment before a huge grin appeared again.

We slipped into companionable silence for a few minutes before a serious look crossed his face again.

"You think we'll be in time?"

I didn't need to ask who he was talking about. "I hope so." I checked to see if Max still slept. Satisfied he did, I continued, gesturing to where he slept. "I hate to think how he'll be if he loses everyone. His entire race."

Brom lifted both hands and rubbed at his eyes before running his hands through his short hair. "It's fucked up, man."

I nodded. "We need to get a handle on these bastards. We don't know what we'll find when we reach the city, but we really need to keep one of them alive long enough to get some answers."

A blush crept onto my friend's cheeks. "Sorry about the whole decapitation thing earlier. Got a bit carried away."

"What's done is done, buddy. Let's just get ahold of one of them and learn what they're after, yeah?"

"You got it, man."

Our conversation came to a close as I noticed the shadow mage's eye droop. He'd readily admitted to pulling hard on his mana, so it was no surprise he needed the rest.

The shrieking of metal on metal sounded out a short while later, and the carriage came to a sudden stop. Max pushed himself to his feet, took a couple of tools from his bag, and climbed the carriage wall, pulling himself over the top and dropping out of sight. I guessed climbing was quicker than getting the large carriage door open again.

A few bangs were heard, then the kwell's face appeared over the top of the carriage again.

"All OK?"

He dropped down beside me, looking a little better off for the nap. "It is now, Great One. Nothing a few taps and twists couldn't fix."

"How long until we reach Yrill?"

Max rocked his head gently from side to side, a bony finger scratching his chin in thought. "Twenty minutes or so."

"And we'll come to a stop away from the fighting?"

"That we will. I will need to open a stone door that will bring us out into the rear of the city, close to the cavern wall."

I paused a moment, a thought occurring to me. "You never mentioned how they are able to keep the attackers at bay."

"Best you see for yourself, Great One."

That seemed like all I was going to get, so I pushed myself to my feet and walked the few steps to Brom, nudging his shoulder and waking him. "Few minutes out, man."

The shadow mage rubbed his eyes and sat up. "Thanks for letting me rest, brother."

I smiled. "You needed it. No thanks necessary."

With no further delays, the carriages came to a stop a short while later, the area brighter lit than the tunnels we had just traversed by rail. Max mentioned it was all to do with contained lava pools. Hestia opened an eye and pushed herself to her feet with no sign of fatigue.

"One moment." Max pulled a tool from his waist, fiddled for a moment, and then the carriage door slowly lowered.

"Thank you, Maxillenitaneous." I nodded my head in thanks, and the kwell bobbed a couple of nods in return. "Let's go and do all we can for your people and pray we are not too late."

Max darted down the line, opening the door to each carriage in turn, griffins and riders stretching as they walked free, out into the well-lit chamber we now found ourselves in.

Ella and Elandra appeared from one, and as I walked over, Sienna joined me at my side from the next carriage down.

"How's Syl doing?"

A slight smile appeared on the raven-haired girl's face. "He's doing OK. Considering."

"That's good."

"We've got some people to save, but we need a catch-up as soon as it's done," Sienna whispered.

Elandra laughed softly as we reached them. "So, three is about to become four…"

I blushed slightly, and Ella grinned at my reaction. The girls must've been talking about me in the carriage.

Own it, Jadyn.

"You got that right," I told them, pulling Sienna, then Elandra, and finally, Ella into a kiss. "Now, let's get this city safe."

I strolled away, leaving the girls whispering between themselves.

Max was already tinkering with a series of small cogs that appeared to be the mechanism that would release the door into the city. I took a deep breath and hoped the scene that would soon greet us was not one of butchery.

The first cog turned, metal ground against metal, and we braced ourselves in a defensive position.

The door slid to the right, revealing nothing but deserted streets.

I wasn't sure what I was expecting the kwell city to look like, but part of me had expected something primitive. I should have realized with all the tool bags that they would have created something special. And special it was.

The buildings were all made of stone, as expected, but each was carved and finished to such fine precision that I suspected earth magic to have been used in their construction. No building sat at more than two stories tall, and the ones that surrounded us now appeared to be industrial buildings: metal workings, repair shops and the like.

What truly set the architecture apart was the way metal had been infused into the designs. Huge cogs and gears pulled platforms both up and between buildings, and smaller versions of the train carriages we just rode sat stationary above us. I could imagine them moving across the cityscape were it not for the fact the city was currently under attack.

The ceiling of the underground city was a good couple of hundred feet above us, sloping downwards further toward the front of the city that remained out of our sight.

Small, practical lamps hung from the ceiling, illuminating the city. There was nothing ornate about Yrill. Everything served a purpose.

Crashes and bangs echoed in the distance, and my breath caught in my throat as I finally saw how they defended against the dark elves.

A huge, curved metal door spanning well into the hundreds of feet across had been lowered through the largest set of gears and chains I had ever laid eyes on. Sections had been fused together and now closed off the city to the entire second floor beyond.

Cracks had started to appear in the defensive blockade, letting through faint flashes of light. The murderers we sought were throwing everything against the city, and if we didn't intervene, and soon, the doors would give in.

I turned to Max. "Lead the way."

The kwell shook himself into action.

I slid from Hestia's back as we moved out, once again moving to carry Syl, joined this time by Mallen, Brom, and Rammy.

Considering the size of the kwell race, I was surprised to find the city's thoroughfares to be as wide as they were, but judging by the size of the multitude of trailers that lined the streets, it was clear they needed to move large quantities of materials around.

We'd only traveled a couple of streets closer to the city's entrance before Max lifted a hand and told us to wait. He disappeared inside a one-story structure with a red cross painted on the outer wall.

Max returned, followed by an older kwell, spectacles similar to Max's resting on their elongated snout. A faint whirring sounded as they walked, and as they moved closer, I noticed small cogs and gears affixed to their right knee, aiding in their movement.

Sars kept his notebook out, scribbling page after page of notes down as he surveyed both the newcomer and the building behind them.

Max gestured toward the figure at his side. "Jadyn, this is..." He paused for a moment. "Well, I guess you can call him Obed."

I nodded respectfully. "Well met, Obed."

The elderly kwell lifted his gaze, nodding in return before noticing Syl behind us. He strode forward, his right hand scratching at this cheek as he moved. "And this is the injured party, I assume?"

"Syl. He got hit by lightning," I explained, stepping aside to let Obed past.

His gaze ran across the tall wind mage's frame, then he turned and headed back toward the building he'd appeared from, murmuring under his breath as he walked.

He paused briefly to give us a puzzled look. "Well, then, what are you waiting for? Get him inside. The griffin, too."

I frowned. Syl we could do, but there was no way Palae was going to fit through the small doorway. As if sensing my confusion, Obed placed a hand against the doorway, humming softly for a moment. The entranceway expanded into a nine-foot-tall hole.

"Well, come on." Obed turned again, striding inside. "We have others to care for, too. No time to delay."

A hand gently rested on my wrist. Max was looking up at me. "It's OK, Great One. Our caregivers will look after your injured."

That was good enough for me.

Six kwell emerged from the doorway, all wearing similar shorts to Max, though each had a small red cross embroidered into the material. A thin bed of sorts on small metal wheels rolled between them as they pushed it toward our position.

I turned, finding Mallen, Brom, and Rammy already poised to lift Syl onto the bed.

"It's OK, sir. Let them help me. You have more important things to do than worry about me. We have a people to save."

I eased a hand under Syl's back and lifted him with the others, placing his damaged body on the bed. "Rest up, OK. We'll be back for you."

Syl smiled as the kwell moved into action, swiftly pushing the bed back inside the building.

Palae limped past, and I ran a hand through her neck feathers. She'd sacrificed her entire wing to save Syl. I hoped the kwell could assist her and provide relief from the pain she must still be feeling.

Further bangs shook the ground beneath us, returning my thoughts to the battle ahead.

I pulled myself back up onto Hestia. "Max. We need to move."

The kwell hurried to join me, before guiding us through the streets towards the huge metal door. A door that was keeping his people alive. For now.

As we moved through what appeared to be a residential district, we started to see more and more kwell. The young cowered inside homes with the elderly as protectors. The females and younger males guided the injured back toward their infirmary.

Seeing such a peaceful race of diligent workers and creators under attack stirred a foul mood in me. I couldn't let their attackers get away with such wanton cruelty.

I was still mulling over a plan of attack when a huge creaking sound shook the entire cavern. One of the cracks in the protective door widened enough for a [Lightning Bolt] to snake through. The blast collapsed a two-story building far to our left, dust billowing into the air.

Fuck...

"What do you have in the way of weapons?" I asked Max.

The kwell turned slightly to face me. "Nothing."

I frowned. "Nothing at all?"

"We have our metal-working tools but no real weapons. We are peaceful and have had no threats to our people on this floor. Until now... Many thought the shield door was unnecessary."

"So, no one is on the other side of the door, battling the enemy?"

He shook his head. "All who were able have been making their way into the city through hidden tunnels. I fear anyone still outside will already be dead." He bowed his head, a look of sorrow resting on his features.

"The shield door isn't going to hold much longer. Can you get us around it and out into the cavern beyond?"

Max nodded. "I can."

That was good to hear. "And what can we expect from the cavern?"

"It's previously mined and shaped stone, around eighty feet high, a couple of hundred feet deep. To the right is the tunnel that leads back toward the lava lake. To the left, the ceiling gradually rises, leading to an area we are currently mining, and the location of the key you seek. The key sits high in the sheer wall, within the second tunnel from the right."

"And to reach that tunnel?"

Max grimaced. "The first thing we would do is remove the ropes and pulleys that we use to scale the wall. Anyone needing access now will either have to climb or fly."

That was actually good. We could still gain access from the air. However, it would slow down our enemy.

"And can we come out into the cavern from multiple directions?"

"I can bring you out to both the left and right of the shield door."

I lifted a hand, and we came to a stop. We'd need to split up to trap them between us. We had no idea of what we were going to face, but we'd have to bring everything we had.

"Charn, will [Ballad Boost] work through the shield door?"

The wind mage tilted his head in thought. "It will. But the shield will dampen its effect. It will be better for me to join you."

I noticed he gripped his lance tightly, his expression resolute.

"I think that's for the best," I agreed.

He gave a single nod. He'd mentioned not wanting to be guarded, protected any longer. Now was his chance.

I glanced around at the others. We barely knew the kwell, but every member of the squad was ready to give their lives to defend them.

"Right, Sienna, Elandra, Ella, with me. We'll head to the left. That way, if the chance arises, or they have already divided their forces, we can head to the key's location. But only if we have the city protected. The kwell's safety is our main priority here. The rest of you, you'll be heading right, coming out by the tunnels."

Fitmigar lifted a hand to get my attention. "A protective [Earth Wall] first me assumes."

The hint of a smile touched the corner of my mouth. "That would be wise. Wouldn't want you getting caught up in the mother of all [Fire Wall*]s."

"And any left standing after that we carve into little pieces!" Brom roared, and I lifted an eyebrow."

"Hells yeah!" Rammy added, and I shrugged. They had every right to want revenge after the slaughtering of the kwell and then Syl's injuries.

"Just try and keep one alive if you can. Preferably one without magic. We need answers still."

Brom's usual grin returned. "You got it, bro."

As the others chatted about tactics, I noticed Mallen hefting a bow from Svendale's side and sliding his war hammer in its place. His elven side continued to flourish after his conversations with Ella. I had hoped she'd encourage this side of him out more. It seemed it was working.

While I ran through the plan with everyone, Max slid off Hestia, only to return with a young-looking kwell. She lacked the usual spectacles, but the tool bag hung from her shorts, her relatively flat, grey-skinned chest as bare as the males.

"This is... well, this is Anoya. She will guide the larger group. I will guide you, Great One."

I nodded in greeting to the latest kwell to join us. "All set?"

Anoya nodded. "I am."

"OK. Then let's go. Good luck, all. Let's show these bastards that they messed with the wrong griffin knights."

A chorus of affirmation replied to me.

We split up, Max climbing back onto Hestia and guiding us through the city to the left, passing the recently destroyed home as we traveled.

The stone wall that marked the edge of the city soon cut us off. Max dropped down again, making his way past what appeared to be a couple of food stores, where he placed his hand against the stone.

A door-sized section of stone shimmered and liquified, revealing a shiny metal wheel sunk into the city wall. Max turned and beckoned me over, so I slid from Hestia's back and jogged across.

"You can likely do this quicker than me. Turn to the left."

I grasped the wheel and turned. It moved effortlessly, the workings all precise and well-oiled. It wouldn't have surprised me if Max could have done this almost as easily.

As the wheel turned, gears and cogs ground inside the wall. A large door slid to the left, revealing a passage through the wall. Thankfully, it was large enough for the griffins.

I turned to find Max already standing next to Hestia, so I ran back, pulled myself up, and paused.

"You're not joining us?"

"No need," the kwell said. "The tunnel leads straight to the cavern. The door opens out of sight and runs on the same mechanics as the one you just opened. It will remain open for thirty seconds before closing itself. Do not let anyone past you before it does so."

"Understood."

I nudged Hestia's flank, and we moved down the tunnel, ready to meet the enemy forces that currently held Yrill under siege.

## Chapter Fifteen

I cursed under my breath as the door closed, securing us within the cavern outside the city. We had no way of knowing when the others were in position.

I turned to Ella, using handsigns to pass my meaning over. We should have considered this before, but at least we could fix it now.

The gorgeous blonde elf nodded and morphed into her falcon form before my eyes. A shimmer followed, and the falcon's feathers turned black. That was new.

Ella pushed off Kelia's back and flew high into the cavern, disappearing from sight. Other than the usual glow from the troughs above, the only light within the cavern came from the magic being thrown toward the shield door.

A brief moment later, Ella returned, reporting that the others were ready. She also shared that our enemy numbered around a hundred cloaked figures.

As I prepared to launch the largest [Fire Wall*] I'd ever attempted, a golden glow to my left caught my eye. There, where Max had informed us, high in the walls, lay the location of the second-floor key.

No time for that now. The kwell needed protecting.

I lifted a hand, looked around at my girls, and then nudged Hestia into action.

Charging from our hidden position, our enemy quickly came into view. Hooded mages threw spell after spell against Yrill's shield door. The cracks we'd witnessed from inside were widening with every new explosion of magic.

I opened by pouring as much mana as I could into a [Fire Wall*]. The drop in mana sent my head spinning as flames roared across the cavern. An earthen wall shot up on the far side as the rest of my squad defended themselves against the tail end of my spell.

In between, cloaked figures took the full brunt of my [Fire Wall*] as the weaker of the dark elves and humans across the expanse dropped to the floor, their cloaks going up like tinderboxes.

Panicked commands were shouted out as those able to survive my first attack gathered, forming groups around certain individuals to try and protect them from the flames. The mages at the centers of groups hurled balls of fire at us.

Sienna threw out a [Wind Wall] that buffeted away multiple [Fireball]s.

Hestia staggered as a prolonged rumble shook the ground, and I noticed Fitmigar's [Earth Wall] crumble to the floor. The squad near the tunnels raced forward, taking the fight to our enemy.

Our plan was to trap them between us, and so far, it seemed to be working. If we gave them nowhere to go, we could whittle them down with minimal risk to ourselves.

Elandra moved alongside me, arm outstretched, using her currently high mana levels to [Dehydrate] three humans as they charged toward us, longswords unsheathed.

My girls were strong and powerful, and I couldn't be prouder.

Flashes and bangs filled the air. Bright sun-like light illuminated the cavern. I gestured to Sienna to take Dawnquill airborne as planned, and Mallen and Svendale did likewise from across the cavern. So long as we bombarded the enemies from above, their superior numbers would mean nothing.

Less than half of our attackers seemed to be mages. The rest were cannon fodder, barely capable of buying the casters a few seconds before dying to spell and griffin talon alike.

At some point, Ella had dropped into her jaguar form. She tore the throat out from a magic-wielding dark elf that she'd caught from behind before springing away toward a second.

We could do this.

[Wind Burst]-imbued arrows streaked across the cavern from above. Mallen frowned in concentration as his shot pierced a human's neck, sending them dropping to the ground in a crumpled heap.

Everywhere I looked, griffin knights were overpowering our enemies. Even Sars, his lance held tightly within his right arm, was fighting well, the tip of his lance skewering an axe-wielding attacker through the chest as Ralartis ran him down.

Rammy and Helstrom fought side by side, timing their fire spells to force the enemy back, the pressure unrelenting. Through the sound of screams, magic, and steel, Charn's [Ballad Boost] reverberated around the cavern, imbuing us with strength.

We were winning.

The city would be saved.

New shouts joined the cacophony, stopping me in my tracks. Cloaked figures streamed from the tunnels behind Fitmigar's position. Alarmed, I realized we'd almost been lulled into an indefensible position, the pincer movement turning the tables in an instant.

I took Hestia forward, her claws clearing the way alongside my [Fireball]s as we pushed those attackers caught between us and the rest of our squad away from the city, clearing a space for Fitmigar and Brom to lead the others to meet us in front of the huge shield door.

The reinforcements rushed straight for our newly formed defensive line, pinning us against the shield door. We could fly off, but that would leave the last shield between kwell's citizens and certain death unprotected.

"We can't let them breach into the city!" I shouted, hurling [Ice Blast]s against those who managed to defend against the [Fireball]s. Bodies turned into pin cushions of icy shards.

Enemy bodies littered the cavern floor, but we were struggling to contain the assault, the number seemingly insurmountable.

Ella appeared at my side again, releasing her jaguar form. I threw out hand signals for the elf to take falcon form and scout at the first chance. We needed to know more.

Three mages approached our line, spell after spell rebuffed by our defensive walls. Sienna and Fitmigar dug deep to prevent serious injury through [Wind Wall]s and [Earth Wall]s.

I was about to begin bombarding the three mages, when their heads fell from their bodies, spurting blood. I assumed a [Shadow Cloak]ed Brom was tearing through their line.

Limbs and weapons crashed to the ground as the bloodthirsty shadow mage hacked and slashed his way across the cavern. He'd left our line and made himself vulnerable. We didn't need to take such risks. Fitmigar was rubbing off on him and not in a good way.

Hestia understood my worry and shot forward to support my friend.

A particularly tall dark elf roared as he unleashed a [Lightning Bolt] that slammed into something unseen, eliciting a cry of pain.

Brom's hunched over form appeared before our eyes a moment later as Shadowtail carried him free of the skirmish, his [Shadow Cloak] dissipating.

I snarled and closed in, [Fireball] after [Fireball] being turned aside as I threw all I could at the dark elf. Hestia battered surrounding figures aside as I unloaded a barrage of spells at the tall dark elf, only for each spell to be denied or reflected.

A feral grin appeared on the dark elf's face as we moved in closer, and then he disappeared from sight, vanishing like Brom...

A shadow mage.

*Fuck*. We were fighting blind.

"Up!"

Hestia shot into the sky, taking us out of immediate danger as we soared toward the cavern ceiling.

My eyes scanned below, looking for any sign of the shadow mage dark elf attacking our line. However, griffin and riders alike were all accounted for, though Brom was still looking the worse for wear.

Charn and Bernolir fought at Fitmigar's side as she bulldozed her way toward Brom's position. She reached his side, hauled him onto her griffin, and began forcing health potions past his lips.

Minutes passed as we continued to repel the enemy. Their numbers dwindled.

I paused while scanning the battle below. The number of cloaked figures had suddenly dropped.

Could there be multiple shadow mages amongst their number? Had more disappeared?

A fluttering from my left caught my eye, and Ella landed in front of me, shifting to elven form on Hestia, her ass pressed up against my hips.

She leaned her head back. "There are multiple figures within the tunnel where the key is located, and more just materialized at the base of the wall, already climbing up. A tall, dark elf stands at the entrance to the tunnel."

"He's there already. Fuck."

The attack on the city had been a distraction. Their real goal had likely been the key all along.

Ella shifted again and flew clear. I cursed the way we'd been played and turned Hestia straight for the far end of the cavern, trusting my squad to deal with the remaining enemies.

I needed to get to the key before the tunnel closed up, just like it had when we'd claimed the first.

Hestia sensed the urgency and flew hard, her huge wings forcing us at great speed across the expanse. Up ahead, the wall came into focus. Ten or so cloaked figures hurried up the sheer incline.

Should I take them out or head straight for the tunnel? The sound of wings drew me to glance behind me and see Sienna and Elandra closing in. The raven-haired wind mage signed that they'd take care of the climbers. I signed back agreement, spurring Hestia to head for the tunnel entrance high in the wall.

My girls could handle anything.

Hestia touched down at the tunnel entrance. I slid from her back, pulling my scimitars free, and strode toward the dark elf leaning casually against the tunnel wall, bathed in golden light from beyond.

I paused as he cleared his throat and lowered his hood, his purple-hued skin, long, silvery-white hair, and pointed ears prominent in the golden glow.

"You're too late, Jadyn."

My breath caught in my throat. He knew my name.

"And you are?"

He laughed without mirth. "Why am I not surprised that you don't know. I'm Drae, and I'm currently the one who stands between you and the riches below. Your need to protect these weak, pitiful creatures has allowed us to claim something that you need."

"So, how about I just come and take it from you, Drae." I strode forward, scimitars whirling, spells primed.

His grin reappeared.

I faltered as I caught the sound of gears turning. His low, raspy laugh reached my ears.

"You have a choice to make, Jadyn. You can follow me into the tunnel and try and take the key back, or you can try and save your friends."

*What?*

"Jadyn, more attackers have arrived!" shouted Sienna. "The shield door's close to coming down. We need to get back if we want to save the kwell."

I clenched my jaw, deliberating it momentarily before admitting I had no choice. I backpedaled, my gaze fixed on the dark elf. "This isn't over."

Drae's smirk remained as the stone rolled across the tunnel between us, and then I turned and sprinted back to Hestia, pulling myself up and taking to the skies again. Fury coursed through my veins as I was forced to let the key fall into enemy hands.

The rest of our squad had remained by the city's shield door, fighting a futile battle. The enemy mages launched [Lightning Bolt]s and [Fireball]s over their heads, avoiding the walls that the knights raised to whittle away at the shield door.

Hestia needed no command to take us into a dive. Mallen guided Svendale to join us in a four-pronged assault from above.

We swooped in overhead, [Wind Burst]-imbued arrows and [Ice Blast]ed projectiles following hot on the heels of another of my [Fire Wall*]s.

Flesh melted. Attackers dropped to the ground full of projectiles. Those lucky enough to avoid the first barrage fell to the follow-ups.

We turned in the air and came around again, picking off stragglers with both spell and talon. The enemy crumbled into a rout. The knights below us took the initiative to hunt down those trying to escape.

Soon, only bodies covered the cavern floor, pools of dark blood reflecting the light from above. They had slaughtered the kwell indiscriminately when they'd infiltrated this floor from above. I liked to think we'd returned the favor.

I landed alongside Ella and Brom. Health potions had brought some life back to the stocky mage's features.

Charn sported a cut to the head. A thin stream of blood had dried down his cheek, but he grinned, pleased no doubt that he'd been involved in the action.

"Everyone accounted for?" I asked Ella.

The elf nodded. "A few cuts and scrapes, but nothing major. Astonishing really after the numbers we faced."

"It's what we've trained for all these years."

"You all OK?"

I glanced to Sienna and Elandra, receiving a soft nod from each to confirm we were all well. "Seems like it."

As we discussed the battle, the others returned from the tunnels, coming straight over to join us before the shield door.

"Get them all?"

Rammy shrugged, and Brom looked almost embarrassed.

The shadow mage spoke first. "Truthfully, we're not sure, man. We caught up with a few, but the tunnels were the trap-filled ones we avoided by using the carriages. It became too risky, too time-consuming to continue."

Sars looked up from their side. "Some may still pose a threat, Jadyn."

I had an idea for a temporary fix and gestured for Bernolir to come over.

"How can I help?" he asked, approaching.

"Going to need a repeat of the floor above. The tunnel collapsing. Hoping this time those responsible for allowing them to tunnel through the floor are no longer with them."

"It be a risk we'll need to take."

Helstrom dropped down next to him, and the pair of dwarfs headed back to the tunnel entrance. We needed to keep others from appearing before the city could repair their shield.

"What happened with the key?" Sars asked.

I shook my head, gaze momentarily down. "They have it. That dark elf. Drae. The entrance sealed itself, and now we find ourselves potentially trapped here."

"We should speak with Max. The kwell may have a way to reach the third floor."

It was worth a shot. I slid from Hestia, made my way over to the shield door, and pounded on the metal.

A minute passed before Max's voice sounded through the door. "Is it over?"

"For now," I called back.

"Good, good. Allow me a moment to let you back into the city, Great Ones."

I pulled myself back onto my bonded griffin's back and watched as the rest of the squad traveled the battlefield, checking that all enemies had expired.

Max soon appeared from the left-hand tunnel out of the city, and we followed the kwell back inside.

"Not one bit of loot worth taking," Brom grumbled from behind me.

"Not everything can be like those books you like," Sars commented, only for Mallen to speak up.

"Not sure there is all that much loot mentioned in those smutty books of his."

Brom guffawed, then started to protest.

We were in dire straits, but the squad, at least, were doing their best to lift each other up. I was glad Brom was doing better. I'd feared the worst when he'd been struck while cloaked.

I had to admit it. My friend was slowly changing. His humor wasn't quite as quick or free as before, and he seemed to take greater pleasure in combat, almost to a bloodthirsty extent. I guessed war changed people, and sometimes it took time to overcome the stress. For now, he seemed to control it well enough. I hoped it stayed that way.

Max led us back into the city. Kwell hanging from ropes and pulleys worked on the shield door, tools banging alongside a constant humming as kwell endeavor met magic. Metal and stone melted like dough, beginning to seal over the damaged sections.

As we alighted from our griffins, walking the streets of Yrill, groups exited the buildings. Adult and elderly grey-skinned kwell led out the young. They all appeared nervous, still, but there was a resoluteness about them. They had prevailed.

At least for now, they were safe.

I dropped down into a crouch next to Max, looking him in the eye. "We still have a problem."

"I assume you refer to the floor below, Great One?"

A simple nod of confirmation sufficed.

"As with yourselves on the first floor, the platform that will take the keyholders to the third floor will take eight hours to ascend to their position, then a further two to descend. If we can gain access to the mechanics, maybe we can slow it further."

"And us? Can we get down there?"

The kwell looked thoughtful. "We have old mining tracks. More carriages. The route is a slow one, though. Ten, twelve hours of travel. It also hasn't been used in centuries, so I cannot vouch for the ease or safety of travel. The track may even be obstructed now in places."

"So, we'll be playing catch up again."

"There is another way."

I glanced left to see Anoya standing at our side. The young female kwell had arrived without us noticing.

"Go on..."

Anoya pointed to Ella. "The elf can shapeshift, yes?"

"She can," I confirmed, not sure where this was going.

"There is a fissure in the ground at the rear of the city. Creatures, rodents, from the floor below appear from it from time to time."

"And you think Ella could travel in reverse. Reach the floor quicker than the platform?"

Anoya tilted her head. "I can't say. I can't even confirm how safe it would be. Just that it's an option for you."

"I appreciate it." I turned to catch Ella's eye. Could I really allow her to risk herself, just to get a jump on those key-stealing fuckers?

I beckoned her over. It was time to find out.

# Chapter Sixteen

"Of course, I'll do it," Ella said, placing a hand on mine and giving the sweetest of smiles.

I'd run her through all the dangers involved, and she had not hesitated for a beat. Brave girl. She would need to drop into mouse-form for the journey, with no idea about time or conditions.

Elandra nudged me from my right, a soft giggle escaping.

I frowned and looked into her dark-brown eyes, wondering where she found the humor.

"You know, Ella doesn't need to go alone, right, Jadyn?"

*What?*

Brom laughed from across the circle. I looked across to see his eyebrows waggling like crazy.

"Oh..."

A soft blush crept onto Ella's cheeks. My breath caught in my throat before a huge grin spread across the beautiful elf's face.

"Does that—"

"No, Jadyn, that would not count as expanding your harem for power," Sienna interjected, and I realized she'd read me like a book.

"You do like me, right?" Ella said, her voice unsure for the first time I could remember. She'd softened and opened up a lot recently, but elves were reserved by nature, more formal than the other girls around me.

"Of course, he does!" Elandra said and shoved me in the shoulder.

I smiled. "Elandra's right."

"Then what are we waiting for? Max, can you..."

If kwells could blush, I was pretty sure Max would be red-faced right now, but he schooled his expression and led us to a building a couple of streets away.

"Visitors quarters," he explained, pointing to a two-story building. "Not that we ever have any these days."

A thought struck me, and I realized I needed to check something.

"Syl! How are he and Palae doing?"

Max smiled. "They are both out of immediate danger. We have kwell already working on potential solutions to their current problems."

"Thank you." I shook the kwell's small, bony hand. The moment I released him, he spun on the spot and headed back to join the others.

Ella's hand slipped into mine, fingers intertwining. I turned to face her, her blue eyes sparkling in the low light. She was gorgeous.

She leaned closer, pressed her lips against mine, and then pulled me toward the building. "Come on, Jadyn. I've wanted to do this since we met."

"You have?"

"I have. I just wanted to make sure you felt the same."

"I do, Ella." I kissed her again, leading her deeper into the building, pushing open a thin, metal door to reveal a bedroom beyond, the bed comfortably large enough for us.

I slipped my hands around her back and pulled her close. She whispered in my ear," I've never…"

"Relax," I replied. We were in a hurry to reach the floor below, but I wasn't here to force myself on her. If it took a little time, then time it would take.

My hands slipped from her hips, sliding up to her shoulders. I began to slip her armor free, revealing the light shirt she wore beneath. Her chest was pushed up by her leather bodice, and I forced myself to slow my racing heart.

Her armor stripped, I stepped away and removed my own. Her gaze flicked down to my waist. She smiled when she noticed how part of me at least was a few steps ahead.

I stepped to her again, pressing my lips against hers, my tongue flicking out, tasting the sweetness of her breath. My fingers pulled the laces through the bodice, and as I slid it open, a grin formed as her breasts remained high.

I pulled her closer, cupping her ass, and she moaned as my cock pressed against her. She fumbled at my shirt, easing it aside, and lowering her head, she ran kisses across my chest.

I did my best to hold back, to take it slow, but she was making it hard.

I leaned back and lifted her shirt over her head, her beautiful elven chest beckoning me in. Her nipples were hard, and I ran a finger across one. A sigh slipped from Ella's mouth. Her thighs squeezed against each other.

"Oh, Jadyn..."

I grinned and ran my hand across the other nipple, circling, rubbing. Her moans increased in volume as I lowered my head and flicked a tongue around her areola.

I dropped my hands to her waist, peeling her skin-tight pants to the floor as I lowered myself to my knees to inhale her scent. I guided a fingertip across her folds before grabbing her soft ass and pulling her onto my mouth. My tongue ran across her pussy and dipped in, tasting her juices.

If this was her first time, I needed to make sure she was ready for me.

I remained there as Ella's hands ran through my hair, gripping hard as I led her toward feelings she likely never felt before. Her panting grew heavier as I slipped first one finger, then a second inside her, my tongue circling her clit. Purrs of delight rewarded my ears.

"I'm ready, Jadyn," she whispered.

I smiled as I rose before her, guiding her back and onto the bed.

Her pristine ponytail appeared disheveled and a rose-colored blush was prominent on her cheeks. She'd never looked more beautiful.

I dropped my pants to the floor and stepped to the edge of the bed.

Her gaze lowered, and she gasped as she took in the size of my cock. I crawled toward her, and her hands clasped around my shaft, pulling me closer.

"Are you sure it will fit?" she whispered.

"I'm going to take it slow. I don't want to hurt you."

"You could never," she replied, lying back again and easing her legs apart, revealing her glistening pussy.

I rose over her and guided my cock against her, dragging it slowly up and down across her slit before gently easing the tip between her folds.

Ella gasped. Her fingers dug into my back.

"I could get used to this..."

"That's the plan," I whispered back, moving inside her, first just the tip, then a little more, deeper with each gentle thrust as she accommodated my girth.

"This is even better than they told me it would be."

I smiled and kissed her again. The girls had already welcomed her into our harem, even if I hadn't realized.

"You okay?" I asked, moving gently back and forth, easing deeper each time.

"I'm okay. I want it all. I can shift around you if I need to."

Fuck yeah. That was new.

I pushed deeper, picking up speed. Her walls tightened and then relaxed, guiding me in further and further until I was fully inside her. Her moans rose to a cry of pleasure. Her breath hitched against my neck.

I ran kisses across the edge of her ear, then down her neck, tasting the faint saltiness of her skin.

"Oh, yes, Jadyn... Fuck, yes."

I moved faster, thrust deeper, and she began to buck against me, her skin glistening as I brought her to orgasm, her cries so loud, so euphoric, as her fingers ran down my back, scratching my skin, her sparkling blue eyes wide.

I wasn't done, though, and I kept thrusting, rocking, pumping into her. She cried out again, her hands grabbing at my ass, forcing me faster, deeper until we came together, warm cum streaming into her as I struggled to not collapse onto her.

"Mmmm... That was amazing, Jadyn."

"Yeah, damn. You felt... so good..." I half-panted back, unable to get myself together. She'd shifted her pussy around me, feeling tighter in moments, then relaxing before going again. I'd never felt anything like it.

I'd barely dropped to her side before a warm feeling flowed through my body, my mana surging back to the level of above ground. Ella gasped beside me.

"My mana..."

"You didn't know?" I couldn't believe Sienna and Elandra had left that little surprise out.

"No. Is this every time?"

"So far," I admitted, leaning over and dropping more kisses across Ella's lips and neck.

"So, do you have it?" she asked.

It took me a moment to realize what she was asking about. I closed my eyes and ran through my spells.

**[Fireball]**
**[Fire Burst]**
**[Fire Elemental]**
**[Wind Burst]**
**[Wind Boost]**
**[Wind Wall]**
**[Water Burst]**
**[Ice Blast]**
**[Dehydrate]**
**[Shapeshift Mouse]**
**[Shapeshift Snake]**
**[Shapeshift Falcon]**

**[Shapeshift Octopus]**
**[Shapeshift Jaguar]**
**[Fire Wall*]**

"Wow."

Ella laughed. "You've got them then."

"I have. You?"

The elf concentrated for a moment, and then a huge grin formed on her face. "You bet. [Fire Burst]."

I laughed and dodged back, momentarily forgetting that Ella wasn't the sort to throw out a spell without careful consideration.

"Do you think we have time to go again?" Ella asked, snuggling against my chest.

I groaned. "We need to get cleaned up and back with the others as soon as possible. I wish we didn't have to."

Ella pushed herself to a sitting position. "Me, too."

"That doesn't mean I can't help you get clean," I said with a wink, and the elf giggled.

The situation was serious, but the first sight that greeted us when we rejoined the others was still Brom waggling his eyebrows. There really was no escaping his teasing.

Ella made a beeline to join Sienna and Elandra while I gestured for Sars to join me.

"I assume it worked. Are you sure you want to try this?" he asked, swinging his left arm out of the way so he could pull his notebook free.

I could always rely on Sars to skirt the sexual aspects of my magical growth.

"I am. Do you have any information that might help us before we go?"

"Like have you ever shapeshifted before, do you mean?" He flipped the pages of his notebook, scanning previous notes.

Ouch. "Well, no. But that's for in a moment. Any clue what we'll face?"

"Jadyn, other than the fact the wind element is involved, I have nothing. I do not even know where you will come out."

Fair point.

"Can I shift with my weapons?"

"You are asking the wrong person, Jadyn."

I was on a roll. "OK. I guess that's it for now."

I ran a hand through my hair, shook away my fuzzy thoughts, and turned to head over to Ella's side.

Sienna and Elandra both smiled as I approached. I pulled them both in for deep kisses before stepping back to kiss Ella.

"You need some time to prepare?"

Ella shook her head. "I've shifted hundreds of times before. It should be me asking you."

"Just tell me anything I need to know as we head to the site. I trust you."

I turned to see Anoya approaching. "You ready?" the small kwell asked, gesturing toward the rear of the city. "It's only a few streets away, but we should get moving."

I noticed that she wasn't as reverential of us as Max was, but I put that down to her youth. She'd been the one who gave us this chance, and for that, I was extremely grateful.

"Lead the way, Anoya," I replied, beckoning for the others to follow.

We needed to confer as we walked, so the griffins walked behind as we grouped together.

"So, what's the plan then?" Mallen asked.

"Ella and I are going to shift and take the crevice through the floor."

"You have any idea where you'll come out?" Charn asked.

I shook my head. "No. I can't even say we'll get there before you. But it is a chance we have to take to get ahead of Drae."

I glanced around the squad. Looks full of determination stared back at me.

"The rest of you, along with Hestia and Kelia, will take the carriages down to the floor below."

"How will we find you both?" Sienna asked, intertwining her fingers with mine, her grip tight.

"I don't know," I admitted. "I'm not even sure we'll know which way to travel. I just have to trust that we'll succeed."

Elandra smirked. "We'll find you, Jadyn."

Mallen frowned. "How can you be so sure?"

"We're connected, Jadyn and me. Sienna, too. Hells, Ella also. We'll follow the bond, and it will bring us back together."

"That's true." I should have already realized. That magical thread that linked girls to me.

Elandra stepped close, grabbed my cock through my pants, and stage-whispered, "And I'll be getting some of this when I find you..."

Brom laughed, and he wasn't alone. Nervous tension in their postures eased.

A cough from ahead caught my ear. Anoya was waiting, hands on hips, next to a jagged opening in the stone floor that appeared to be a smelting factory of some sort.

I led Ella over to the young kwell's side, Max joining us.

As the older kwell fixed his spectacles that had slid down his nose a fraction, I crouched before him. "Thank you for all of your help, Maxillenitaneous."

The thin, grey-skinned kwell scoffed. "It is I who should thank you, Great One. Thanks to the knights, Yrill is safe. The enemy at our door is no longer a threat."

I tilted my head. "I'd say we both helped each other."

"If it pleases you to think so."

"What will you do now?" I asked. "Will you travel down with the others?"

"I have much to help with here in the city. Anoya has volunteered to guide them down, and I have accepted. The sense of adventure prevalent in the young is one I have long forgotten."

Anoya laughed. "Pah, Maxillenitaneous, you speak like you are ancient."

"Sometimes I feel it."

Satisfied all was in motion, I held out a hand and shook Max's, careful to soften my grip against his brittle bones. "Thank you again, friend."

The kwell struggled to keep his head held high as he returned a single nod. "Friend."

I turned to Ella at my side. "Ready?"

"When you are, Jadyn," the elf returned.

How hard could this be?

Sienna smiled at me, blinking away something from her eyes before walking over and pulling me into a tight hug. "Be safe, Jadyn."

I pressed my lips against hers. A second set of arms wrapped around me. I turned and kissed Elandra on her silly grin.

"Right. Time to shift."

I stepped back, lifted a hand to the others in departure, and sensed [Shapeshift Mouse] slide its way into the forefront of my mind.

"Jadyn, you can't take your weapons."

I paused, retaining the spell's proximity while passing my scimitars to Sienna. That would make any fighting tougher when we reached the floor below, but with magic, we should be fine.

Mana moved from my core, taking a hold on my latest spell and sending a warm feeling through my body.

I'd seen Ella change often enough to know there was no pain involved, but the sensations caught me off-guard, nonetheless.

My limbs felt fluid, almost liquified, as they shrank, slowly at first before accelerating. My vision blurred, and I squinted. The soft light of the cavern started to hurt my eyes.

The floor rose to meet me, and the dexterity of my fingers, my arms and legs, all shifted. Suddenly, I found myself on all fours, with huge silhouettes towering over me. For the first time ever, I understood the true fear of being prey.

A squeak came from my side. Squinting, I could make out another mouse beside me. Ella.

Ella nodded and dropped into the crevice. I followed, clumsily at first, but soon easier as I grew familiar with my new form.

Darkness closed in around. As I ventured deeper underground, I found that my vision clarified. Ella's form appeared ahead of me and I followed after her, my tiny claws clacking against the hard stone.

I'd never considered myself claustrophobic, but as we delved deeper, and the crevice narrowed, brushing against my fur, a bit of horror crawled in my guts at the thought of being trapped in here until my mana ran out. Forced shifting back to my human form would surely be a horrible way to die.

I shook my head, trying to clear away the morose thoughts.

I lost all sense of time as I followed Ella's fluid movements. She had an astonishing way of navigating the passages smoothly as if she'd been a mouse her entire life. Meanwhile, I bumped my head against every other corner and stepped on my tail a couple of times.

More than once, we came across other tiny critters. Each time I found myself on edge, ready for combat, But these creatures meant no harm. They seemed completely unaware of the magic-wielding mages that traveled amongst them.

Little by little, the heat of the floor above was replaced by the chill of a soft breeze almost. We were likely closing in on our destination.

How long had we traveled? An hour? Two? Ten?

I couldn't tell. I just had to hope we'd be in time.

It would have been nice to have been able to chat while shapeshifted. I made a note to consult Sars or Therbel, our casting instructor, to see if that was something we could learn.

I relaxed slightly as the passage widened.

A squeak from ahead gave me pause. The brightness forced me to squint again. We'd reached the end.

I joined Ella's side. She was peering over the edge and into the floor below. I couldn't actually see the floor. We were perched in the ceiling, and the world beyond looked like a blurry mess to my mouse eyes.

Ella bumped my nose to gain my attention. She then pushed herself from the hole, falling into the space beyond. I gasped, panicking for a second, before the faint outline of a bird appeared.

I fought that feeling of terror again. Of being prey. I cycled through my spells, pulled forth [Shapeshift Falcon], and dropped from the hole.

# Chapter Seventeen

Air streamed past my face as I plummeted from the ceiling. My tiny mouse limbs morphed into wings, sprouting feathers. My vision sharpened, revealing the towering islands that rushed toward me, each landmass connected to the next by thin stone walkways or precarious-looking rope bridges. The plethora of glowing fauna bathed the entire level in a permanent twilight.

I moved my wings and felt the wind beneath them. The feeling was unlike anything I'd felt before. My movements were jerky, and I threatened to spiral out of control.

Fuck...

I tried not to panic, running through ways to slow my fall if I couldn't get a quick enough grasp on flight.

I relaxed a bit when Ella dove to catch up to me. She unfurled her wings and guided me through the motions to slow my fall.

I concentrated on her wings, pushing all thoughts of the fast-approaching ground from my mind as I copied her movements. Gradually, my descent turned into a semi-controlled glide as the air beneath my wings settled.

And as the dregs of panic faded, euphoria surged. I felt free. Fast. Damn, flying was awesome! If a falcon could laugh, I'd have giggled like a child as I soared through the underground 'skies' deep beneath Atania.

Ella took us down, guiding me to land on the nearest of the landmasses beneath us.

No sooner had we touched down than Ella shifted back into her elven form. Her hair was pristine and her clothing flawlessly clean.

My change wasn't quite so smooth, a barrage of coughs leaving my throat, a shower of dirt I didn't know I carried billowing free as I returned to human form—the only form that had sufficed for the first nineteen years of my life.

Ella laughed and approached, gently brushing the dust from my clothes while I swept my hair from my eyes. My head rang, and I realized I'd carried over the bumps from the passageway, a slightly discombobulated feeling threatening to slow me down.

Rubbing the bruises, I turned to inspect the island that we'd landed on. The stone we stood upon was slick, covered with moss and plants that cast an eerie flickering glow over our surroundings.

The actual floor of this third and final level was far below the island we stood upon, the land here perched at the top of a natural stone column that appeared too thin to hold us aloft. As I scanned the third level, each of the islands in view was similarly held up, though in the distance I thought I could make out more than one that had fallen.

"Which way?" Ella asked.

"Your sense of direction is likely better than mine. We're looking for the settlement hinted at on Sars' map."

Ella frowned in thought. "We got turned around more than once on our way down." She looked left and then right, her ponytail blowing in the wind.

I didn't interrupt, content to let the ranger use her skills to guide us. Truth be told, my mind was still a little scrambled, so I'd have only confused matters anyway. A minute passed before a look of assuredness crossed the elf's face. "This way." She pointed left, toward the fallen islands in the distance.

I slipped my hand into hers and squeezed, pulling her into a kiss. "Thank you."

"For what?"

"For the risk you took in guiding us down here."

She smiled. "For a minute I thought you meant for the bit before that."

"Hah. Well, that, too, I suppose."

She bumped against me. "I'm teasing, Jadyn."

"I'm still getting used to that," I admitted.

"I realize I might have been a bit standoffish at first."

I shook my head. "You had every right to be like that. You just need to be you, okay."

She kissed me again, the warmth of her breath and the softness of her lips threatening to make me forget all about the keys and our current issues.

Pulling back, she smiled. That shy look returned briefly before fading beneath a confident grin. "Shall we?"

"Absolutely." The others would be able to fly to join us when they eventually arrived, even in the stronger winds above, but having to make our way by foot, we needed to get started. "What are your mana levels like?"

Ella thought for a moment. "They started higher than ever before after... well, you know why. The passage took it out of me a fair deal, and then moving straight from mouse to falcon uses more than moving from mouse to elf to falcon, which I'll never really understand, so I could do with a break."

"Let's take a breather then." My levels were still pretty high, but I had a much larger pool than Ella to begin with. We headed for the thin stone walkway that led to the next island.

Ella led the way across the stone path that couldn't have been more than a foot and a half across. I was halfway across when the constant wind buffeted me off balance. I grasped for a handrail that wasn't there, and for a moment windmilled my arms as gravity tried to tug me off the bridge.

Ella threw a look back over her shoulder. "You okay there, Jadyn?"

"Um... yeah... fine," I lied, my cheeks heating as I tried to hide my near accident.

"Remember how I descended in the arena, down to the door?"

I smiled as I recollected the way she had seemed to slide down the dirt, almost skating across the ground. "Got it!"

I slid my left foot back, my boot gliding across the shining stone surface and propelling me forward, before I pushed with my right, moving me again. Soon I was sliding toward the next island, only the frequent crosswind proving an obstacle as it continued to threaten to push me off, sending me plummeting to the ground below. That and the couple of times I foolishly decided to look down.

We continued to travel between the islands, heading toward where we hoped to find a settlement and the third and final key, but I couldn't help thinking we were missing something. Where was the threat? We were only walking and had encountered no issues. On griffinback, there'd be no challenge at all. Something wasn't right.

We drew closer to the first of the collapsed islands. Here, the plant life grew taller and their light was brighter.

Something stopped Ella in her tracks. She bent down close to a glowing fern-like plant, inspecting the leaves.

"Something wrong?"

"Jadyn, we're not a—"

A deep, guttural growl cut her off.

A head appeared from behind a rocky rise ahead of us. Was that a panther?

No need to panic. We might not have our weapons, but we were both mages.

"Want me to [Fire Burst] it?" she asked from my side.

I lifted a solitary eyebrow. "Only if you have to. If it's just the one, and it poses a threat, I'll take it out, and then we can do a quick lesson as we walk to bring you up to speed on your new spell."

If Ella was disappointed she didn't let on, her gaze never leaving the panther ahead of us. "If it becomes a problem, we can always fly, right?"

"I wouldn't be so sure."

The panther stepped out from behind the rocks, and Ella gasped as two four-foot-long wings appeared, joined to the panther's back, tucked in against its sleek body.

Not panther. Pantherine.

Fuck.

The beast tensed its back and bellowed out a silent roar. A magically-imbued gale threatened to blow us over the edge of the island.

I tensed my legs, leaning into the wind. Ella faltered a step beside me, and I threw out a hand and grasped at her sleeve.

Wind eased. The beast prepared another bellow, and I threw out a [Fireball] to interrupt, singing some fur off the creature's flank.

I followed up with a second, then a third.

The beast backed off, evading the spells.

I closed in, another fireball forming on my palm. The pantherine suddenly leapt forward, catching me by surprise. I threw myself to the ground. Claws whistled past my face as I rolled to the side.

Turning, the pantherine yelped and slunk away after catching a [Fire Burst] with the side of its face. Ella stood before it, palm out.

No need for practice it seemed.

Stuck between us, the pantherine unfurled its wings and pushed off into the air, where it released a toe-curling screech.

A screech that was answered across the islands ahead.

While the beast was trying to gain altitude, I cast [Dehydrate]. The pantherine let out a mewl of pain, its form shrinking and twisting. Its withered corpse dropped from the skies, plummeting toward the floor far below.

"Others will be on their way soon," I called to Ella.

"This way! We need to find somewhere more defensible." She was already moving across the island.

I ran to catch up.

Passing the rock formation that the pantherine had hidden behind, Ella pointed toward a cave hidden behind one of the few non-glowing plants. It was likely the pantherine's lair.

Ella lifted a finger to her lips and crouched before the entrance, brushing the plant aside. Appears empty, she handsigned back. I moved up to join her, creating a [Fireball] in my hand to light the space and confirm her initial conclusion.

As Ella slid inside, I glanced around. The silhouettes of more pantherines approached. We were about to have company.

I entered beside Ella and rested a hand on her thigh, giving it what I hoped was a reassuring squeeze.

Okay, what options did we have? We couldn't go airborne. As falcons, we might be able to escape, but we would be severely outmatched in the air. Jaguars only made sense if they landed.

Come on, Jadyn, think...

We were weaponless. Ella's bow would have been perfect right now.

If only there was a way to fight them in the skies without putting ourselves at risk.

The wind whistled beyond the entrance of our hiding place, and I cursed. We wouldn't know how close they were until they fell upon us.

Wind spells didn't make a whole heap of sense with conditions as they were, and [Ice Burst]s and [Fireball]s would lose some of their accuracy when launched into the winds.

A thought came to me, drawing my lips into a smile. It might not work, but now felt like a good time to test it out.

I hadn't merged any spells since prior to the wolf attack near Riverhaven. I'd actually tried to merge another Fire and Wind spell together since, but nothing happened. It wouldn't take. It was like I had one shot with each pair of elements, and so I held back, until now, wary of wasting this ability.

I didn't pause or second guess my decision now, though. This felt right.

I furrowed my brow in concentration as I selected [Fire Elemental], holding it in place, not yet drawing mana into the spell. Instead, I pulled on [Shapeshift Falcon] easing it across and then locking it into place next to the first spell.

This had better work.

I pulled on my mana, slowly at first, increasing the volume until a click sounded, and the letters blurred, shuffled, and reformed.

[Shapeshift Elemental*]

Oh, yeah.

It looked like I could use the same spell for all the animalistic forms. That was an unexpected bonus as I'd only been focused on the falcon.

"I assume you've had some success?"

I grinned at Ella. "We're about to find out."

I mentally selected [Shapeshift Elemental*] and pulled mana from my core. Magical energy suffused my body, growing denser. I found I could mold the spell into my desired form.

Ella gasped as a fiery falcon formed before us. Edging closer and lowering its head into the palm of my hand, the flames washed over me without injury, despite the searing heat, and I nodded in satisfaction.

The pull on my mana was lower than that required by [Fire Wall*]. I assumed that was due to the size of my creation. I made a mental note to not test creating fiery dragons any time soon, but I'd likely try something bigger in the days to come.

If we survived to see them.

I focused again and tried to produce a second elemental falcon, but the spell wouldn't take shape, meaning I'd have to run them one at a time. Hopefully, as soon as one dissipated, I'd be able to conjure another one.

I looked into Ella's blue eyes. "You ready?"

"Shouldn't we stay hidden a little longer?"

"That will allow them to group up and surround us. We'll have a better chance if we can take the fight to them before they all arrive."

Ella nodded. "I suppose I'm ready then."

"We'll fight back-to-back. That should prevent anything from sneaking up on us. You're going to need to utilize [Fire Burst], and only shift to escape—unless we can trap them on the ground."

"And you can fight while still controlling the falcon?"

I looked within. "My other spells are all active, so yes."

"Then I guess we do this."

I pulled her in and kissed her, smiling as I stepped away. "Follow me."

I edged to the entrance and pulled the plant aside. Two pantherines circled above us, scanning the ground.

"Two above. Maybe more nearby."

Ella rested a hand on my shoulder. "Let's do this."

With a flick of my wrist, I sent the falcon out. The pantherines screeched as it streaked toward one of them.

Ella and I shot out hot on its heels, a [Fireball] striking the first from behind where its wings met its back as it tried to evade the falcon.

It plummeted to the ground, and Ella immediately [Fire Burst]ed its face.

I focused on the other airborne pantherine while flying the falcon through the air, evading swiping claws before sending it straight through the pantherine's wing.

Nice. It wasn't a one and done.

Ella's back pressed against mine. "Got another three incoming, Jadyn."

"How long?"

"Thirty seconds at most."

I went to turn the falcon for another pass, only to find it had already done so, sensing my need before I even expressed it. This was a gamechanger.

Sensing my desire, the falcon shepherded the pantherine toward our position, harrying it left and right and forcing it back. I launched [Ice Blast] at its rear. Sharp ice lanced through its chest. The beast fell from the skies.

With the first two dealt with, the falcon shot across the underground sky. The first of the three incoming beasts swerved the falcon's attack, but the second was too slow and received an elemental to the face. The falcon exploded in the shower of sparks.

The pantherine crashed to the ground, twenty feet from Ella, allowing her to finish the beast off while I conjured my next falcon.

No sooner had it formed than the falcon shot into the air again, primed without order to assist in our attack.

The two pantherines landed, claws extended as they charged us.

Ella began to shift into a jaguar form, but I placed a hand on her shoulder. "There's no need."

I exhaled deeply and went to release [Fire Wall*], only to find it wouldn't come forward. Multi-elemental-branched spells could only be used one at a time it seemed.

I cut my connection to the falcon, allowing it to dissipate, and threw a [Fire Wall*] forward.

Flames tore across the ground, incinerating both the fauna and the pantherines. Their charred corpses fell to the floor, smoke blowing in the wind.

The other pantherines in the air started growing smaller. The smart cats had decided that we were not worth hunting.

Ella exhaled beside me. "Wow."

I rubbed my eyes and ran my hands through my hair. "That could have been a lot worse."

"There are definitely more ahead, and who knows what else."

"There's no sign that Drae has been this way, and the squad hasn't caught us up yet, so why don't we take a few minutes to rest up and assess our best approach."

Ella took a seat on the floor, and I dropped down beside her. She leaned across and rested her head on my shoulder, and I smiled.

The whole underground situation was properly messed up, but I still treasured a chance to spend some time alone with Ella. If Sienna and Elandra were here, too, well that would be perfect.

"So, do we wait for the others or keep going?"

I slid a hand around her back and held her close. "We've no way of knowing who'll reach us first. If we can locate the third key we can at least guard it from Drae if he reaches its location before the others."

"And what if something already guards it from us?"

"Truthfully, I'm not sure. I'm sure as a ranger you had to think on the fly at times. Being a griffin knight is no different. We'll decide if and when it happens."

Ella seemed to be okay with that, dropping a kiss on my cheek before asking, "You got the hang of falcon-form enough for us to reach the next island?"

"I think so," I admitted. It had felt pretty alien at first, but I'd mastered it enough to land safely. Guiding the elemental falcon had helped me appreciate the movements more, too.

"On we go?"

I rose to my feet and offered a hand to pull Ella up. "On we go."

"Race you across then," the elf said, a glint in her eye before she shifted and surged into the air.

# Chapter Eighteen

I wasn't sure if the pantherines were wary after our previous fight, or if they were lulling us closer, but we didn't encounter any issues with them in the hour or so that followed. Another island had collapsed in the distance at one point, and it occurred to me for the first time that it might be part of the third floor's challenge.

"You see what I see?" I asked Ella, gesturing into the distance.

"Appears to be a city hanging from the ceiling."

"After all we've seen so far, it wouldn't be the craziest thing."

The elf nodded. "I guess not, but what do we do? We can take falcon form and fly up there, or we can continue to approach by foot."

"It makes more sense to..." I paused, a feeling tugging at my mind like a couple of threads had been pulled, gently catching my attention. Sienna and Elandra were nearby. I could feel them.

"What is it?" Ella asked, resting a hand on my arm.

"The others are coming."

"That's good, right? We'll be better equipped to face whatever this next challenge throws at us."

"Absolutely. I just have no idea how close they are."

"I'll go and check."

"OK. A quick look. Any danger and you get yourself clear. Understand?"

Ella smiled and pressed her soft lips against mine. "Message received, Jadyn. Don't worry."

Ella shifted again, her falcon form pushing into the blustery winds. A gasp caught in my throat as she struggled to maintain flight for a moment before she shot away, back the way we had traveled.

Alone for the first time in an age, I turned away, heading on to the next island. The wind was intensifying the closer I traveled toward the city.

I'd expected Ella to return quickly and began fearing the worst when another two islands collapsed one after the other. Thankfully, the thread that linked me to my beautiful elf still tugged at my consciousness. She was safe.

Approaching the city, I started to make out the details of dark, ornate towers hanging four or five stories down from an ancient castle. Numerous smaller buildings surrounded it, a deep wall enclosing it all within.

Considering the kwell had used this floor in the past for mining, I found it odd that Max hadn't mentioned the city. Maybe they'd just never made it this far?

One thing stood out as I studied the settlement. The place was completely pitch black. Was this another deserted ruin of a city?

I hoped so.

"It's better guarded than it appears you know."

I spun on the spot, unable to locate the source of the voice. My heart pounded against my chest. I felt naked without Hestia or my weapons to hand. Pulling forth a [Fireball], I rotated it in my palm as I continued to scan the island.

"If I wanted to kill you, you'd already be dead."

"Show yourself then, Drae," I growled.

The dark elf appeared before me, hands raised. Four more purple-hued elves materialized behind him, weapons reflecting the flickering light. Slowly, Drae lowered his hood. A scar across his right cheek caught my eye.

Fuck. Outnumbered by a group of murderous shadow mages.

I steeled myself. Once I had some answers, I'd go down fighting. "If you're not here to try and kill me, what do you want?"

"What you see before you are all that remains of the force dispatched to retain what was once ours."

Was he talking about the contents of this ancient vault? "You're doing this for books?"

The dark elf shook his head. "There is so little you know, Jadyn. So much you have to learn. Everything is bigger than you could ever imagine."

"I've learned enough to kill you," I spat.

Drae laughed. "Perhaps you have. But then you still need the key we possess. Kill me and you'll never claim it."

"Maybe I'm OK with that."

"We both know you're no fool, Jadyn. With ancestry like yours, I know you better than you know yourself."

What the hells was he talking about?

"So, if you're not here to kill me, what do you want?"

A brief look of uncertainty crossed his face. "I'm here to propose a truce."

I laughed and shook my head. Had I bumped it that hard in the tight passage? Was I hallucinating now? "You're serious?"

Drae's face hardened. "Deadly."

"And what would this truce entail?" I asked, the ball of roiling flame still rotating on my palm.

"We need to work together when we reach the city."

I shook my head. "Work with you? After what you did to the kwell?"

"An unfortunate situation. Collateral damage if you will."

"I suppose some things are more important?"

"So, you do understand."

I scoffed. "I've read enough to know all about people like you. You're all the same. The end justifies any means."

Drae stepped closer, and I tensed, ready to react. "We work together, or we all die."

I paused. "Tell me what we're facing, and then maybe I can decide whether to kill you now or later."

Drae laughed again. "I knew I'd like you, Jadyn."

I stepped toward the dark elf, easing more mana out, the ball of flame growing in intensity on my palm. "Tell me."

He lifted his hands again. Palms out. "You've already met the pantherines, I suppose?"

I nodded. "A few. Dealt with them easily enough."

"They have an entire army of them, you know?"

"Who's *they*?"

"The golems, of course."

I lifted a hand to my temple. I didn't need Sars here to tell me how fucked we were. Stone golems were immune to all types of magical attacks. Blunt damage was the only way. "How many golems?"

Drae shrugged. "Ten? Maybe more. With the time they've been allowed to strengthen down here, they'll be more than a challenge for you knights, griffins or not."

As much as I hated the idea of leaving this bastard alive, ten golems would be a problem. We'd need all the help we could get to take them down.

"How will we know you're ready to start the attack on the city?"

"You won't miss the sign."

Great. Suitably vague.

A tugging on my connections to the girls broke me from my thoughts. Glancing to my right, I could make out the outline of griffins rapidly approaching.

"I'll trust you'll make the right decision when the time comes..."

The dark elves had cloaked themselves again, vanishing from view as my friends approached. How was I going to explain this one?

Hestia landed first, lowering her head to nuzzle my neck before pausing and peering around as though sensing something. She tilted her head, and I ran a hand through her feathers.

"It's OK, girl. They're leaving."

She remained wary. Then, as though it had never happened, she nuzzled my neck and chirped affectionately.

"Everything OK, man?"

I smiled to see Brom and Fitmigar approach.

"It's good to see you all, brother, but we are going to need to have a quick conversation before we can be on our way."

"If it's about mousing your way along those passages before almost falling to your death as a bird. As a bird, man. Well, Ella already filled us in."

Fitmigar grinned. "Woulda been a stupid way to go, Jadyn."

I glanced at Ella. A faint blush spread across her cheeks. I smiled to show I didn't mind the ribbing and turned back to Brom.

"Something else. Let's gather around, and I'll see if I can surprise you."

Word spread through the squad, and soon we were gathered in a circle, all eyes on me.

Sars leaned to the left, his damaged arm moving to allow him to pull his notebook free. Once he'd balanced it on his thigh, writing implement poised and ready, he nodded for me to proceed.

I took a deep breath and addressed the others. "In Ella's absence, I spoke with Drae."

An immediate cacophony of shouts and curses sprang up.

I lifted a hand to quell them. "Let me explain."

---

Elandra shook her head. "I don't like it."

"None of us do, Elandra." Sienna placed a hand on her friend's shoulder, squeezing gently.

"What's to say he isn't still here, listening in?"

She had a point. They'd arrived without me noticing, after all.

"They're not. I'd sense them."

I turned to Brom, eyes wide. This was new.

"It's how he was able to strike me when I was cloaked."

"So, your [Shadow Cloak] doesn't fool another shadow mage?"

Brom shook his head. "Depends on your mastery. Drae looks old as fuck, right?"

I frowned. "I wouldn't say that, but yeah, he's definitely a bit older than we are."

"Means he likely has a stronger grasp on cloaking spells."

Sars scribbled away as we spoke. I was surprised he hadn't already known this. I was also disappointed Brom hadn't shared this information earlier.

Sars looked up. "So, if he is stronger, I get how he can sense you, but how come you can sense him?"

Brom shrugged. "Nothing special involved. Drae is the stronger shadow mage, at least how I see it, so where I can sense if he's in the vicinity, he can pinpoint my location exactly while I'm cloaked."

"It be better than nothing, me love." Fitmigar rubbed Brom's shoulder from next to him.

It was an advantage I didn't know we had. "It'll be of huge help to us," I said. "Seems like we need to take this truce at face value, but if we've got you to ensure they keep to their word... well, that's half the battle, right?"

"I suppose," Brom replied, looking a little sullener than I'd hoped.

"Jadyn is right. You will be an invaluable help in the future conflict."

I nodded in thanks to Sars. Brom's spirit needed the boost. That alone was unusual, but then since Brom and Fitmigar had got together... well, unusual had become the norm.

"So, we mount our griffins, prepare our spells, and shoot for the city?"

I glanced at Rammy, noticing how tightly he gripped his greatsword. He was keen for another battle, but then that was nothing new.

"We're waiting on a sign, but yeah, we should prepare."

Helstrom huffed from across the circle. "Long as they don't be meaning to just get a head start. Get the third key."

I had considered the possibility, but I still held the first key, and they had ample chance to try and take it from me before.

The city was still a good hour or two away by foot, much closer by wing. We couldn't, however, dismiss Drae and his cronies having some alternate means of travel.

"Let's fly until we're two islands away from reaching the city. We'll land there and wait for the signal."

"That seems like our best option," Sienna agreed, and nods of agreement appeared around the squad.

"Charn, you OK to [Ballad Boost] us as we travel?"

"Already on it, Jadyn," the wind mage confirmed. I realized I hadn't even been aware of the gentle warmth flowing through my body. "I'll boost us further as we close in on the city."

"OK. So, pantherines will go down to our magic, but we'll need blunt force to defeat the golems. Everyone ready?"

"Born ready!" Rammy shouted.

The circle broke up, and I pulled myself back onto Hestia, checking that Orcgrinder and Dragonkiller were sheathed along her side. Time for Galen's combat lessons to show their worth.

Mallen moved alongside me. I smiled as I noted both the bow and the war hammer that he carried. His conversations with Ella had really helped him, bringing his ranged attack skills alongside his melee abilities. I wouldn't readily admit it, but it left me feeling a little envious of his talents.

That said, Mallen would likely point out the four branches of magic I now possessed.

I caught Helstrom's eye and nodded. The dwarf spoke to Rammy at his side, and the pair moved forward. It might only be a short flight, but they'd really taken it upon themselves to remain our vanguard.

As we moved, picking up speed, the ground beneath us creaked and rumbled.

Ah, fuck...

"Go, go, go!" I roared as the island began falling away beneath our feet.

I pushed Hestia on, following in Helstrom and Rammy's wake as we moved closer to the city.

Our plan to land on one of the islands closer to the city collapsed. Literally. All remaining islands crumbled, leaving only the one directly below the city intact with a stone stairway to the settlement above.

Plumes of dust and rock were stirred by the increasing winds, swirling across the expanse. Tiny shards peppered our skin and reduced visibility. Our advance turned into a struggle.

A psychic link would have been good about now.

Gradually, the obstruction dispersed, blown to all corners of the level, and the city loomed large above us. Ominous. Unwelcoming.

What do we do? Sienna signed.

No option but to enter city, I signed back. Movement from the towers ahead caught my eye.

Drae hadn't been lying at least when he spoke of a pantherine army.

Dozens of winged panthers pushed off across the city, heading to intercept us.

I launched [Shapeshift Elemental*]. The fiery falcon surged toward the oncoming swarm, cutting a path through the stormy winds.

I pushed Hestia forward, the squad following right behind me.

I raised my right hand and spelled out the signals that would send Charn, Bernolir, and Fitmigar toward the base of the third level. They'd be responsible for finishing off any injured pantherines that we sent spinning from the air. Fitmigar's earth magic would be incredibly useful in confirming the kills.

The rest were to follow me, taking down airborne felines with magic.

Hestia screeched as the pantherines closed in. Several griffins echoed her rallying cry, talons out, prepared to rip and tear their way through this horde.

The fiery falcon reached the lead pantherine, burning a hole straight through a wing before surging on through the pack. A couple pantherines fell—an early task for Fitmigar and the others below.

The moment the elemental falcon exploded, I created another. The flaming bird shot off again, reaping destruction through our enemy's ranks.

The pantherines had closed to within range now, and I threw out a series of [Fireball]s, joined by Rammy, Helstrom and Sienna. Many winged panthers tumbled from the skies.

Surviving ones used their wind attacks to rebuff our spells, and for a moment at least, their losses slowed.

The distance closed in an instant, and the pantherines now flew amongst us, weaving between us, evading [Ice Blast]s and [Lightning Bolt]s.

I focused on a group of four pantherines surging toward us and pulled on [Dehydrate]. Unleashing the spell, the group faltered, their flight arrested, their bodies shriveling. My head spun, and I was momentarily forced to grip harder with my knees as I swayed on Hestia's back, the drain on my mana deliberating.

Too many at once, Jadyn, I admonished myself.

[Fireball]s and [Ice Blast]s cut through the commotion, the smell of singed panther filling the air, but we were far from safe. Blast after blast of super forced air was blown our way as our enemy fought back, the focused blasts of three enough to send Brom failing from Shadowtail, the griffin forced to dive to catch her rider as the ground rose to meet them.

It seemed they'd had enough of fighting defensively.

Though pantherines were quick and agile, they were no match for our griffins. Any that came to close were torn from their flight, wings removed from bodies, throats cut in mid-air, arterial blood blown across this aerial battleground.

Still, they came in wave after wave. Our squad spread out beneath the city. Some chased down targets, others were pursued.

Sienna must have been running low on mana as she'd turned on Dawnquill's back and was firing barely-imbued arrows back at the two pantherines that chased her down.

I moved to assist, only to find Elandra and Veo already closing in. [Dehydrate] dropped the first before an [Ice Blast] took out the second.

I beamed with pride at the strength of my girls. They were relentless.

Flashes from the stairway caught my eye. Drae and the others had arrived. [Lightning Bolt]s sparked through the air, felling any pantherines that had flown too close, unsuspecting of the danger.

Their numbers were finally dwindling.

Time and again I utilized [Shapeshift Elemental], the falcon working without thought. Still, Mallen took a glancing blow, and Sars almost lost his seat in a desperate evasive maneuver, twisting under a flashing, claw-tipped strike.

I surged toward the pantherines again, holding my spells back for a moment as Hestia took over.

Pantherine after pantherine was snatched from the air, torn asunder and dispatched as I unsheathed Orcgrinder, slicing into the underbelly of a couple that managed to somehow evade Hestia's talons as they passed.

If Sienna's mana was getting low, others would likely soon run out, too. I leaned forward and whispered in Hestia's ear.

"Going to need you to drop me at the entrance to the city, girl. The others need to do the same."

We darted towards the tower. Hestia screeched, calling the others to join us, and then she led the flock of griffins up toward a landing platform amongst the upside-down hanging spires.

"Drop us and go. Take the fight to these fuckers, and we'll deal with the golems."

The doorway would not allow griffins to travel within. We'd be going on without our bonded companions.

Hestia let me slide from her back and turned, screeching defiantly as she raced across the claw-marked stone floor and took off to rejoin the battle below.

The squad arrived in twos and threes. Charn, Bernolir, and Fitmigar were the last to join us. Brom moved to my side, resting a hand on my arm.

"We've got company, bro."

# Chapter Nineteen

Brom gestured to the left, where four dark elves materialized before us.

I lifted an eyebrow. Only four?

Drae noted my expression and shrugged. "He didn't make it."

While he spoke, I noticed a faint golden glow emanating from a gap in his cloak and frowned.

Drae laughed. "Ah, yes. I forgot you'd be able to see that. Quite the gift, Jadyn. And one I'm sure you don't yet understand."

"What's the murderous bastard talking about?" Brom asked.

"The golden glow from the keys and the exits. Seems like I'm the only one who sees it."

Drae shook his head. "The only one here, perhaps, but not the only one who has this ability."

Enough with these fucking riddles already. "Let's just get this done, shall we?"

The dark elf mocked a bow. "I thought you'd never ask."

Our squad approached the gate into the city, wary of the murderous elves around. The feeling was reciprocated. The three elves behind Drae rested hands on their weapons, gazes flicking between us all. Only Drae appeared at ease as he turned his back to us and sauntered on ahead.

I stepped alongside the dark elf, keeping a close eye on his movements for any sign of deceit.

"Have you fought golems before?" I asked.

Drae shook his head while focusing on opening the gate. Clicks sounded as he worked, a series of tumblers on an ancient lock.

I frowned again. Hadn't the pantherines all flown from this courtyard? If that was the case, shouldn't the gate still be open?

"How do you even know they are here?"

The dark elf rolled his eyes at me. "You have your books, and we have ours."

"And what do yours tell you?"

"They tell us that this city is guarded by a family of stone golems. Tall, brutal rock-born creatures. They are not allowed to leave the city, only charged with preventing the unworthy from gaining the final key."

"And that's why you need us? Because we are worthy?"

Drae scoffed and shook his head. "I need you to help fight. You are no more worthy than I, Jadyn."

"You probably even believe that."

The gate clicked open, and the dark elf deemed the conversation over. He strode through the entranceway, nonchalantly flicking a ball of flame onto a nearby sconce, illuminating the deserted city. Dark, internal corridors guided us between outer buildings, occasionally reverting to precarious open-air paths.

Drae led our unlikely entourage, remaining relaxed as though walking through his home.

A hand slipped into mine. I turned to see Sienna's beautiful smile. "You OK?"

"I am," I admitted. "My mana levels are slowly recovering. How about you? Saw you looking a little light back there."

She squeezed my hand. "Better now. Charn's voice truly works wonders. I wouldn't say I'm ready for a magical showdown anytime soon, but I feel steadier, at least."

"That's good."

"Going to need my mana boosting as soon as this is all over, if you know what I mean, Jadyn," said Elandra from behind me.

I laughed. Despite our current situation, a part of me stirred at her flirt. "You got it, Elandra."

Brom laughed behind us.

Drae lifted a hand, and we came to a stop. I wasn't overly comfortable playing second fiddle, following his lead, but he knew more than we did. Letting him lead was the best call. For now.

"Vorg, to the front."

A smaller dark elf barged his way through our ranks to join Drae.

"Vorg, I need you to [Shadow Cloak] yourself and inspect the room ahead."

Vorg looked less than enthused, but he did as ordered, disappearing into the room beyond.

Drae paused in the doorway, casually leaning against the dark stone wall and picking at what must have dirt under a fingernail.

A building-shaking thud broke the silence.

Pained screams echoed from the far end of the dimly lit room, then cut off abruptly. For a moment, silence. Then, lumbering footsteps approached.

We readied our weapons as a humanoid silhouette appeared in the dark. In one hand, it seemed to be dragging something – a body, I realized.

No. Half a body.

Someone dry-heaved behind me, and I found myself glad I'd not really eaten much.

Drae remained nonchalant, leaning against the wall as he turned to look at me. "That proves that magic will not aid us."

"You couldn't have found another way to demonstrate it?" Brom asked.

"Vorg was weak. Weak and stupid. He won't be missed."

I scanned the others, checking weapons. We might have to be creative to find sources of blunt damage.

I only had my scimitars, and Elandra and Sars also carried swords. Rammy held his greatsword at his side, though his muscles would've been perfect for a war hammer right now. Mallen and Fitmigar had perfect equipment. And then we had Brom with his daggers. My shadow mage friend would be as good as useless here.

Sienna and Ella had bows...

Helstrom's axes...

Fucked.

We were fucked.

Movement from the back caught my eye, and Charn and Bernolir shuffled forward.

"Got these on our way down from one of the carriages," said the dwarf.

"Thought they might be useful if we had to clear anything along the way," the wind mage added.

My eyes widened, and a grin threatened to spread across my face. The pair held sturdy iron pickaxes. Maybe this wasn't the disaster it first appeared.

"I think you might have just saved the day, here."

The pair both beamed with pride as Charn held his forward. "We'd be honored to pass them along to anyone who might better wield them."

Bernolir nodded. "Aye. We want to be more useful in battle, but we're not stupid, Jadyn."

"Like Vorg," Drae added dryly from ahead, and I refrained from rolling my eyes.

"Do we have a moment?" I asked the dark elf.

"A moment, yes, but I have no doubt that it knows we gather here."

That would have to suffice.

"OK. Before we move on, we don't know if we face one or multiple threats here, so let's get our heads straight before we enter."

Serious faces looked back at me. If we fucked up here, there would be no tomorrow.

"From what I just witnessed, the golems are slow. If we are quick, we should be able to stay out of their range. It's crippling and killing them that we are going to have to work hard to achieve."

Nods of agreement came back at me.

"Good. Now, who wants to kill the baby?" said the dark elf.

*The what now?*

Drae exhaled and shook his head. "You didn't think that was an adult golem, did you?"

Rammy forced his way forward. "Baby or not, that monster's about to meet its maker."

Drae bowed theatrically and gestured into the room beyond. "After you, my red-headed friend."

The fire mage grimaced as he headed past the dark elf, Mallen and Fitmigar hot on his heels. I doubted he appreciated being called friend by the leader of the very group we came here to stop.

"Wait up," Brom called, following on behind.

Charn's song carried across the corridor, the boost filling us with vigor.

Rammy strode straight at the baby golem. Its seven-foot-tall frame was hunched over as it snacked on Vorg, unaware of the danger approaching.

The red-headed fire mage swung his greatsword. The huge blade whistled through the air and bounced off solid stone with a reverberating ring of steel.

Mallen followed in behind, cracking his huge war hammer across the golem's temple. A part of its head collapsed in, and it staggered. Fitmigar followed up with her mace to the back of the head, knocking the creature to its knees. The three fell upon it as one blender of swinging steel. The stone guardian soon lay motionless at our feet.

Brom paused mid-step, the pickaxe he'd taken from Charn raised. "That wasn't really a baby, right?"

"Of course not," Drae replied dismissively as he strode past the corpse and on toward the next corridor.

I jogged to his side. "How do you know where to go?" We were inside the fortress, corridors branching off as we walked, but Drae walked his route with purpose.

"Do you not think I have studied the layout of this fortress? I know where these creatures locate themselves."

Fair enough.

"Are you going to join us in these fights, or are you only here to spectate?" I asked.

He waved me away. "I didn't see you strike a blow back there, Jadyn."

"Then I guess we both need to get involved."

The dark elf slid his sword free, balancing its weight, swishing it through the air a couple of times. "As you wish."

The next doorway approached, barely lit in the low light afforded by the few sconces that lined the corridors. Drae entered the room and immediately fell into a fighting stance. He glanced toward the doorway. "Join me, Jadyn. Let's show them how it's done."

I was interested in seeing how Drae made a blade work, but it made more sense for me to use something blunt, so I asked Mallen to borrow the war hammer.

Brom went to follow us in, but the dark elf waved him back. "The time for us all to fight will be upon us soon enough."

The sound of something big moving in the darkness reached my ears, and heavy footsteps pounded across the room. The dark elf spun out of the way of the first blow and raked his blades across the back of the golem's knee. I charged to join him.

I'd always felt relatively tall at six-two, but the stone guardian towered over me by a foot at least. Its stone fist flew at my head at skull-shattering speed.

But land it did not.

Sparks flew as I crashed Mallen's war hammer against its arm. A deep dent appeared. Rolling away, I turned to face the golem.

Drae was quick to follow my attack, his curved blade hitting the joint on the guardian's arm.

We circled the golem, evading its clumsy attacks, and landed blow after blow against the same joint until the lower part of its arm fell free.

Sweat poured down my back, and I brushed my hair from my eyes. "One limb down, three to go."

The golem made a lumbering grab for Drae, but the dark elf flipped backward and over its arm, landing in a crouch, one knee against the stone floor.

Drae straightened up and grinned at me from across the room. "It's all about the dance you see. What say we remove a leg next?"

It made no sense to me in a life-or-death battle to drag things out.

Hefting the war hammer, I cracked it across the golem's chest, forcing it back. Relentless, I struck, again and again, its chest crumpling as it fell backward to the floor. I brought the hammer down on the center of its skull, obliterating it in one forceful strike.

I sighed and tossed the weapon back to Mallen.

"I'm not here to dance, Drae. Can we just keep moving."

A flicker of annoyance crossed the dark elf's face, but he shrugged it off. "Maybe we're not so alike after all."

"I'm not here to toy with the guardians. I take no pleasure in killing them. We pass the challenge, we collect the key, and we move on."

Drae rolled his eyes. "So dramatic, Jadyn."

I didn't bother replying. The dark elf sheathed his sword and turning, heading deeper into the fortress.

A couple of times we had to traverse the fortress's open walkways. The wind remained strong, forcing those crosses to be slow and steady, but it did give me the chance to make out the griffins far below, feasting on their kills.

They'd done their part well.

Within the fortress, the golems were attacking us individually without any strategy or wits. These guardians would only be an issue in greater numbers.

And then we came across a room that made me curse my wandering mind.

Multiple rumbles and thuds sounded from within the room before us. The very walls around us shook. Even Drae hesitated.

As griffin knights, we moved as one. The challenge we'd been expecting was finally here.

# Chapter Twenty

Charn's haunting melody filled our bodies with warmth as we stood in the doorway to the golem-filled chamber.

Sturdy stone tables edged the dimly lit hall, and large pews had been hewn into the very walls themselves. At the end of the tall space stood a huge stone slab altar.

My first thought was that we were in their church. Then I spotted that the desecrated carcass of a butchered pantherine covered the stone altar and figured it might be best to not think too deeply on what this place was.

Eight bulky stone golems stood sentinel-like in the middle of the room, all taller than the two we'd faced so far by at least a foot or two. We had the numbers, just, but they had the size and the power.

If all eight came at us in one wave... well, we were likely fucked.

I clenched my fists and took a deep breath. This was a challenge we were going to win.

"I'm going to create a distraction. Fitmigar, I need you to create a pit. See if we can't lower the number we'll be facing, at least temporarily. Anyone with a blunt weapon, we'll need to finish them off. Everyone else, do what you can with what you have available, but stay safe."

I found Bernolir in the crowd. "I'm going to need that pickaxe."

The dwarven earth mage nodded and passed the weapon across.

Satisfied, I conjured a [Shapeshift Elemental] in jaguar form and sent it in, gaining the attention of several golems. The floor rumbled and shook, and Fitmigar grunted with effort as the pit opened in the floor behind the end of the golem line.

I directed the elemental jaguar to pounce on the two guardians at the end of the line. Their clumsy swipes missed, and the elemental crashed into them, throwing them off balance and into the pit. They didn't die, but it would take a moment for them to rejoin the battle.

The remaining golems came forward, huge stone fists swinging wildly through the air.

I moved to meet them, reaching the line with Drae. The dark elf's weapon sliced across the side of a golem's knee joint, and I crashed the pickaxe into its shoulder.

The rest of the squad joined the melee around us. The loud strikes of Mallen's war hammer and Rammy's greatsword were matched in intensity by Brom's pickaxe, delivering blow after blow.

I weaved my way through the golems, striking chests and backs before twisting away. Though deadly, their movements were slow.

Arrows flew across the hall, pinging ineffectively off stone.

I continued to whittle away at the silent golems around me. One strike of my pickaxe cracked a hole in one, but it rushed at another target. Seemed their heads were the only weak point.

A pained cry drew my eye to the gruesome sight of Drae's cloaked subordinate getting pummeled to a pulp and thrown against the wall. Their fractured body slid to the ground in a broken heap, dead. Other than their leader, the rest were hardly the great fighters I'd assumed them to be.

Magical prowess over combat skills it seemed.

I sidestepped a stone fist whooshing past my face and spun my pickaxe to return the favor. Strike after strike struck true, and the golem's movements slowed as stony fragments flew free.

My jaguar elemental distracted the golem long enough for me to land a blow on its head. Its movement slowed a fraction, but still, the golem refused to go down.

I sidestepped a punch and rolled beneath a crushing hug, evading its sweeping arms while staying close to hammer away at the cracks. I ducked under another blow that would have been my end and hefted my pickaxe again, only to have to dodge a different golem.

Before I could return to the one I'd been fighting, another was in my face, fists flailing, driving me back. The wall was fast approaching at my rear, and although I had speed on my side, I couldn't afford to let it get too close, trapping me.

My elemental jaguar came barreling in from the side, momentarily unbalancing it but leaving no lasting damage. The jaguar disintegrated, but it had brought me an opening.

Shooting forward, I hacked into the golem, striking body and head. The golem fell to a knee, the force of its fall shaking the hall.

I lifted the pickaxe again, intent on keep its focus on me as Brom leapt into the air behind it. The shadow mage brought his own pickaxe down on the back of its head. Life left the golem's eyes as it crumpled forward.

Elandra and Fitmigar fought at my side, keeping a golem occupied long enough to allow me to leap onto its back. Stone hands grasped at me. Too late. I sank my pickaxe into its head, again and again. Its life force was extinguished with the series of brutal strikes.

Grunts and cries of frustration reached my ears. Across the room, I saw Drae dancing between two golems, narrowly evading their blows as he twisted, turned, and rolled between them. He'd slowed them somewhat, but he was struggling with actually finishing them off.

"Brom!"

The stocky shadow mage caught my gesture as I pointed toward the battling dark elf. Shaking his head, Brom gripped the pickaxe handle harder, knuckles white, and reluctantly sprinted across the room.

I advanced to my next target.

Charn's voice rose with a new song reminiscent of one of Brom's favorite tunes but with new words to accompany it. Maybe I'd been too quick to judge. Had the pair been working on strengthening Charn's tunes? Energy rushed through my body.

With renewed strength, I battled throughout the hall, striking blows and forcing guardians back.

Our speed was keeping us alive, but one wrong move could still spell the end for any of us.

Another pained cry drew my gaze to Sienna holding her arm as she retreated across the hall, back toward where Charn and Sars took shelter. The pair had health potions ready to treat any injuries.

I paused. Where was Bernolir?

A dwarven roar answered the question. A section of the ceiling caved in above Fitmigar's pit, trapping the two guardians beneath the rubble.

We'd whittled them down to a manageable number, and Brom had managed to assist Drae in taking down one. His dance was slowing, though. The dark elf wasn't getting the [Ballad Boost]ed benefits that we all did.

Still, he battled on.

The last of Drae's cronies had grown distracted, and he now found himself flying across the room. His body slammed against a door in the wall I'd not noticed before, nudging it open a fraction.

A golden glow seeped out from beyond.

The final key.

The others remained oblivious. Rammy took the fight to the killer of the dark elf. Mallen jogged to assist as a booming rumble shook the hall.

The largest golem yet staggered through the doorway at the far end of the hall.

"Boss!" Brom shouted.

I rolled my shoulders and took a deep breath.

This fucker was almost twice the width of those we were still fighting and a few feet taller, too. Lives would be lost here.

Unless...

I threw out a series of handsignals behind my back, laying out my plan.

"Understood," came back from Sienna.

I had to trust they'd take care of it.

Mallen roared as he brought his war hammer down, obliterating the golem he fought in one swing. At the same time, Drae and Brom finished off their own assailant.

Only the largest golem remained. It stood motionless as though considering the threat we posed.

Silent.

Brom and Drae joined my side. Mallen and Rammy did likewise, keeping their eyes on the boss. A low cough from behind confirmed that Fitmigar was still present.

More of the golden light now illuminated the room, and I relaxed slightly. The others had done as requested and left through the side door to search for the key.

The golem beat its fists against its chest.

I sent the jaguar first. An alarmingly swift punch from the golem obliterated it instantly.

The golem shook its head and charged, faster than any of the others, at Fitmigar. I sprinted after it, hacking my pickaxe into its back. Drae followed behind me, adding his own effort, but the guardian boss didn't slow at all.

Fitmigar rolled left, catching a glancing blow from the golem's foot. It sent her rolling end over end toward the entrance to the hall. Her mace flew free, crashing into the wall and bouncing off the floor.

Dazed, she scrambled back into the confines of the corridor beyond. The guardian stomped after her, shaking its head in frustration when it found itself too large to exit the room and get to the dwarf.

It turned as we closed in, deflecting an over-shoulder blow from Rammy and throwing him off balance. The attack left barely a scratch.

Rammy backed away, eyes wide, head shaking. His greatsword rang in his hands as his foot kicked against the mace.

"Rammy!" I called, gesturing for the fire mage to kick the weapon across to me. He flicked the spiked weapon across the hall with his foot, spinning it end over end until I plucked it from the air, a spike stopping a fraction from my eye.

I blinked.

Slowly.

Fuck, that was close...

I hefted the mace in my hand, feeling its weight compared to the pickaxe. These were the weapons that would bring down the guardian boss. Now, I just had to work out how to wield both simultaneously.

Mallen and Drae were frustrating the golem, darting in, striking, and then retreating, keeping one step ahead. Brom was sidling around the room to join me.

While the golem was preoccupied with the others, I came in from the side, sliding low and crashing the point of the pickaxe straight through the guardian boss's right knee. Shards flew from the joint.

It shuddered in pain but kept moving forward.

"The head!" Drae called, evading a sweeping punch from the golem.

I used a [Wind Boost] to launch myself up at the golem's head, bringing both pickaxe and mace down toward the back of its head.

It turned before I reached it, batting me away, the strike flinging me into the wall. Momentarily dazed, I shook my head to clear my thoughts.

I hadn't killed the golem, and it now only had one focus: me.

It turned and ignored the others. Striding toward me, its very footsteps shook the hanging city's foundations. I scrambled back, hands searching for the weapons that had been knocked from my grasp, my heart pounding in my chest.

Any hope that others would come to my rescue was extinguished when the guardian boss threw its huge stony fists into the ceiling and brought a huge section down, trapping me with it.

The golem closed in. I found myself defenseless, weaponless, and with an abundance of magic that I couldn't hurt it with.

I'd had a good run, right? The others could go on without me.

Right?

No, fuck that.

An idea formed.

Why hadn't I thought of it before?

Just because I couldn't use my magic to damage the golem, it didn't mean I couldn't use it at all.

A huge stone fist came barreling toward my face, and I pulled on [Shapeshift Mouse]. The fist flew over me as my tiny claws found purchase, and I shot between the golem's legs.

I released the spell immediately. Shifting back near my pickaxe, I dove it into the golem's head with all my might before using [Wind Boost] to dodge its backhand swing.

This boss was fast, but I could be faster.

Large shards crumbled from its head as it turned to chase me.

I backed off. [Fireball]s flew from my hands. They bounced off it, but a face full of fire makes you blind, immune or not. I had mana to spare, and I threw everything I could at the golem to confuse and disorientate, [Ice Blast]s and [Fire Burst]s batted away as it searched for its target.

Each time it closed in, I boosted to the side or shifted and evaded. The golem's frustration grew as it failed to lay a strike on me.

This wasn't enough. I couldn't just buy time forever. It seemed that no one was coming to help me.

It was time to try something a little different.

If this didn't work, I might not make it out of this.

No, I *would* not make it out.

As the guardian boss came at me again, I tossed the pickaxe high and cast [Shapeshift Falcon], flying after it.

Catching up to the spinning wooden handle, three feet above the golem's head, I returned to human form and brought the weapon down, full force, into the top of the guardian's head. The pick pierced deep.

The golem collapsed with a rumble of stone.

I landed a few feet past, turning and raising the pickaxe high as I skidded to a stop. I had to make sure it was over.

A stony fist rose shakily into the air.

It wasn't.

Not yet.

I dodged past the weak movement, bringing the pickaxe down on its face like I was trying to tunnel through a mountain, refusing to let up until only rubble remained.

Faint shouts gradually pulled me from my frenzy. I realized the others had no idea what was happening and called back, letting them know I was OK. Then I set about finding a way back.

There was a small crevice near the ceiling. I considered shifting into mouse form to squeeze through, but then who was to say if we'd need the pickaxe again.

I sighed as I climbed the rubble, reaching the top and pulling rocks clear, even using the weapons to lever some free until the space was large enough for me to crawl through.

The others sat on the ground, catching their breath. Drae leaned against the wall behind them, the nearest thing to a content look on his face.

Two more broken golem bodies now littered the floor. They must have climbed from the pit in my absence. No wonder they hadn't been working to get to my side.

Chatter came from the open door as I slid down the rubble. The others were returning. Sienna appeared fully healed and had a golden glow emanating from her fist.

Meeting me at the base of the blockade, she pulled me into a hug, pressing her lips against mine. The moment passed all too quickly. She stepped back, opened her hand, and offered me the key.

"I hope it wasn't too hard to find?"

"Nothing we couldn't manage."

I smiled, took the key, and slid it into my pocket next to the other. Only one more needed.

I turned to face Drae. The dark elf stood, hands raised, and shrugged.

# Chapter Twenty-One

"I say we just kill 'im."

I glanced at Fitmigar. She likely wasn't the only one with that opinion. Drae needed to pay for his crimes, but he'd answer to the highest authority.

The issue was containing him.

We had enough of us to guard him, now that the threats seemed to have passed, but if he used shadow magic only Brom would be able to locate him.

For now, rope would have to do.

Once we had him tied up, it was time to move. The first floor's cavern had collapsed after we found the first key, and if the same happened again, we could find ourselves plummeting to our deaths.

We continued through two more rooms within the fortress, both empty of threats. A familiar golden glow appeared ahead. We'd reached the edge of the city, and our way out lay before us.

Ahead, a thin, glistening walkway led to an open area carved into the far wall. The end of the third floor. Beyond this courtyard lay an illuminated tunnel. Illuminated only to me.

I whistled loudly from the city's edge. Twelve griffins appeared, screeching euphorically before as they landed on the courtyard opposite our position.

We shuffled our way across the path. I walked with Drae before me, keeping a close eye on the dark elf. The urge to kick him over the edge lurked at the back of my mind.

"Any idea what happens now?" I asked Sars when we grouped up with the griffins.

The wind mage didn't even bother to pull his notebook out. "Not a clue, Jadyn."

"If I may?"

I groaned. Of course, Drae would know.

I gestured for him to speak, and that smug grin of his appeared again.

"There's no safe area on completion of the third floor. This tunnel leads to tracks, and those tracks will deliver us directly to the vault."

"So, no platform up to the surface?"

"No way back up until you reach the vault."

That ruled out half of the squad taking Drae back up while we continued without him.

"And then?" I asked.

He shook his head and rolled his eyes. "You have the keys. What do you think happens next?"

He was insufferable. "OK. So, we open the vault, and that's it?"

"That is it. I mean, there could be threats between here and the vault, but I wouldn't know anything about that..."

"Can I kill 'im now?" Fitmigar asked. I almost allowed it.

Instead, I turned to the others. "Keep your weapons close. Charn, Bernolir, that includes you both."

They stood proudly gripping their pickaxes again. They might not have swung them, but their quick thinking on the journey down had been the reason we'd defeated the golems.

Helstrom and Rammy guided Mossrik and Chiron into the tunnel. We followed, Drae walking in the middle of the column, myself and Brom riding immediately behind. He might be restrained, but that didn't mean we could relax.

The tunnel thankfully meant we were out of the wind. Once Rammy tossed a [Fireball] into the first sconce, we could make out more of the paintings we'd seen in the chamber leading to the underground network.

That felt like an age ago now.

I followed the images of titanic beasts battling griffin knights too numerous to count, wars fought across land, sea, and air. They likely told the story of events that had transpired years before.

Maybe events that hadn't happened yet at all.

Was this our future?

Sars sighed from behind. I knew without looking that he wanted the time to document it all.

"We'll return, Sars."

"I sincerely hope you are right, Jadyn. This is priceless. Absolutely priceless."

"If it's possible, we'll do it."

That seemed enough to satisfy Sars who went back into silent contemplation.

"You know, you've not said how you killed the golem boss yet, man."

I took a moment to talk Brom through my battle, doing my best to downplay how close to death I'd been.

---

No threats materialized before we reached the tracks. Pristine open-top carriages awaited our descent. Someone had to be looking after these. But who?

Unlike the carriages we'd ridden with Max, these could hold four or five griffins in each. I pushed Drae in first, then followed with Sienna, Elandra, and Ella before pulling the large door shut. I'd hardly had the chance to speak with them lately, and even if we had to endure Drae's presence, I'd take the opportunity while I could.

The griffins all sat and closed their eyes. Full stomachs probably left them needing a nap. It was a feeling I assumed Rammy felt most days.

Drae leaned against the far wall, declining the chance to take a seat. He seemed as nonchalant as ever.

The girls gathered near me, each kissing me before dropping down, waiting for me to take a seat beside them.

"Oh..."

I sighed and looked at Drae. "Oh, what?"

"You're the original kind of creation mage."

I assumed he was talking about my harem, but I couldn't resist trying to learn more. "The original kind?"

"I'm sure you'll discover more in the vault, but yes, the way the ancients grew in power. Carnal..."

His thin lips curled in distaste, and it was my turn to grin. "I assume you do things differently?"

"Very much so," he replied, dryly. "But you'll have to read up about that, too. I'm not here to make the rest of your knights stronger for you."

Oh... so the others could grow stronger, too. Now, that was interesting. I'd need to let Sars know as soon as we disembarked.

For now, I chose to recline with my girls at my side, our hard work hopefully done. We'd completed the challenges on all three floors. We had dispatched the dark elves and humans that had murdered the guards and infiltrated the tunnels, capturing their leader in the process. We held all three keys, ready to unlock the secrets of the vault.

Gentle snoring reached my ears. I smiled as I noticed all three girls sleeping around me. As soon as we were done here, we had some catching up to do. Mana levels were still low, after all.

I still had to pinch myself sometimes. These three beautiful girls were all connected to me now. We were stronger together. If we could unlock more of the secrets behind multi-wielding, soon maybe we'd all be more powerful.

Hours passed. I remained alert, unwilling to relax even when the dark elf opposite finally slid to the floor and closed his eyes.

The tunnel wove ever downward, and at one point, small drops of water formed on the tunnel above us. The odd drop fell into the carriage. Could we be traveling under a lake. The sea?

I pondered where we could be, but with all the switchbacks I soon gave up. Hopefully, all would be revealed soon enough.

Eventually, the gradient evened out a little, and when the carriage rocked, I assumed we were at our destination. I glanced across the carriage to see Drae staring at me, a smile spreading across his face.

Something was up.

The carriage rocked again, and the girls woke. Alert.

"What's happening, Jadyn?" Ella asked.

"I'm not sure."

The carriage rocked a third time, more forcefully than previous. Hestia screeched. The griffins rose, heads swiveling, alert for danger.

"I hear scratching," Sienna whispered from my side, slipping her hand into mine briefly before pulling her bow from her back and rising to a crouch.

A purplish glow fell over the tunnel, casting the inside of the carriage in an eerie light. The color deepened until legs appeared over the top of the carriage.

Elandra shouted, and I grimaced as dark black spiders as large as dogs dropped into the carriage in numbers too vast to track. Their eyes were deep purple, glowing with an unnatural light. They came toward us in a wave, fangs twitching.

I unleashed a barrage of [Fireball]s, picking off spiders as they fell towards us.

The spells flew true, abdomens bursting open in a spray of gore, but there were too many.

Razor-sharp legs cut into my arms as they threatened to overwhelm us. The griffins snapped their beaks and raked their claws, but the carriage was too small to let them go all-out.

Mindful of the others and the flames, I switched to my scimitars, cleaving a path through the arachnids towards Drae. This was the dark elf's doing, of that there was no doubt.

I was bumped and knocked as the carriage continued to rock. The waves of spiders threatened to push it off the tracks.

I sliced through head and abdomen alike, roaring in fury as I dispatched one after the next, clearing a path to Drae.

I found him still sitting, a smirk on his face, not a scratch on him.

The spiders' numbers were dwindling now, the floor of the carriage sloshing with innards. The griffins snapped up body parts and swallowed them whole. I sliced through those that remained, continuing even after Ella and Sienna's arrows riddled their bodies or Elandra had run them through.

"Jadyn!"

I shook my head, clearing my mind. Sienna gestured toward my pocket. "Do you still have the key?"

I patted myself down, feeling the outline. "I do."

I'd divided the keys amongst the carriages before we'd set out to make sure that if Drae tried anything on the journey down, he'd find himself unable to claim all three.

He'd definitely tried something here, but he hadn't made any effort to leave.

I stood beside the girls, my gaze remaining on Drae as he slowly rose to his feet.

"I did warn you."

"I'm not sure what your aim was there, but the games stop now, Drae. You live still because we allow it."

"Very dramatic," the dark elf replied.

Part of me thought it would be easier just to kill him where he stood, but justice had to mean something. If no one answered for the slaughter of the kwell, for the killing of the king's guards, then what was the point of it all?

The carriages slowed to a crawl. It appeared that we'd reached the end of the line.

The carriage stopped, and I turned the metal handle to open the door. A ramp led us to the platform dimly illuminated by a luminous moss on the ceiling.

Drae moved slowly, tempting me to shove him along, but I wouldn't lay a hand on the dark elf lest he have a trick up his sleeve.

The griffins followed, content to leave the rest of the spider parts to rot where they lay. Soon, Rammy located the usual run of sconces and gave us light.

"Which way?" Brom asked, checking out both ends of the platform.

"I'm going to guess not back up the tunnel we just traveled down," Mallen replied.

Brom nodded. "Fair point."

I joined in to save the shadow mage from any further embarrassment, gesturing to our left. "The golden light is coming from the end of that tunnel there."

I pulled myself up onto Hestia, and together, we led the way down the short tunnel. It led to a large circular chamber covered in more of those mysterious murals.

That wasn't what caught my attention this time, though.

It was the two doors.

The first was a large stone door, matching the style of the platforms from earlier levels. Images on the door left me in no doubt of where the platform would likely rise to.

"Is that what I think it is?" Elandra asked, inspecting the door up close.

"Sure looks that way," I said. The image embossed on the door fairly easy to confirm.

"Right where I judged us to be," Sars added.

I turned and lifted an eyebrow. "You knew?"

Sars frowned, looking a little nervous. "I would not say I knew, Jadyn, but my calculations did have us moving under the Eilerin Sea."

Fuck. So, the platform did lead up to Eilerin Island. Home of the Beastkin. Hence why the image of a cat girl decorated the door. My question now was did the beastkin know?

Actually, my main question was how soon could we open the other door?

The second door was a dark, wooden door, and wide enough to allow multiple griffins to pass through with ease. The image of a griffin far taller than even Hestia had been burned into the wood. Centered in the door were three golden keyholes. The vault.

Gesturing for Rammy and Fitmigar to keep a close eye on Drae, I nodded to Brom and Helstrom. The pair dismounted and stepped forward, pulling keys from their pockets and holding them toward the locks.

Time to unlock the secrets of the ancients.

# Chapter Twenty-Two

As one, we slid the keys in, taking a deep breath before turning them. Clicks sounded out in unison. The door eased open.

This was it.

The vault.

What ancient treasures might lie within?

Brom nodded to me, and I pushed the heavy wooden door.

It being called a vault I had expected a small room with a few shelves of dusty books and maybe a legendary weapon or two. I had been wrong. The room had books—so many books that Sars would not live long enough to read half of them—but that was just the start.

Detailed maps hung from every wall of the timber-framed room. Some were of landmasses that I didn't recognize, others barely recognizable as what Atania may once have resembled. Images were dispersed between them, of animals, of races, that bore no resemblance to any I'd ever seen before.

I'd seen horses before, but I'd never seen them flying through the skies. Female riders wielded weapons from their mounts, their wavy hair blowing in the wind.

I exhaled and stepped into the room, looking up to see a starscape detailed across the ceiling above me. I was no scholar of the night skies, but there appeared far too many stars to compare it to what I'd seen those few times I'd studied the night sky above Atania.

We could spend a lifetime in here and never learn all the vault's secrets.

Wooden tables lined the center of the huge room, and doors were interspersed along the wall.

The others filed in behind me, conversations whispered, almost revered. I smiled as Sars took his notebook out, wide-eyed. He would need a few more if he hoped to even start to understand what we'd discovered.

I patted him on the shoulder as he passed, but he barely noticed. His gaze flicked around the room, the reward perhaps greater for the wind mage than anyone else here.

Bernolir ambled past, mumbling about dwarven heritage. Helstrom and Fitmigar followed him to a section full of iron-forged weaponry.

Ella appeared at my side, dropping a quick kiss on my cheek before pulling Mallen toward an area that I assumed was elven-centric, images of sprawling tree cities towering toward the stars catching my gaze.

How could this be? Wherever I looked I saw the chance for us to be something more. Something stronger. More learned.

"Your section is at the rear."

I glanced across, already preparing myself for more of the dark elf's games. "Humanity?"

"Not exactly," said Drae, and I paused. I couldn't trust the dark elf any more than I could tame a wyvern, but he'd sprinkled some truths in with his lies and deceit before now.

"It's just a shame you'll not get to see it."

I stopped dead. What?

The very walls of the vault began to shake, pictures crashing to the ground as shadows passed over the room.

I sprinted back toward the entrance and gasped. The chamber outside had become a hive of arachnid activity. Spiders triple the size of the ones in the carriage now forced their way toward the vault door.

Where the hells had they come from?

No doubt Drae had lured these spiders here somehow, just like he had attacked the carriage before.

We couldn't let them inside. The treasures within couldn't be allowed to be destroyed.

"Form up!" I roared. The squad dropped whatever they were looking at and charged across the room to join me. I hauled myself up onto Hestia, tapping her on the flank. "One more time, girl."

Hestia reared up, talons gleaming in the firelight, and charged to meet our latest foe. These weren't the worst we'd faced, far from it, but we couldn't let them take the vault's secrets from us.

Everything we'd been through these past few weeks, from our first mission to the border to our journey to the depths of the land, strongly hinted at a great evil intent on destruction. I'd be damned if I wasn't going to give all I had to discover it and eradicate it once and for all.

[Fire Wall*] surged from my hands, tearing through the giant arachnids. I was tired of being attacked at every turn. I was tired of being chased down. Here we would stand, and here the spiders would fall.

Twelve griffins screeched, their riders launching spell after spell. Spiders dropped far faster than I could ever have hoped for. If they'd planned on stealing or destroying our discovery, they'd severely underestimated us.

A second wave skittered in from the tunnels. Magic and steel of Griffin Knights met them with violence, decimating the creatures.

As Charn sang loudly, our mana replenished almost as quickly as we used it, Bernolir concentrated, and I expected the ceiling to come crashing down at any moment, [Rock Fall] his only current spell as far as I was aware, but then he placed his hand against the stone floor and hummed.

The sound was familiar. One I should have learned myself. It was the sound of kwell magic.

The stony floor shimmered, liquifying, and the spiders' legs sank into the floor. The humming stopped, and the floor solidified again, leaving the spiders trapped. We fell upon them, slaughtering the trapped, helpless swarm.

Only when all were dead, did I realize what we had done.

We had left Drae alone in the vault.

Cursing, I rode Hestia into the vault, scanning left and right as I searched for the dark elf. Unable to see him, I slid from Hestia's back, pushing open door after door until I found him.

Drae stood near the rear of a stone-walled chamber. One scone burned brightly, casting plentiful light across the barren space. A huge silver oval frame was positioned at his side, and that godsforsaken smirk was on his face once again.

He continued to smile as I closed in, his hand coming forward. I pulled on my mana, preparing for a fight.

Instead, the dark elf slowly opened his palm, revealing a series of smooth white stones.

*What...?*

Drae's lips moved, whispering softly in a language I didn't understand. The interior of the silver frame at his side began to shimmer, the effect like a pebble into a pond, and my breath caught in my throat.

With a single nod, the dark elf stepped back into the frame and disappeared.

# About the Author

Travis Dean is an author of progression fantasy with more than a touch of spice. Griffin Academy: Knights of War is his debut novel.

Travis hopes you've enjoyed meeting Jadyn and the griffin knights of Atania and are as excited to follow his journey as he is to bring it to you.

Amongst other places, you can find Travis on Facebook and X (@TravisDeanGA), so do come by and say hello.

# Check This Out !

**Thank you for reading!**
**If you enjoyed this book, please leave a review.**
**Reviews are so important to authors.**

★★★★★

**Join the Royal Guard Publishing Discord to participate in tons of giveaways, extra content, and chat with all our authors and narrators.**

Check out

For more Harem Lit / LitRPG Adventures:

*Check This Out !*

www.royalguardpublishing.com

https://www.facebook.com/RoyalGuard2020

https://www.facebook.com/groups/dukesofharem

https://www.facebook.com/groups/haremlitbooks

https://www.reddit.com/r/haremfantasynovels/

https://www.facebook.com/groups/LitRPG.books

https://www.facebook.com/groups/litrpgforum

https://www.facebook.com/groups/LitRPGReleases

https://www.reddit.com/r/litrpg/

https://www.facebook.com/groups/LitRPGsociety

Printed in Great Britain
by Amazon